Inside The Magic Circle

The ability to establish rewarding relationships is one of the vital ingredients for
success. Knowing your personal pattern of
action and response in relation to others
gives you a big edge in the game of life. The
more intimate the relationship, the more
powerful the effects of the basic Sun Sign
influences, whether positive or negative, and
the more our basic character traits are
exposed to view. Interaction of these basic
traits in your love1sex relationships can
undermine the most compelling and
magnetic surface traits between two people
if they are not recognized and dealt with
effectively.

A knowledge of basic Sun Sign traits and
their interactions can set the stage for fulfillment in every other department of your
life₁

We will send you a free catalog on request. Any titles not in your local book store can be purchased by mail. Send the price of the book plus 50¢ shipping charge to Tower Books, P.O. Box 270, Norwalk, Connecticut 06852.

Titles currently in print are available for industrial and sales promotion at reduced rates. Address inquiries to Tower Publications, Inc., Two Park Avenue, New York, New York 10016, Attention: Premium Sales Department.

LOVE CIRCLE

OF

THE SUNS

Paige McKenzie

TOWER BOOKS   NEW YORK CITY

A TOWER BOOK

Published by

Tower Publications, Inc.
Two Park Avenue
New York, N.Y. 10016

Copyright © 1980 by Marje Blood

All rights reserved
Printed in the United States

LOVE CIRCLE
OF
THE SUNS

Foreword

The Magic Circle of the Suns

Your natal horoscope, more personal than a finger-print, can tell an astrologer your individual potential for success, wealth, happiness, love, and sexual fulfillment. It can also indicate trouble area, and ways to lessen or to avoid the negative impact of these times, by channeling your energy in more positive directions.

Centuries of observation have shown the heavenly bodies in Earth's solar system influence our lives in specific ways. These influences are reflected in the arrangement of the Moon, Sun, and every planet, yet each of us feels these influences in different ways.

The principle focus of a chart, however, is channeled through your Sun Sign. In your relationships, the basic traits of your Sign will indicate the way you express the attractions you feel to and from others, the way you express love and friendship, and of course your sexual responses, modified by your unique chart pattern.

But knowing your own responses and reactions is only part of the picture. Basic Sun Sign traits will be expressed differently in relation to each of the other Signs, and the full portrait of your Sign will emerge from this *total* interaction.

Relationships form the foundation for every area of your life. The ability to establish rewarding relationships is one of the vital ingredients for success. Knowing your personal pattern of action and response in relation to others gives you a big edge in the game of life. Understanding the how and why of *others'* motives can help assure fulfillment in life.

The more intimate the relationship, the more powerful the effects of the basic Sun Sign influences, whether positive or negative. Most of us cultivate the attractive qualities that draw others to us and enhance them to work well on the social level. The closer the relationship, the more our basic character traits are exposed to view, without the protective personality cover on the surface. Interaction of these basic traits in your love/sex relationships can undermine the most compelling and magnetic surface traits between two people if they are not recognized and dealt with effectively.

For most of us, a fulfilling love relationship lights the way for success in all other relationships: career, family, friendship. A knowledge of basic Sun Sign traits and their interactions can, by pointing the way to joy and happiness in your intimate relationships, set the stage for fulfillment in every other department of your life.

YOUR SUN SIGNS

The Sun Sign descriptions used in this book must, of necessity, be general. Since the heavens are in constant motion, no two individual horoscopes can be exactly alike, and basic Sun Sign traits may be modified or intensified by planet placements in individual birth charts according to the exact time of birth, the

Ascendant Sign (the Sign on the horizon at birth), and the Sign in which the natal moon is placed.

Birth dates for individual Signs are:

ARIES	March 21 - April 19
TAURUS	April 20 - May 20
GEMINI	May 21 - June 21
CANCER	June 22 - July 22
LEO	July 23 - August 22
VIRGO	August 23 - September 22
LIBRA	September 23 - October 23
SCORPIO	October 24 - November 22
SAGITTARIUS	November 23 - December 21
CAPRICORN	December 22 - January 19
AQUARIUS	January 20 - February 18
PISCES	February 19 - March 20

ARIES

Aries-Aries

Two Aries coming together—if indeed they manage it at all—will result in spontaneous fireworks. What appears to be blazing love at first sight is more likely to be flares and sparks thrown off by two fiery personalities in competition over which will be the conqueror.

Aries does not submit easily to subordinate roles, and love will not make submission any more appetizing. In fact, Aries' willingness to see an element of sexual teasing in every contact with the opposite sex makes it easier for the Ram to keep testing until a mate of another Sign is found who will follow, rather than try to outshine the brilliant vibrations of another Aries.

Competition will be the base of the conflicts that besiege this relationship almost from the start. Who will be president; who will be office boy? Who will drive; who will ride? In every situation—momentous or miniscule—the battle will be fought with heat and aggression. Many Signs can develop give-and-take through confrontation by learning from experience, starting each round from an adjusted viewpoint. But Aries starts from scratch with each encounter. The launching pad will be the same; the explosive reaction will be the same; the result will be the same—instant conflagration.

The dynamic energy of Mars, the Aries ruler, does not make for easy approaches or exploratory advances. Aries rushes into relationships head on, assuming others will make the adjustments to achieve mutually satisfying interactions. Not so here. Each Aries mate will blast off in a pre-programmed launching and, as often as not, will come together on a crash course.

These two Suns can manage a relationship only if they can synchronize their explosive starts and pace their brilliant leaps in harmony, so that they run out of steam side by side—on target—instead of clashing head on in the air. And it would require highly developed, idealistic Aries types to pull it off even then.

Ascendant Signs will be extremely important here: Aries characteristics filtered through a softening effect from the rising Sign may allow leeway for these two Suns to work out some kind of compromise; perhaps to develop a set of ground rules where they take turns being first.

If this union survives to the point where there are children, some such understanding will be mandatory to keep the younsters from being consumed in the conflicts of the parents. A parent with a Cancer Ascendant might use strong protective orientation to restrain the high-handedness of the other parent in dealing with the children. A Pisces Moon in one Sign could allow more understanding in that parent than is usual with Aries. A Libran Ascendant could give a balancing effect.

The chances of these two Signs coming together and staying together are about the same as those between two maverick roman candles. But they may keep trying from beginning to beginning to beginning.

Aries-Taurus

The basic incompatibility of fiery enthusiasm and patient acquisition here is focused through a common trait of ambition. When the relationship endures it will be largely through this overlapping sense of purpose in achieving a common goal. There may be a problem of finding a common goal, but if that is accomplished, Arian self-confidence and executive ability can compliment the Taurean ability to build on the ideas of others, and build enduringly.

Other traits which they share are to the detriment of one Sign or the other—usually Taurus, whose greater sensitivity in personal matters leaves the Bull vulnerable to Aries lack of finesse in personal relationships. They may be drawn to each other through a social encounter which, in both these Signs, will have sexual undertones. But once they enter an intimate relationship the conflicting personalities often clash. Sex will carry the day for a while, but in time Aries tendency to give the most casual meeting a sensual flavor will play havoc with Taurus emotions.

Taurus sensuality runs deep, but once it is centered on a loved one, remains fixed. Taureans are possessive of their loves. They do not understand Aries flirtatiousness, which can lead the impulsive Rams into dangerous waters before they realize it. Taureans, knowing the depth of their own sexual responses when aroused, can forgive indiscretion but will not look kindly on habitual romantic flings. Taurus may try to save the relationship; Taurus resists change all the way. But once pushed to the point where rage is activated, the Bull will be unyielding in the decision to end the union.

Aries will truly not understand this Taurus determination until it is too late. Once forced to take action, the Bull will not relent until the matter is settled. Taurus forgiveness is genuine, but once the affair goes beyond the bounds of forgiveness, Taurus will stand stone-still until a just settlement is achieved. Taurus will always even the score, waiting years if necessary to accomplish this.

Aries will be surprised at the tenacity with which Taurus clings to grievances once they have been established. Aries, quick-tempered as a firecracker, thinks nothing of angry words and slamming doors; they are simply a means of emphasizing a strong-willed outlook. Aries wouldn't recognize a grudge if one identified itself by name, and cannot realize the extent of Taurean endurance in this direction. Once Taurus has reached the point of slamming a door the wall will go down with it.

Aries aggressiveness may delight Taurus briefly in the relationship, but will probably become nerve wracking after a time. Taurus works steadily to shape a particular corner of the world to personal comfort. The Bull is uncomfortable with all change; must plan far ahead and move slowly in taking new directions; cannot function in an environment which shifts from hour to hour. Aries, to the contrary, soon feels as if moving through hardening concrete when dealing with Taurus in a close relationship.

The Taurean trait of clinging to a losing proposition long after everyone else has walked off the field is particularly galling to Aries. The Ram makes two or three head-on efforts at solving a difficult problem and then walks away to look for an easier way.

Aries is always looking for an easy route to the top of the mountain; in fact, will often spend more time trying for quick success than would have been demanded by taking more traditional paths. Taurus, if there is no obvious way open, will patiently *build* a road to the top, leaving an enduring highway behind for the next person to follow. If Aries could allow Taurus to go first, the way could be smoothed for both, but this seldom happens. Aries is impatient, and does not like to follow anyone.

Conflicting Sun Sign traits seem almost to conspire to separate these two. Aries generosity comes to confrontation with the prudent self interest of Taurus. Taurean generosity comes to the fore to include loved ones *after* the Bull has acquired the good things of live for personal use. And Taurus possessiveness in intimate relationships lacerates the independent Aries spirit.

Aries, argumentive to the end, will explode at Taurus reasonableness. Reason is not what Aries wants in conflict; the Ram desires head-on confrontation that will bring peace after a good fight, win or lose. Taurus will try to avoid an all-out confrontation, perhaps fearing the unleashing of the deep fires of anger that lurk in the Taurean personality. Taureans are disciplined people who do not like the feeling of losing control—particularly self-control.

Children of this union fare better than either of the parents most of the time, combing the best of each in a way that produces well-rounded, capable individuals with enough of the Taurus stability to keep the Aries precociousness under control.

In the end it will probably be Taurus who suffers most in this union. Taurus is ruled by Venus, the planet of love and beauty and attraction, and is willing to work slowly to achieve the compromises that will bring the relationship closer to personal ideals of enduring beauty. Standing dead center, trying to follow the erratic patterns of Aries behavior, will leave Taurus first confused, then simmering, until anger finally erupts with the force of Etna blowing its top. And that will be THE END.

Aries-Gemini

Sextiled Suns are supportive of each other, and these two have much in common. They work well together. Each prizes freedom of movement and allows the other *carte blanche* to move about in the relationship without penalties. Both are self-confident and move ahead with assurance to get their enthusiastic projects off to a running start.

Both Aries and Gemini communicate well, not only with each other but with everyone. This partnership makes a good team; they share the quality of whole-hearted involvement in whatever they undertake—at the moment. Aries appreciates Gemini versatility and creativeness; Gemini can use Aries aggressiveness to get moving in the right direction. If Aries has a tendency to assume leadership and direct the operation, it won't bother Gemini, who will be happy to let Aries run the show as long as the Ram doesn't interfere with Gemini restless consideration of first one aspect of the project, then another.

The life style of this couple will resemble the proverbial three-ringed circus. There'll always be something happening. Both these Signs are easily bored and will usually have several projects in various stages of completion (or noncompletion). Children will be encouraged to do their things as well. This household will be overflowing with sporting equipment, craft materials, animals, causes—and people.

Both Aries and Gemini will gravitate to the scene of the nearest action. They want to be part of what is going on. The difference will be that a time will come when Gemini, lacking the robust energy and stamina of the Ram, will have to withdraw from contact with other people in order to recharge emotional and physical batteries. Aries, a veritable dynamo, can keep going long as the excitement continues. But neither will go into a fit if Gemini says, "I'll take the car and go on home; you catch a ride with someone when the party's over."

The intimate side of this relationship can be a fascinating interplay of passion and detachment which brings out the best in both these Suns. The whirlwind Gemini personality can fan the Aries fire almost at will; at the same time Aries fire will kindle an answering flame in unemotional Gemini. A fire arrow can generate a lot of excitement on a merry-go-round. Aries idealism sometimes gets lost in the lusty Arian passions, yet Gemini versatility can activate Aries positive traits almost without effort. There's no predicting what will happen next with a Gemini in the house. Aries boredom never really has a chance to surface with Gemini for a partner, and vice versa.

Gemini manages to counter mental activity with physical invovement, and intuitively evokes a balancing atmosphere when the impulsiveness of Aries gets out of hand. Sometimes Gemini will be drawn into a whirlwind of indignation by Aries fiery resentment, but usually falls back on natural skepticism to keep from being blown too far off base.

There will be times when the sensual side of the Aries character is dissatisfied with the lesser physical demands of Gemini; when the Twin's moodiness leaves something to be desired in the romance department. Gemini nervousness suffers under aggressiveness; Aries will grow irritable at chronic health problems that might result. Aries has little patience with illness—personal or someone else's; anything short of a severed limb will arouse little sympathy for Gemini.

But Gemini detachment in emotional matters allows acceptance of Arien irritability more easily than most

Signs. If things get too hot, Gemini will get in the car and take off alone, knowing that once Aries cools down the whole matter will be forgotten. Neither of these Suns demands a strong emotional involvement from the partner and usually they can weather conflicts because nothing holds their deep interest for long—not even a rousing marital battle.

They agree down the line on the raising of children; each treats children as people and urges them to grow up as fast as possible. Birthday parties often wait until the children are old enough to plan their own. Doing ''for'' children is more chore than privilege with either of these Signs.

Yet their children will learn self-reliance and self-confidence early; will be encouraged to try new experiences. They will also be expected to obey a few strict house rules laid down early in their lives. Both Aries and Gemini have the detachment to discipline their children if it is for the benefit of the youngsters, although Aries may spout off first in an angry outburst. Indulgence is seldom seen in their relations with offspring.

All in all, this is a fulfilling relationship in spite of differences that would seem to be more corroding than they usually prove to be. For whatever reason, there is enough give and take to keep this romance alive for a long, long time.

Aries-Cancer

The Aries-Cancer love affair is a pressure cooker: elemental fire and water combine here to produce anger and tears and heated passions with very little that is beneficial to either Sign. Their strongest common traits —industriousness and ambition—are not supported from other sources; and while each may admire the other's dedicated approach to getting ahead in the world, in terms of personal relationships even this trait may work to keep them at cross purposes.

Both Aries and Cancer have strong executive abilities. Fine. But neither is prone to subordinate his own personality to that of another. Cancer, although seeming always to put the family first, is only playing out basic character traits in so doing.

Even when they divide the areas of their lives, with Cancer running the affairs of the home and Aries handling other areas, there will be a strongly competitive atmosphere which will bring emotional confrontations. Cancer possessiveness in a woman will resent the slightest intervention in domestic matters, but will also resent Aries willingness to leave all such details to her; worse, she'll brood and sulk over Aries' lack of interest in the family. The Cancer man, while nominally agreeing to let Aries run the household, will find it virtually impossible to hide resentment when Aries makes impulsive decisions regarding household purchases without consulting him.

The Ram's recklessness, generosity, lack of concern for the rainy day, horrifies the frugal Cancer individual, whose fear of being without funds can be traumatic. Aries couldn't care less about tomorrow; the Ram lives for the present and takes care of each day's needs as they become evident. Money is made to be spent, in Arien eyes. Aries can usually improvise if funds are short; but can't understand the philosophy of doing without today for fear of possible need in the future. Aries enthusiasm and optimism assumes that the future will be better—not worse—than today, and sees Cancer frugality as selfishness.

Cancer will work patiently to achieve desires. Aries wants instant gratification of desires, and the greater the yearning the greater the impatience. Aries is strictly a fly now—pay later person. Aries will often borrow money and use credit cards to take trips if they find themselves between jobs, on the theory that there is plenty of time without work schedules to meet; and there's always the possibility that opportunities for new jobs will come more quickly by moving around rather than by sitting still and waiting for jobs to come to them.

Cancers' inclination under these circumstances is to retreat into their homes, lock all doors, and go on half rations until they are assured of steady incomes again. Whichever they decide to do, one of these Signs will be frustrated; sooner or later the accusing silence of Cancer will set off Aries' quick temper and the pressure valve indicator will move into the danger zone.

Aries, self-confident to a fault, never quite realizes the extent of the Cancer inferiority complex. Lack of self-esteem remains strong in Moon children no matter how successful they become. Their moods fluctuate with the changing of the Moon (literally) and they brood over imagined defects, intangible failures, when in fact their affairs are progressing with a smoothness that calls up envy from those around them.

Fearful of shadows no one else can see, Cancer will be hurt by what seems to be Aries recklessness and lack of concern for mutual security. Cancer cringes as Aries barges ahead, seemingly inviting disaster by challenging superiors or throwing good money after bad in an attempt to recoup losses. The best traits in either often brings out the worst in the other. No matter what they do they seldom find their good traits meshing to ease the grinding of the gears in their relationship.

Underlying irritations carry over into their intimate life. There can be moments of fulfilling love between the two. When Aries focuses drive and ardor on the loved one, Cancer response is all-encompassing. Cancer protectiveness, so galling to Aries much of the time, can be comforting when aggressive challenges in the outside world have backfired on the Ram. The most venturesome warrior needs to have bruises bandaged and spirits soothed at intervals.

But Cancer protectiveness, with any encouragement at all, blossoms to possessiveness. And the Aries need for love and comfort ends quickly. Cancer efforts to hold Aries close by constant hovering will result in angry outbursts and a quick departure by Aries, leaving Cancer to nurse personal wounds alone.

Aries in an amorous mood will have forgotten angry accusations made during an earlier quarrel, and will be impatient with Cancer coolness and hurt silence. Aries will *never* really understand that for the water Signs, sex is interwoven with emotional response. Cancer will find Aries earthiness under the circumstances distasteful; Aries will see Cancer rejection as sexual blackmail. Neither will be right—although there is an element of truth on each side of the question. Worse still, there is little chance to achieve understanding between them, since Cancer becomes more reticent as Aries becomes more demanding.

Children will further aggravate the problems of this relationship. In fact, children of Aries-Cancer marriages may learn to play the parents against each other. Aries impatience with Cancer possessiveness in the name of "mother love" will bring about monumental outbursts from Aries, who wants more than anything to see children be self-reliant, self-confident and resourceful; and who sees these qualities submerged by the emotional tides of Cancer protective instincts.

Sooner or later Aries will probably seek solace from the confining Cancer personality in extra-marital affairs. Sooner or later the Cancer partner will probably come face to face with evidence of Aries infidelity. And whatever chance of success the marriage has can disappear in one final, fatal eruption as the pressure cooker explodes.

Individual charts may have planetary placements which allow these two Suns to come together in a working relationship, but they will seldom allow for an easy relationship.

Aries-Leo

The union of Aries and Leo Suns can set the world on fire! Aries idealism feeds the steady flame of Leo high-mindedness. Both are strongly oriented toward getting to the top in career and personal affairs. There is not much doubt that success in terms of material wealth and position in life will come to them.

Both Aries and Leo are very much aware of their public images; both want to impress. Aries enthusiasm moves aggressively toward dazzling goals—attaining a palatial home, moving in elite social circles, advancing career enterprises. Leo yearning for affluence backs this focus all the way. These two Suns represent the temperament that believes the way to become a millionaire is to live like one—especially when you're broke. Whatever they do will be done with a combination of Aries flair and Leo style, and onlookers will be dazzled by the performance.

Neither of these Signs can bear to be second in anything, and therein lies the main obstacle to their happiness. This relationship will have an underlying tone of competition. Each partner will have and desire to use executive leadership traits. Neither wants to bother with burdensome details. And each will be adept at delegating routine chores to others. As partners in a mutual enterprise they will divide authority between them and work together to get the job done through worthwhile subordinates.

In an intimate relationship this process doesn't work too well. Here there are only two—one must lead and the other must follow. Neither Leo nor Aries likes looking at another's back. Practically, it may be difficult for the courtly Leo to move fast enough to surpass the impulsive Aries. The Lion will not make the effort willingly, nor be happy doing it. Royalty cannot maintain dignity while chasing a rocket. Inevitably Leo self-importance will emerge in moments of intimacy, and not even Aries flirtatiousness will be able to overlook this completely. Self-importance in a Leo mate is fine with Aries—as long as it is directed toward someone else.

Woe betide the Leo mate who brings the imperious public manner home at night. One does not *order* an Aries to serve the dinner, or to clean out the bathtub; nor, in reversed roles, does one *order* an Aries to be home at 7:00 sharp for dinner, or to stop by the store for a loaf of bread. For that matter, one does not *order* a Leo to do any of these things either.

The household of this pair may, in fact, resemble a deserted field camp most of the time. Neither can bring energy to spend time on trivial details like dusting or making beds. It's a sure bet that the Leo-Aries couple will hire a cleaning woman whenever the budget permits. They'll eat out often, and they'll eat at progressively finer restaurants as they move up in the world. They'll have charge accounts at the best stores. Leo, at least, will dress well and expensively; Aries, unless Leo exercises the prerogative of purchasing clothes for the partner, will dress in a combination of haste and taste, expensively if possible.

They will travel as often as they can manage it to the

places people talk about. Leo and Aries both have a tendency toward name-dropping; they'll give the impression of being on close terms with public personalities a little sooner than they actually make it. But they'll get there if their minds are set on it; with Aries to get them moving in the right direction and Leo to keep the show on the road, their success potential is high.

If only they could manage their private relationship as handsomely as they conduct their public encounters! But Fire Sign egos burn hot, and frequently these two emerge as two separate high-blazing bonfires instead of one steadily glowing fire.

While the intensity of the love that binds them will seldom be in question, differing attitudes and means of expression of love may spark some spectacular explosions. Leo love is a reflection of basic fire qualities; once a mate has been chosen, Leo love burns with a pure, steady flame forever. While Leo will not be above a back door escapade now and then (the king may enjoy such royal pleasures if discrete), fidelity and loyalty from the mate is expected at all times. Leo will be deeply wounded if the mate is discovered in extra-marital involvements, and kingly disappointment will not be alleviated one whit by knowledge of the Lion's own clandestine amours. (The king is *entitled*.)

Aries flirtatiousness will be a constant source of misery to Leo. Although able to look the other way when Aries is twinkling at a prospective client or someone who can further their personal ambitions, Leo will have moments of doubt which will be expressed heatedly when these two fiery personalities collide head on.

Leo is generous with love, but is also possessive; generous as long as the loved one is following Leonine wishes. Aries generosity makes no such demands; Aries shares with whoever is near. And Aries finds Leo posessiveness only a little less cloying than the Cancer variety. If Leo demands are too restrictive, Aries will begin to look on the lavish gifts which accompany them as expensive bribes and will be tempted to demonstrate independence that much more strongly.

Still, while the emotional clashes of these two generate a lot of heat they usually end in a flare-up of passion and the air is cleared—until the next time.

Most often, Aries and Leo combine their complimentary traits when dealing with their children. They will want for them the things that signify importance in the public eye. These children will usually have clothes a little more expensive than others in their classes; birthday parties a little more lavish than those of their friends. They'll have their own cars a little earlier than their peers; they'll be the ones who take the special trips, the ski lessons, the summers in Europe, to the extent that the budget can be stretched.

At the same time, these parents will expect of their children certain standards of behavior. Leo particularly will demand that the children not embarrass the parents in the eyes of the world—and Leo will decide where the limits lie. Both Leo and Aries want children they can be proud of, and while indulging them on the one hand will set strict standards on the other. The children don't usually find it too hard to live within this framework.

All in all, this will be an exciting, fulfilling marriage of two highly dramatic Suns who will command attention from those around them as they move together from success to success. Their failures can be spectacular, but are soon lost in the rosy glow of more successful fires they've lighted. This relationship may seem to be built on a base of exploding firecrackers, but the flame that sets them off will be one of enduring passion.

Aries-Virgo

An unlikely union, this: Cardinal Fire and Mutable Earth. What would a fire arrow see in a dragonfly? How could a dragonfly survive near a fire arrow?

But potent physical attraction can work between these two in spite of character traits that seldom mesh. Some of these traits are in direct conflict, but most just miss touching at any point.

A strong supportive bridge for contact between the two, along with a magnetic physical attraction, is the bond of accomplishment. Aries executive abilities recognize the worth of Virgoan dependability and efficiency. Aries wants nothing to do with irritating details of their enterprising activities. Aries happily delegates details to Virgo, who may not always enjoy the nitty-gritty of keeping the show on the road, but who would prefer taking care of these chores to taking a chance on having someone else botch things up.

And this interchange of talents works only so long as Aries is on the road with the show and Virgo is behind the scenes handling logistics. They don't work well in close proximity in a long-range situation. Virgo cannot forego the urge to try to re-educate Aries with a few well-chosen critical comments after observing the harum-scarum Ram at work. Aries feels covered with plastic spider webs when subjected to Virgo criticisms.

The irritations generated by too much togetherness will spark frequent explosive scenes between these two Signs: both Virgo and Aries tempers ignite easily. The difference lies in the dying sparks. Once having erupted, Aries forgets the matter which caused the explosion; Aries seldom holds grudges. Virgo, an intellectual Sign for whom words have precise meanings, will brood over exchanges made in anger and will find it hard to overlook statements which Aries forgets almost as soon as they are spoken. Further, Virgo memory banks store these statements for analyzing, and for drawing on for future reference. Aries lives for the moment; is never comfortable confronted by carefully detailed ideas and statements tossed out at some brainstorming session, especially while being asked to honor as commitments these irrelevent spin-offs.

Virgo may envy Aries aggressiveness from a small distance; up close the reticent Virgo is apt to be appalled at this routine rushing in where angels tiptoe. Virgo is a planner, relying on logical analysis of facts and situations to solve problems. Enthusiasm is not Virgo's long suit. But the two Signs can be supportive and work to the common good, if Virgo can restrain personal squeamishness toward Arien over-reaction; and if Aries can endure unemotional evaluation of enthusiastic ideas. Virgo moodiness acts like swamp water on Aries optimism; after so much of this Aries will probably dash off to look for a more responsive climate in which to promote exciting projects.

Aries is idealistic. Virgo idealism is there, but hidden beneath a thick hedge of critical objections and practical observations. Aries will search for a place where idealism can flourish without having to battle its way through a jungle of ifs, whys and wherefores. Virgo practicality can be a heavy hand upon the Aries spirit.

Yet Virgo loves to serve others, and within limits will labor loyally to place strong bracings under the adventuresome Aries undertakings. Aries generosity also desires to help others. There is a wide divergence in concepts here, however. The Virgoan desire to help others usually begins with a critical countdown which will show the other person how to operate more efficiently, establish productive routines, and to run a tight ship. Worthwhile goals, of course—but Aries doesn't

26

function too cheerfully under the conditions imposed by Virgo. And Virgo logic and prudence can be thrown into a panic by Aries impulsiveness.

The truth is, both Virgo and Aries are *Peanut's Lucy*: both are quick to see how the *other* person should implement improvements. And both are inclined to communicate their findings to the lucky (?) person to whom they are being of service. This inspires a pleasant glow of self-satisfaction when their attentions are turned to a mutual subject, or even on separate but unrelated subjects. The rub comes when they turn these talents on each other. For neither Aries nor Virgo is receptive to personal criticism. Many a friendship has cooled because those who have accepted untold amounts of helpful advice from one of these Signs (and profited from much of it) have *presumed* to return the favor, no matter how tactfully. A romance usually has a short life under these conditions.

On bad days this relationship can seem to sprout thistles are not easily controlled. Aries is an ardent Sign responds to Virgo nit-picking. And once sprouted, thistles are not easily controlled. Aries ia an ardent Sign while Virgo is reticent and reserved. Aries aggressiveness in sex may startle Virgo, but at the same time fascinate. Virgo, whose conservative facade seldom reveals the depths of the personality, can be equally ardent, providing the mate can get past the armor with which Virgo protects the innermost self. And, in truth, it may take the dynamic Aries approach to activate Virgo responsiveness. If Aries idealism works overtime to unite with Virgo spirituality, this can result in a beautiful relationship based on physical rapport and mutual respect.

As parents they function well together. Their children will probably grow up to be capable, well-rounded, self-reliant individuals equipped to deal with whatever situations confront them. As babies they may miss being cuddled, but they will be treated as people rather than as playthings, and self-confidence can be a fulfilling quality for a child to have.

The relationship would probably be most rewarding as a brief and passionate affair. But if the Aries-Virgo pair want to try for permanence, there is a potential that would make success worth every minute of their efforts.

Aries-Libra

The attraction of opposites works to weld a bond between these Suns that can be virtually unbreakable. Opposing Sun Sign traits that seem more divisive than attractive compliment and fill out qualities that are lacking in the individuals. By blending their strengths and weaknesses, opposing Signs become a balanced whole.

Indecisive Librans are attracted in spite of themselves to self-confident Ariens who make up their minds quickly and let the sparks sting where they may. Aries devil-may-care attitudes and impulsive actions may startle the gentle Libran, but at the same time inspire admiration for the sureness with which Aries moves ahead once a goal has been set.

Librans are as ambitious as Aries behind the genteel facades which often suggest they are somewhat above the hurly-burly of active efforts at personal advancement. Libran tastes border on the luxurious, and being strongly self-oriented, they usually assume that if they want something strongly enough the funds will be forthcoming to acquire it. Practically speaking, this sometimes leaves them short on pocket money—an embarrassing situation for Librans. They will appreciate Aries resourcefulness in such circumstances.

Aries goes after what is desired without looking to right or left, so caught up in an impressive take-off that consequences are seldom considered. Libra can stand to one side, saying neither yes nor no. If Aries pulls it off, Libra will cheerfully claim a share of the benefits; if Aries crash lands, Libra will ignore the whole affair.

Libran inability to take a stand, to make decisions, can drive Aries to a frenzy. Aries doesn't want to listen to endless pros and cons that, with Libra, can sometimes continue so long the situation is inoperative before a decision is reached. Aries knows better than most the meaning of "strike while the iron is hot." Aries enthusiasm frightens Libra, who has a basic need to put every situation in perfect balance. Libra's litany of reasonable objections will direct a stream of cool logic over Aries projects and cautiously counter Aries over-optimism, but will never show open opposition. This reluctance to become involved in outright conflict over issues allows Aries freedom to maneuver within this potentially limiting relationship.

Where Aries sees any difference of opinion as a challenge, and rather enjoys the conflict, Libra cannot endure confrontation, preferring to insinuate objections (and for every positive there *must* be a negative) in quiet ways. Aries brainstorms; Libra holds briefing sessions. Each can learn from the other's methods. Aries *needs* a restraining influence when preparing to launch dazzling enterprises. Libra *needs* Aries ebullience to build a fire under equivocating judgments. Spontaneous fire steadies down with a controlled oxygen supply.

These Suns work well together by balancing out on broad, basic areas. The irritations which afflict this union will be of the elbow-rubbing caliber. Quick-tempered Aries will become argumentative under Libran pressure to explain every move. Libra loves to be consulted; not from a desire to take over—Libra doesn't really want that much responsibility—but to keep aware of everything that is going on that affects the partnership.

Aries only wants to be first. In order to get ahead of the crowd Aries is willing to sacrifice time-consuming subtleties in relationships. Libra, needing to be first in relationships, applies gentle pressure until the Aries temper explodes, then quickly backs away to put space between them, thereby minimizing the conflict.

But it'a hard to move quickly enough to escape the falling embers when Aries temper flares. Aries in trouble lashes out, blaming the closest person for whatever has caused the outburst. Libra cannot—will not—accept criticism, and must rationalize and counteract the accusations down to the most minor detail. And the cycle repeats itself.

But Aries and Libra communicate beautifully in the bedroom. Libra is an ardent Sign, and Aries has a lusty approach to sex, and on the physical level these two will resolve their differences. Neither is emotionally oriented toward love; Libra, who is likely to have rather exaggerated romantic ideals of what a mate should be, accepts a very earthy substitute when fired by the Aries provocative approach. And Aries idealism is inspired by the romantic charm of Libra while the physical side of the relationship is being satisfied.

Both Aries and Libra lean somewhat to the double standard in marital matters. Libra finds marriage a natural state, but appreciates beauty and can be led down the garden path by a very gentle tug. The marriage relationship is never threatened by this delight in romantic encounters along the by-paths of life. Libra will not make too much of Aries flirtatiousness in public so long as it is not carried too far—balance is *all* in Libran relationships, and fair is fair. Aries, for whom almost any encounter with the opposite sex contains an element of flirtation, accepts the Libran equivalent as part of the natural order of things. The rapport they achieve in their intimate relationship is usually too strong to be threatened by momentary indiscretions.

As with other areas of their lives, they balance beautifully in the rearing of their children, who seem to receive the best qualities of each Sign and blend them to full potential. Agreeing on basic concepts and goals for their youngsters, minor problems are kept in check by Libran ability to arbitrate all views to a point of common agreement. Ariens want their children to achieve; Librans want children they can present to the world with pride. The children usually live up to both these expectations.

And each Sign has the quality of letting bygones be bygones. Aries may make rash statements during heated arguments but does not cherish hurts. Libra is too forgiving, enjoying the balancing aspect implicit in the sinner-forgiver relationship (no matter which position Libra is holding).

If this gets past the initial stages the opposing traits will gradually blend to a complimentary balance which brings out the best in both Signs: Libran dedication to the marriage supplying the eternal flame which lies at the heart of the Aries heat wave of enthusiasm and optimism.

Aries-Scorpio

The intensity of this Sun combination will suggest a tropical atmosphere: Fire is the mover, Water the stable element, and the result is a heavy, moisture-laden heat which can be oppressive but magnetic. Sex is the magnet. This is an aspect which attracts and holds incompatible elements together by overpowering force, and may produce the kind of fated love of which legends are made.

The original attractions will be strengthened as much by the negative as by the positive traits of each Sign. Both are forceful Signs; both tend to have trouble blending the positive-negative forces within themselves to a satisfying whole. Scorpio, especially, produces many individuals who never manage to blend these two opposite sides of the personality completely. Thus the prototype Scorpio comes in two distinct models: the sublime and the demonic. Aries too must work hard to combine the two opposing sides of the personality, but will be more likely to fluctuate between two natures—a devil one week, an angel the next.

The two Signs, brought together by compelling sexual attraction, often blend their positive-negative qualities to a strong and splendid union; Scorpio sexuality uplifted by Aries idealism; Aries sexuality uplifted and regenerated through Scorpio devotion.

But there are so many qualities which seem to work at cross purposes here! The negative traits which aren't duplicated work hand-in-glove to emphasize weaknesses. These strong-willed Signs are almost impossible to sway once the course is set. They may be headed in the same direction toward the same goal, but their paths do not—cannot—coincide. The only point of contact is the steam generated through their elemental qualities of Fire and Water, as the equatorial atmosphere is laden with humidity because of the interaction of sun and river.

Ambition is the bridge which strengthens the physical relationship, providing channels for communication and allowing them to function in some sort of harmony in outside encounters. Scorpio, a jealous Sign, does not enjoy sharing the partner with others, even in casual social meetings. Aries is independent all the way. Not being jealous nor overly empathetic, Aries often does not realize the pressures which jealousy places on the Scorpio mate at parties where an element of flirtation is often present. For Aries, flirtation is usually an automatic amenity; the Ram may not even be conscious of this trait which is so much a part of Arien character. Scorpio tends to be almost antisocial in private life.

Yet it is virtually impossible for Aries and Scorpio to be together with activating the ambition present in both natures. And ambitions are usually realized by contacts with those who can help in the long climb up the success ladder. Thus, motivated by desire to succeed, Scorpio may be drawn into participation in social situations; and Aries may learn to control impulsive flirtations in deference to Scorpio jealousy.

This pattern of getting positive results through negative motivations seems to explain the power of the relationship to endure. Scorpio moodiness and secretiveness are the antithesis of outgoing Aries attitudes. Scorpio operates best in shadows and hidden places; Aries, like a jet, functions to best advantage when marking a trail across a clear sky. Yet somehow shadow and light unite here and co-exist, locked in a battle of opposing strengths where neither can dominate but neither will set the other free.

This combination suggests the clandestine affair which holds two people in a love-slave relationship rather than a creative marriage. Children of such a union would probably suffer severe pressures, torn between two forceful parents absorbed in their own conflicts. There would be danger that the Scorpio parent, jealous and possessive, would transfer intense personal involvement from the mate to the children. The Aries partner, needing more freedom of movement in order to survive, might encourage this transfer. It would not be an easy home for children to grow up in.

The highly evolved Scorpio and a highly idealistic Aries could build a marriage of enduring power. In less ideal circumstances this might prove to be a battle to the death between Scorpion and Ram.

Aries-Sagittarius

From beginning to end this Sun relationship will have the excitement of a carnival, probably starting with a teen-age marriage and lasting through to the Golden Wedding celebration. The supreme self-confidence of this pair will keep them zooming above the crowd—an arrow towing a striped balloon—while acquaintances and relatives watch from below with admiration and envy.

Caution is a word neither recognizes; there is a strong gambling instinct in both Signs which combines to produce recklessness. With Aries to lead the way Sagittarius is game to follow anywhere. Fortunately, Jupiterian luck seems to protect them from the consequences of risks which for most people would set red lights flashing and sirens screaming.

But red lights—which signal STOP for most of us— seem to function as GO signs for these two. Sagittarius cannot bypass a challenge (this is the original "dare me" kid). The Arien sense of competition generates a desire to be first in everything. Together they home in on goals like runaway fire engines, laughing every minute.

There is little of the malicious about these Signs, alone or together. What turns them on is Fire energy and optimism that doesn't end. As ruler of Sagittarius, Jupiter's expansive qualities infuse the Archer personality and feed on Aries optimism. The best way—practically the only way—for others to deal with them is to get out of the way as they whiz past.

Often this excess of energy and initiative will be syphoned off in activity for the sake of action. Ariens are prone to scatter their efforts; Sagittarians scatter enthusiasm. The result can be many projects which die untimely deaths through pushing the starter button too soon, or overshooting the mark. But for Aries and Sagittarius this is all in a days work. They walk away from a crash landing, brushing the dust from their jeans, too deep in plans for their next take-off to feel for broken bones.

Surprisingly often these impetuous launchings hit the target dead center. Jupiter is a veritable horn of plenty for Sagittarians; and Aries never gives up on new ideas. Here Aries ambition burns white hot and simply overpowers the Archer's what-the-hell attitude. There is often a longing for status in Aries which is more native to the Capricorn Goat than to the Ram. Sagittarius, while decrying the quest for status, enjoys the high living that accompanies same. Certainly the Archer isn't about to upset the applecart when Aries is homing in on a jackpot. In down periods, when failure dims the power source for a time, Sagittarius may give in to black depression that eclipses the sun for a few days, but will soon be drawn back into the race by Aries initiative.

Both Signs are industrious. The main problem in this relationship will be lack of persistence for specific projects. Impatience plays a major role in failures. Both Aries and Sagittarius demand instant results, and they don't mean thirty seconds later.

They are remarkably well suited to each other physically. They share a fun-and-games attitude toward sex that gives each the feeling of freedom they need in even the most satisfying relationship. Still, tolerance stretches only so far. Sagittarius can carry the buddy-buddy roll-in-the-hay approach too far for Aries idealism to accept sometimes. Aries is adept at drawing a fine line between teasing and open invitation, but if this goes too far, Sagittarius may make displeasure known.

Hot tempered, both, it is not usual for these two to talk out their differences. Sagittarian bluntness will be the abrasive against which Arien argumentativeness sparks in a running reaction, releasing in relatively harmless flareups the energy which burns in both. When there is major discord between the two the inevitable eruptions of anger can resemble twin volcanos blowing their tops. These two can survive monumental battles that would send others to the divorce courts. A basic honesty allows them to accept faults in each other which they recognize in themselves. They are not resentful; once the battle is done, it's over.

These are fun parents. As soon as the kids learn to hang on they'll be encouraged to climb on the band-wagon and come along for the ride. They are not hoverers, yet they are not indulgent either. Aries will probably apply more steady discipline, but Sagittarius will allow children to suffer the consequences of their actions no matter how painful. Sagittarius learns by experience and feels that tossing the children into the lake is the best way to teach them to swim. Aries takes the executive approach, delegating jobs and demanding performance according to ability. They seldom get in each other's way in the matter of child rearing.

Once each has learned to accommodate the other's profile they tend to fit together well. Aries provides the light, Sagittarius the heat, for this relationship. As it matures, Aries tends to settle down, absorbing some of the Sagittarian glow; while Sagittarius gains something from Aries direction. The Arien tendency to over-react benefits from the philosophical attitude which Sagittarius uses to recover from misfortune.

In the end, what begins as one more adventure may become, almost without these Suns realizing it, a union welded together by physical compatibility which is synonymous with the steady flame of enduring love.

Aries-Capricorn

Suns in square have many obstacles to overcome in establishing sustained relationships with one another; most of these relationships do not endure, once the initial attraction fades. But Aries and Capricorn are doers, and they recognize in each other the ambition that is a prime force in both their makeups. Here negative traits can reinforce each other to produce strength. Aries lacks staying power and gains from Capricorn persistence; Capricorn materialism is softened by Aries idealism. Both travel toward lofty goals: status at the summit.

Thus we see the unlikely picture of the Aries fire arrow stinging the glacier to move a little faster and take a new direction; to warm a little and soften its stern profile. The Saturnian Sun accepts this nagging from Aries more readily than from most Signs. Without this prodding, Capricorn tends to set course and move implacably forward, as a glacier moves.

Aries precipitates from take-off to target, following a trajectory that flys over obstacles. Both Aries and Capricorn realize that the shortest distance between two points is indeed a straight line. Each is determined to establish a visible silhouette against the skyline. Desire for a place at the top is basic motivation for either of these Signs, and there is an interacting element of mutual admiration for this forward movement.

Even their shared minus quality—lack of empathy—reinforces here: it is virtually impossible for either Aries or Capricorn to get inside another's skin. Capricorns are too intent on establishing their own rights and privileges; Ariens, always impatient, measure others' motives against their own and judge accordingly. This makes it easy for them to ignore obstacles. The net effect furthers a "it's my way or the wrong way" double standard. Aries and Capricorn understand each other on this.

A broad-based foundation of understanding holds these two together more firmly than most squared-Sun combinations. Self-oriented, self-willed—when these two take stands against each other the opposition can be overwhelming. The most basic source of conflict will probably be over who will give the orders. Neither of these Signs is strong on give and take. Each has built-in executive ability and functions well in the role of General. The good feeling that comes from moving chess men around the board to achieve an advantageous position adds to Cardinal Sign conviction in both that since it's so right for the mover it has to be right for the ones being moved. Without empathetic rapport, they carry out their plans without malicious intent, unaware of frustrating consequences for others.

In an intimate relationship involving Aries and Capricorn, the result can be a long-drawn battle to achieve supremacy, with one dominating one situation, the other the next. This emotional tug of war would exhaust most people, but Aries and Capricorn have great vitality and, in fact, may enjoy the competitive atmosphere even in marriage.

There is strong physical attraction between these two Suns. Capricorn, usually inhibited in casual relationships, has a deep-down sex drive that responds to Aries earthiness; can be aroused by the fiery flirtatiousness of Aries to break through the glacial inhibitions which protect a very sensitive inner self which longs for interaction with others. At the same time, Capricorn dignity may tone down the Aries tendency to pull out all stops if given the slightest excuse. It is in this one area that they may approach diplomacy and tact with each other, not wishing to endanger a union that is physically exhilerating.

Even so, Aries will find the sometimes brooding self-centeredness of Capricorn a burden. The Saturn rulership of Capricorn comes on strong in the area of personal interaction: Saturn demands performance before reward, and rewards according to performance, and judges by stern Saturnian standards. Capricorn is apt to show love by slaving long hours to provide luxuries the fast-moving Aries accepts in passing, then *demands* love and respect and admiration in return. Aries will despise Capricornian insistence on brooding over past hurts and demanding recognition for favors Aries didn't want in the first place. Aries seldom looks back, being more interested in new experiences than in pressing the tongue in the hole where the tooth was pulled to see if it's still hurting. There is a part of Capricorn that enjoys self-pity.

While leery of Aries impetuosity, Capricorn allows leeway in this partner's behavior that would not be acceptable from most other Signs. Capricorns are akin to Virgos in awareness of the public image and in demanding meticulous observance of conventions. Status comes at too high a price to risk getting on the wrong side of public opinion. Ariens are equally aware of the importance of status and public opinion, but may be tempted to indulge in clandestine flings now and then if they think the public is looking the other way.

Capricorn's rocky facade is not chosen voluntarily.

The Goat longs for affectionate rapport with others. While suffering from the unconventional behavior of the Aries partner, Capricorn will find it difficult to risk upsetting the basically rewarding relationship. And while the shadow of saturnine reserve hangs heavy over the Arien spirit at times, the Ram will think twice before deserting the support offered by this mountain of strength.

Their children will profit from the cross currents their parents create. However stern, the Capricorn parent will be a Gibraltar in times of trouble; a source of strength without question. And Aries will offer excitement and adventure to liven the inhibiting atmosphere. Children of Earth and Water Signs will find security through Capricorn; Fire and Air children will relate to Aries. And all will profit.

If these two endure the pressures of opposing wills during the early years of the union, the later ones will be tremendously rewarding. Aries gains steadiness with maturity without sacrificing the adventurous, enthusiastic spirit that adds color to the partnership. In the later years Capricorns usually come into their own. Their conservatism is supported by material evidence to show their chosen route through life was indeed the correct way—whatever anyone else has said. As self-confidence grows to balance sensitive inner doubts, the Capricorn personality loosens up. Aries Fire burns steadily from the shelter of the Capricorn mountain, proclaiming status achieved and shored up by successful ventures which could not have gotten off the ground without Capricorn's strength to back them up.

Aries-Aquarius

At first encounter this is a potent combination of idealism and intellectual curiosity. Aquarius will be drawn by the enthusiasm with which the Aries personality approaches a new relationship, and will react with delight as Aries, always aware of the exciting possibilities of a new liason, makes the opening advances almost automatically.

Aries will be attracted by Aquarian's enthusiastic reception to a new relationship, and will appreciate the indiscriminate curiosity with which the Aquarian considers what Aries proposes, and the lack of concern with details which many other Signs impose on Arien ideas.

There will be a strong physical attraction which Aries will find satisfying and the Aquarian will be happy to explore as Aries leads the way. Aries flirtatiousness supported by idealism will excite in the Aquarian partner an answering response, which will be all the more challenging to Aries because of the Aquarian's apparent detachment. (Later, however, Aries may find that the mating dance is not the come-on but the game itself as far as Aquarius is concerned, and the intriguing "other world," which promises unknown enchantments is, in reality, reserved for the Aquarian alone. Aquarius, willing to allow the Aries fire freedom to burn at white heat on its own ground, will not chance a conflagration in the Aquarian domain.)

From the beginning the attractions will be based as much on ideas and convictions as on physical stimulation. Aquarius will respond eagerly to the innovative Arien ideas; will be impressed that the Ram has initiative to pull these ideas into focus and launch projects in a spectacular manner. Aquarius is not always able to put futuristic concepts into a form that fits contemporary needs.

Aries will appreciate the keenness of the Aquarian partner's understanding of the possibilities of proposed projects. Aries will accept Aquarian suggestions right up to the kickoff, fully expecting the Aquarian to be at the goal posts to complete the touchdown. This may or may not happen. Aquarius is as easily intrigued by the passing stranger as by the intimate companion; more easily, perhaps, as the partner becomes familiar.

In any event, the beautiful spontaneity of the first encounter may fizzle and die as this pair moves into a relationship demanding closer interaction. The tempting fire of Aries magnetism may, in intimacy, rise to a roaring flame from which Aquarius draws back in alarm. Experimentation is one thing; lustiness is another matter. Aries directness in sexual matters may affront the Aquarian. The Arien character is always oriented toward fulfillment and self-satisfaction. There is no holding back. Aquarians always reserve part of themselves no matter how deeply they are involved with others. For Aries, love and sex are one; for Aquarius, sex is a very real part of love, but the exciting involvement also includes intellect, and intellect gets lost in the shuffle when sex and Aries come together.

Once the initial enchantment begins to wear thin the small differences will rub holes in Aries-Aquarius congeniality, and the irritability shared by both Signs will flare. Aquarius, while maintaining tolerance of Arien attitudes, may drift to other relationships now and then to escape the heat of Aries fire. Aries, lacking in understanding of the inner workings of others, is not known for tolerance. When things go wrong the Aries temper explodes all over the landscape, and the partner knows *exactly* where the blame is being placed. It won't be of much help here that once Aries temper cools, the angry accusations will be fogotten because Aquarius probably won't be around to hear the apologies. And Aries, never one to hold a grudge, will be surprised to find that Aquarian memory is photographic. Aquarius cannot abide criticism and will simply withdraw from the situation which calls forth critical comments.

Both these Suns are aggressively independent. Aries, of course, is aggressive in almost everything; for Aquarius, independence is the avenue through which aggressive qualities are channeled. Each will work with another as long as the relationship challenges and the situation stimulates. Neither is adept at working to preserve a partnership that shows signs of disintegration. Aries, under these circumstances, is prone to nag and blame. Aquarius will dig in and resist.

Both Signs make loving parents however. It is here the Aries idealism shines at its best. Aquarius will instill strong ethical concepts in the children. Both will enjoy their youngsters as individuals.

Physical closeness, which for many Suns will be the ingredient that holds the partners together, is not powerful enough here to work its magic. Their mutual concern and love for the family may fill this purpose instead. With Aquarius and Aries it would be possible to maintain a marriage for the sake of the children with a mutual understanding that each would be free to find fulfillment on their own.

It will take strong empathetic emphasis in both individual charts to counteract the abrasive elements that prolonged intimacy brings to the surface when these two live together. If positive interactions between the personal charts are strong enough, the Aries-Aquarius union can be dynamic.

Aries-Pisces

Beginning with Aries, adjacent Signs borrow qualities from preceding Signs, with an underlying continuity of progression around the Zodiac Wheel. But Pisces, being the last Sign, brings an end to the cycle. In Aries a new cycle begins—Aries is always a beginning point. Thus bridges existing between Aries and Pisces are more tenuous than those of other combinations.

This does not mean there is no attraction between the two; only that channels for interaction are not obvious. The Aries personality is aggressive, eager to move into action, supremely self-confident. The Pisces character is basically withdrawn, unsure, often without vitality to move into action even when there is desire for action. Thus, in a sense, the two traits compliment each other in close relationships. Perhaps the Aries fire longs for the cooling effect of water; perhaps the Pisces water yearns for warmth. Properly balanced, the steam generated whenever these two Signs meet can fuel a dynamic union.

The Aries desire to dominate—to be first, to give directions—can be attractive to Pisces who, often finds it almost impossible to reach conclusions. Nor does the Aries urge to be the center of activity unduly upset Pisces, who fluctuates between needing to be around others, and needing to be alone to restore vitality drained by intense emotional reactions to others.

But this action-reaction pattern can also become the shoals upon which the relationship founders. Aries responses are expressed in action: attracted, the Ram makes immediate, positive moves that do not leave feelings in doubt. Pisces too moves with purpose when attracted to another, but more subtly; coming near the person desired—then moving away, then reappearing—

until they are finally united.

Aries will soon tire of this elusive game, for Aries purpose is to take the prize as rapidly as possible. But Pisces may get so much pleasure from this emotional hide-and-seek that the actual surrender or capture becomes an anti-climax.

Empathy is elemental with Pisces, who doesn't always realize that not everyone possesses this ability to see inside another personality at will. Aries bluntness in intimate moments seems willful callousness to Pisces. And Aries is uncomfortable when Pisces intuition slips behind the blustery activity to the center core of Aries character.

Increasingly, this results in explosive outbursts from Aries, with Pisces struggling to appease the angry Ram by reacting to statements and accusations which, as often as not, are forgotten as soon as they are uttered. Chances are good that Aries will develop a habit of spouting off on the slightest excuse, for it won't take long for the Ram to realize that Pisces assumes guilt almost automatically when it is tailormade to fit.

These outbursts are corrosive to the Pisces temperament. Pisces will go to any lengths to avoid confrontation. Pisces feels discord and reacts constantly to set matters right by intuitive changes, trying not to disturb surface interaction. Since Aries meets even the most trivial problems head on, the Ram may become contemptuous of what is seen as Piscean refusal to act on problems.

Aries conquers moodiness by action; Pisces needs solitude to restore inner equilibrium. Aries has little sympathy for the shifting moods of Pisces. Aries acts upon the environment; Pisces reflects the surrounding scene. When the relationship is not in harmony, however calm it may appear to be, Pisces absorbs the unhappy vibrations; may become ill from frictions that barely brush Aries awareness.

The ingredients that hold the relationship together will be idealism and generosity. And large doses may be required to salve the psychological wounds these two can inflict on each other unknowingly. As Pisces persistently evades confrontation, Aries may deliberately provoke a reaction by apparently innocent comments and questions, until Pisces rises to the bait.

Aries may not realize there is risk of succeeding too well. The Pisces personality is at least tinged with martyrdom and will be accepting long after most other Signs would have fled. But once pushed to extremity, Pisces fights back with ferocity, and the surprised Aries may find it necessary to pull back from this unexpected ability of Pisces to go into action when escape is impossible.

The result may be a stronger relationship balanced by a growing respect on the part of Aries, and Pisces intuitive understanding that this is taking place. Since Aries seldom broods, and Pisces forgives almost too easily, it is possible for them to pick up the relationship with a new set of ground rules.

In this relationship as in all others, Pisces reflects the qualities presented by the partner. Once Aries learns to respect Pisces sensitivity, the Fish responds idealistically to the changed situation. The main bridge to togetherness must be through shared idealism. Both Aries and Pisces will support their principles to the last ditch— Aries by leading a crusade; Pisces by a kind of nonviolent opposition. Convinced that the other is action from conviction, either will grant generous leeway in working out difficulties.

Children of the Aries-Pisces unions will probably combine the best of the traits of the parents. Pisces compassion and Aries idealism may produce children of great sensitivity, with initiative to take action on the concepts which they support. The Aries parent will encourage offspring to try their own wings; Pisces will dust off their crumpled feathers when they fail. Both will urge them to keep trying.

Still, with Pisces, a little aggression goes a long way (a heat wave soon shrivels a rainbow); and Aries grows restive very quickly when exposed to Pisces sensitivity for any length of time (fire is uncomfortable with a rainbow for a halo). Except in very rare cases, chances are better for a short-term relationship than for a long-term alliance, unless the situation allows for plenty of solo time away from each other.

TAURUS

TAURUS-ARIES (Page 12)

A firecracker trying to stimulate an alabaster statue.
And succeeding too well.

Taurus-Taurus

This is the stuff of which Golden Weddings are made:
Venus ruling here through the persistent Taurus Sun
makes for eternal love. Taureans build empires patiently, enduringly, to house items of beauty and value by
which they measure their security. Possessive, yes.
Acquisitive, yes. But with love—the binding ingredient
that softens these qualities to a benevolent self-interest
in both partners.

They may have to wait to experience this blissful
union for second time around. Many Taureans have to
fight their way through an unsuccessful early marriage
to learn the hard lesson of give-and-take. Since both
men and women of this Sign tend to be charmingly
inflexible in their early years, they find it extremely

difficult to manage the compromises demanded from marriage. Taurus resists minor concessions with the same implacable determination shown in facing portentious issues. Often drawn into early marriages through the earthy sensual qualities in their characters, they find it almost impossible to accept oposition to their points of view.

But Taureans hate arguments with the same inflexible attitude. As they grow past the early adult years—and having learned from bitter experience that there are indeed two sides to every story—they once more find themselves drawn to permanent relationships. Taureans are not given to temporary structures; they do not feel comfortable without substantial homes of their own. For Taurus the home is indeed the castle; it is needed to provide inner security. For the same reasons, the Taurean love nature is not long satisfied without a permanent mate.

The Sun Sign qualities most basic to Taureans are those which imply permanence, status, financial security. Involved in long-range programs for security, most Taurus couples will not often stub their toes on hidden obstacles. The one area where these two might experience problems is through taking opposing views on an important project, perhaps one involving money. If one Taurus digging in for a stand is stubbornness personified, two Taureans taking a stand is stubbornness squared. It isn't likely to happen, especially if one or both has gone down for the count in a previous marriage because of inflexibility. But if it *should* happen! Stories of married couples who refuse to speak to each other for years of an otherwise working marriage probably relate to Taureans.

This Sun combination may choose to have few children—or none at all. Taureans must first provide for themselves, and well; only then do they enlarge the personal circle to care for loved ones generously. Thus they may wait too long to consider parenthood. Taurus individuals settle into routine more easily than most, and they do not look forward to the changes which babies inflict upon the home situation.

Still, these are loving parents when they do have children, and care for them with benevolent responsibility. Air and Fire Signs may feel a heavy burden living with Taurus parents, but there will always be love to hold the family together, even during trying situations which plague these relationships.

A solid, beautiful union that simply goes on forever.

Taurus-Gemini

Taurus-Gemini seems an unlikely combination: mutable Air and fixed Earth can't even whip up a successful dust storm together. At best Gemini will be an irritant to Taurus, tossing dust in his eyes and confusing him with constant motion. Gemini efforts to influence the stolid Taurus will resemble a firefly attacking Ferdinand the Bull.

The attraction here is a longing on the part of each to find a quality they sense lacking in their own personalities: Gemini longing for roots, and Taurus yearning to be a butterfly. Whether or not, on a practical level, they can indeed draw on these qualities in each other is debatable. The Gemini need for movement to satisfy the curiosity is so basic that roots made of cobwebs would chafe at times. And Taurean need for a solid base would induce vertigo at the mere thought of flying. Still, the impossible dream is the attracting force. Individual planet placements strongly modifying the basic traits of these two Signs would have to be in effect to give much of a chance for a positive relationship.

Sincerity of purpose will help them make an honest try. But the opposing traits are so many and so well defined that it seems fruitless for these two to try to come together in a permanent relationship. The keyword for Taurus is *endurance*; for Gemini, *versatility*. Taurus needs to possess and make permanent; Gemini needs to move and think. How does one make thought and movement concrete without destroying them? A cement block cannot be flexible. Sincerity will find it hard going to blend these qualities.

An appreciation for beauty may bring these two together in the first place; sociability may hold them for an evening. Attempts to build a lasting relationship may be a series of frustrations. Slow-thinking Taurus may be fascinated by the wit and sparkle of Gemini chatter—but how does communication take place? Gemini talks better than listening, and Taurus listens better than talking—and briefly this will pass for communication. But Taurus must develop ideas methodically from concept to finished product. Gemini is not interested in broad or in-depth concepts. Gemini delights in lots of intriguing bits and pieces of information.

Gemini is creative; Taurus is practical. Taurus borrows ideas from others and develops them to fruition. It is not that these two cannot agree on a good idea. But before Taurus can find the shovel to begin the spade work, Gemini is bombarding the Bull with spin-offs from the original thought. The result is either confusion for Taurus or boredom for Gemini. You can't hitch a butterfly to a plow any more easily than you can send a telegram by pony express.

Change is a way of life for Geminis: they move from job to job; from house to house; from town to town; from school to school almost on whim. Taurus makes thorough plans, and then moves patiently to bring these plans to reality. In trying to establish a home together they would have little more than their appreciation for artistic beauty as a common denominator. And this love of beauty, like almost every other trait, will be expressed in conflicting ways.

Gemini's appreciation for beauty is abstract: Tel Star circling the earth and admiring its awesome majesty from the depths of space. Taurus' love of beauty expresses in a desire to accumulate attractive and valuable surroundings which are permanent. Taureans build houses of beauty for themselves in the most literal sense of the word. Geminis make any corner in which they light into attractive homes of the moment.

While Taurus is willing to wait to acquire the desired treasures—doesn't substitute something of lesser value for quick possession—Gemini is prone to take whatever can be found when the mood strikes.

Gemini nervous energy is used to maintain the level of constant activity, and the Twin works well against deadlines. Taurus can't be pushed. It will almost take an atomic explosion to hurry Taurus through the morning shower and toothbrush routine. Taurus resists change with stubborn strength. Gemini stimulates change. Taurean efforts to hold surroundings intact once they have been arranged to satisfaction will make Gemini feel like a caged hummingbird. Gemini rearranges furniture at each cleaning; may decide at 2:00 A.M. to wallpaper the entry hall, or start painting the ceiling an hour before dinner. If either Sign tries to accommodate the other's wishes it automatically locks them into intolerable roles. Taurus digs in and refuses to budge; Gemini may have a nervous breakdown.

The one area where these traits modify and compliment is in their intimate relationship, perhaps because the attractive elements are intensified. Gemini curiosity will keep the Twin trying to stimulate a response from

Taurus; and Taurus acquisitive desire to capture a butterfly may express itself through ardor. But Gemini sexuality has the same quality of detached curiosity as the basic nature; sooner or later Taurus ardor becomes jealousy.

As often happens, children of this combination will probably blend the qualities of the parents without much trouble; it is as if the blending of most Signs must be achieved one step removed from the contact point. In the end these nicely balanced children may end up counseling their parents in the arts of interaction.

Self-confidence and basic good will may keep these two trying to achieve the impossible dream by coordinating the qualities of the two Signs into a rewarding whole. Taurus hates to admit defeat, and both Signs have strong familial loyalties. But marriage is a blending—a union—and the closest this Sun duet is likely to come will be symbolized by a butterfly perched on the shoulder of a marble statue.

Taurus-Cancer

This can be one of the loveliest of Sun combinations for lasting love and happiness in marriage. Even the opposing qualities blend and support each other. The major area of conflict will come through shared negative personality traits, but the pluses so far outnumber the minuses here that, except for potent afflictions in individual charts to planets occupying these areas, it would be difficult to bring permanent disruption to this relationship.

Both Taurus and Cancer have strong roots in the past: conservative Taurus appreciates Cancer's traditional viewpoint in all matters. Material security is vital to both these Signs. Cancer's very real fear of being without resources is allayed by the visible evidence of material success with which Taurus supports emotional security. Their goals are almost identical. They value money, and are agreed that the proper use of it is to supply themselves with attractive possessions that give daily proof of their ability to acquire wealth. They are ambitious. Cancer demands status and Taurus finds it very pleasurable. They are willing to work hard and patiently to build an affluent life. They are both extremely reliable in handling money to get the best from it—for others as well as for themselves—and they are usually able to command excellent incomes with which to provide the life they enjoy.

The home will provide their greatest pleasure. Cancer is the natural Sign of the fourth house of domestic affairs, ruled by the Moon—the Mother. Cancers immerse themselves in the home and family affairs. Their emotional involvement will always be through home and family, whether man or woman. Taurus finds the home the natural nucleus around which to build a storehouse of treasures. Taurus will appreciate Cancer's love of antiques and will enjoy working to restore them, while being pleasantly aware of their value as investments.

Hospitality will be the focal point of this home, and will always include excellent food. The dinner party will rank high on the list of preferred entertainment: Venus rulership gives Taurus appreciation for good food served in attractive surroundings. It also endows charm and graciousness as host. Taurus likes to care for others. Most Cancers are good cooks. They also love good food served invitingly. This hospitality will be offered to close friends and relatives (both Taurus and Cancer have strong feelings for family), and relatives are usually welcomed with loving kindness).

Cancer and Taurus will continue to build and enjoy the rewards of their efforts as long as they live. These two do not have to set an arbitrary retirement age in order to find time to do the things they enjoy. They are both geared to taking their pleasure as they go along. In later years they simply change emphasis, with more time for leisure, and perhaps a shift in career which allows them flexibility of hours but insures adequate income.

Self-reliant Taurus lends strength and support to Cancer to shore up the Moon Child's deficient self-esteem. Cancer moodiness—reflection of the Moon rulership—can play havoc with the ego of the sensitive Cancer partner. The presence of Taurus can be a mighty comfort to Cancer when inner foundations seem to shift with the tides.

Cancer is a worrier, and calm reason (the bright side of Taurus stubbornness) helps anchor Cancer's runaway emotions in times of stress. Cancer over-reacts to problems; Taurus finds practical solutions. While Taurus practicality may irritate the emotional Cancer partner at times, this annoyance is a small price to pay compared to the obvious benefits of having a personal tower of strength on which to lean.

The thorn on the rose in this relationship will be hidden beneath the charming exteriors in personality traits that tend to duplicate each other. Cancer tenacity toward family and domestic affairs can be an awesome problem. Cancer possessiveness can smother when it gets out of hand. The emotional intensity which Cancer turns on home matters, colored by the moodiness which reflects the Moon's phases with such painful accuracy, can be a burden even for broad-shouldered Taurus to handle. Cancer will be hurt by slights that haven't been invented yet; and when hurting, doesn't bring the subject out into the open but retreats into some distant emotional environment which Taurus cannot reach.

The Cancer capacity for self-pity easily spawns a martyr complex which, once developed, is particularly galling to Taurus. The brooding silence of Cancer will be accepted to a certain point; pushed too far, Taurus may startle the mate with a volcanic eruption of temper over some seemingly petty point. Once a stand has been taken, the Bull's stubbornness can go on forever. They may refuse to speak to each other for days; in such an impasse it will probably be Cancer who makes the first move toward reconciliation.

For Cancer is sensitive, but beneath the sensitivity is a hard core of practicality; hurt feelings, weighed against material benefits, will almost always ease. Taurus is practical too, but can be pushed to the place where inflexibility will win out over obvious disadvantages.

Most of the time the intimate relationship between these two is fine—Cancer enjoying being the focus of Taurus ardor; Taurus appreciating the Cancer hovering and mothering. Taurus charm delights in catering to the sentimental Cancer. At times of discord, however, Cancer is apt to withdraw physically as well as emotionally. For Cancer, sex is so interwoven with emotion that there can be no separating the two. Taurus finds it much easier to distinguish between them. The Bull's strong devotion to home and family is translated to ardor for the mate when things run smoothly. But the sex drive is strong in Taurus, and if Cancer withholds bedroom privileges, the Bull may seek out discreet extra-marital partners as a means of gratifying physical appetites.

Cancer's withdrawal into a shell to nurse emotional wounds will entice Taurus to the edge of this sensitive inner personality of Cancer, but the Bull will not risk drowning in the tides of Cancer emotional upheavals.

Children will play a happy part in the marriage, being loved and cared for; supported emotionally, materially, and in all other ways. The strength of the family will be a powerful psychological foundation for these children. These two Suns will note and respond to evidence that their personal problems may be harming the children. Abandoning their solid stands will be hard for both Taurus and Cancer, but once they turn their tenacity to a mutual problem—saving the home—the stubbornness and persistence will work as strongly for them as against them.

Their efforts will be shored up by their basic beliefs in the inviolability of family ties, and from the difficulty of dividing mutual assets. But deep down will be a foundation of steadfast love which binds them more completely than they know, and this will be the deciding factor if this union is in jeopardy.

Taurus-Leo

The Bull who marries a Lion may feel the Leo has a red flag tied to his tail most of the time. These fixed Signs, squaring, will frequently give others the impression they are engaging in a gargantuan duel—a colossus challenging an atomic reactor. What saves the conflict from becoming a battle to the death is the equally impressive power of the physical and spiritual attraction that only those extremely close to them are aware of.

Taurus and Leo are foundational Signs, and the traits that others see are apt to be the qualities of strength: self-confidence, benevolent self-interest, and arrogant sureness of movement; plus presumptive belief in their right to an affluent life. These Suns are not leaners in any sense of the word; they care for others—as lavishly as their resources permit. And both are possessed of Vesuvian tempers that can seem to set the world afire when the eruptions coincide.

Give-and-take in this relationship is virtually non-existent. Any situation will be characterized as all give or all take. The Bull *will not* be pushed around; the Lion *will not* be put down. This is fine, if they are united against an invading army. In marital arguments over who is going to take out the garbage it becomes a question of overkill.

The Lion is a born executive (*naturally* Leo belongs at the top of the administrative chart) and seldom hangs this authoritative attitude in the closet at the end of the day. Giving advice to a Taurus is like pelting a stone wall with marshmallows. And Taurus can refuse to listen forever, once the choice is made. If it's hard to persuade a Taurus, it's impossible to order one to do something. Combined, these tenacious traits can sustain a difficult business campaign against great odds and end in victory; making constructive domestic decisions under such circumstances is like cracking eggs with a jackhammer.

But even this public view of these two Signs, which can overpower those of lesser strengths, seems to be softened by their obvious sincerity. They *do* care for others—they just want to express their caring in their own ways. In their private relationship, this same love and sincerity allows these Suns to channel their powerful love for each other into something resembling a give-and-take experience.

For love is the magnetic force that holds the Taurus-Leo combination together in spite of many solidly opposing character traits. Venus, planet of love, is the ruler of Taurus; and Leo is the natural Sign of the fifth house of love and creativity. For each, love holds a special meaning, and this sets up a mutually receptive flow of love which has force to equal the titanic nature of their conflicts.

For Leo, the vital energy of the Sun rulership is expressed in the love experience, even when the imperial personality insists on dominating the relationship. The attraction and beauty of Venus is expressed in the basic Taurean personality. Yet there is an elemental sexual force in the aggressive Leo, in common with all Fire Signs; and a slight shift of emphasis activates sensuality in the Venus influence in Taurus. Together these Signs reach an ecstatic union of sensuality combined with the essential purity of love that transcends the unyielding confrontations of other levels of their lives.

As long as they remain in the privacy of the home, little can threaten this idealistic union. When they move into social situations problems can arise. Leo cannot resist the pull of the spotlight—and stars attract admirers. Subject to flattery more than most, Leo easily gives in to the temptation to respond to advances. Taurus is one of the most social of the Signs, but is a jealous lover. Any expression of jealousy will only get the Bull more of the same from Leo, who will not abide opposition. And even while demanding privilege in this matter, Leo will be possessive of the Taurus partner. At which point Taurus may turn on the charm for one of the available substitutes nearby. In turn, Leo will turn up the magnetism a few notches. And the cycle repeats itself with increased intensity until it culminates in a spectacular explosion of temper from both sides.

But somehow the love itself seems not to be diminished in the process, although neither Taurus nor Leo is above an occasional casual affair (while demanding the partner be above reproach in such matters). This does not seem to touch the solidity of the basic relationship. Leo claims the right of *lese majeste*, and Taurus may indulge in a liason because an attractive opportunity presents itself, and each will feel free to do so as long as discretion is maintained. Both Leo and Taurus have a strong need to retain an unblemished public image. Leo kingliness must not be sullied; Taurus dignity must not be impaired.

Children of the two will be cared for, provided for, loved to excess, indulged, and love will redeem any minuses engendered by the less constructive forces. Love will be the keyword in the family relationship.

In small ways Taurus and Leo can balance each other's personalities: patient Taurus can sometimes restrain impatient Leo; Leo tendency to indolence can sometimes persuade the hardworking Taurus to slow down. Leo impulsiveness can often be in harness with Taurean refusal to be hurried into decisions. But by and large these Signs will battle and love with equal passion, and through it all preserve a larger-than-life relationship that endures.

Taurus-Virgo

Suns in trine are in harmony, with qualities offering strong foundations to the relationships, and which bear up well under stress from less compatible traits. For Earth trines, practicality will almost play a strong part in settling differences. Emotionalism runs a bad second in marital disputes; seldom does one of these partners act impulsively to the detriment of the union.

Both Taurus and Virgo have a reliable sense of responsibility; when they undertake the marriage it is with the understanding that duties are part of the package as well as pleasures. For Earth Sign people, happiness is often a sense of achievement.

A working relationship for these two is literally that— each partner *working* to bring about a fulfilling interaction.

And these are patient people where long-term goals are concerned. True, Virgo can be testy and nit-picky over the small details of togetherness, but for the long haul Virgo is as willing as Taurus to plan and build and painstakingly put together a solid structure, in relationships as well as in careers.

Virgo and Taurus do not enter relationships lightly, especially the institution of marriage. They are reasonable people who solve the problems of relationships with the same careful logic they use on blueprints—in fact, will see the marriage ceremony as a sort of blueprint to help work out differences. Both have good memories and will remind their mates of promises and agreements, quoted word for word, if matters seem to be veering from balance. This does not mean there is never a flare-up; far from it. Virgo has a quick temper that ignites easily and subsides to sulkiness; Virgo is the partner who can go for three days without speaking if feeling slighted. Taurus, being patient, will take a certain amount of this, but can be pushed too far. Once experienced, Virgo will not easily forget the Taurus temper, which makes Virgo irritability look like a Fourth of July sparkler trying to square off at an erupting volcano.

There will be many abrasions in the daily lives of these two. Nagging will be one of the worst faults the Virgo partner will bring to the relationship. The Bull does not take advice well, especially in the home environment. Taurus has a basic desire for peace and harmony in the home, and wants to enjoy the attractive furnishings carefully gathered for the comfort and pleasure of the family. But Venus rulership not only creates the need for gracious surroundings in the Taurus character, it also endows a sensuous need to *use* these luxuries. Taurus will not tolerate a hospital-neat home environment which does not allow a footstool out of place. Not that Taurus is a slob—the Bull is in fact an orderly person—but one who believes that the comforts of home are acquired for enjoyment, not for display purposes.

The main difficulty between these two may come about if the overly-logical Virgo partner does not respond to Taurus sensuousness. Taurus is romantic; never crude. But there is a strong physical accent in the Taurus character. Taurus enjoys the interludes which set the stage for romance—and then desires the love-making. Virgo's fastidious outlook, carried to excess, becomes rejection to Taurus, who will simply not accept it. Virgo, while not the detached sexual introvert often delineated by astrologers, is nevertheless less dependent on the physical side of love than many Signs. Virgo is inclined to accent a spiritual quality in the love relationship that relegates the physical to a sort of health routine—a necessary part of a cycle required by the body for wholesome functioning. Taurus cannot—*will* not—accept this. And Virgo sharpness can verge on the sarcastic; it must be curtailed during romantic interludes if this relationship is to survive without damage.

Virgo moodiness is legendary, and lucky the marriage partner who can accept it as a part of the Virgo character that must be lived with. Taurus will accept it to a degree, and if the trait is not too obvious, these two will weather these periods without undue stress. But Virgo should curb the temptation to indulge too sharply or too frequently in critical sarcasm. For Taurus, once hurt, holds grudges forever. Taurus forgives, but does not forget. Sooner or later the Bull will demand retribution for these hurts.

Yet even in this vital area of interaction patience and practicality will work a sort of holding magic. Taurus is pesistent in efforts to build; Virgo too has staying power. If these two really love each other—and chances are they do, for each is cautious in choosing a life partner—they will channel this persistence toward a workable solution of problems. For each will be aware of the material advantages that go with the partnership, and each will take time to weigh the assets against the liabilities and attempt to change the disruptive conditions if at all possible.

They function together beautifully as parents, with Virgo providing the intelectual stimulus to help children grow mentally, and Taurus to supply a measure of indulgence to soften the Virgoan detachment. Both will demand standards of behavior that will stand offspring in good stead as they reach adulthood; each will guide their children without keeping them dependent on the family. Taurus has a strong sense of family unity and strives always to preserve the solidarity of this relationship no matter how severe the stress. Virgo will, from the beginning, work to help children reach independence and maturity, and in times of trouble will give concrete guidance for solving problems.

From the start Taurus and Virgo will assume a lasting relationship, and will work harmoniously in most cases to build a partnership that will withstand outside stresses while overcoming internal differences. Almost always they will achieve a happy, fulfilling union.

Taurus-Libra

A powerful attraction exists between these two Suns, much of it generated by the Venus influence from the common ruler. There is a charm about both Taurus and Libra that eases the way for them in most situations. And here, where there's a surface magnetism that has little to support it at deeper levels, the Venusian influence will allow harmonious interaction to a much greater degree than seems possible.

The initial attraction will probably come through mutually interesting social encounters, and will enlarge as a common love of all that is harmonious and gracious is disclosed. Even the minus qualities of these two Signs are of a gentle, insidious nature. There is little violence in this union with the exception of Taurus temper, which is aroused only after long and continued provocation from an outside source.

But minus traits which manifest under the guise of virtues are hard to cope with and hard to identify; and troubles here will come from unwillingness of either Sign to recognize the roots of the conflicts—either personally or in the partner. Too often the minus traits of one reinforce and enlarge the minus traits of the other so easily that the union is in trouble before the possibility reaches the awareness of the partners.

Both of these Suns value public opinion, so much so that they may drift to cutting corners to preserve a facade of status and public esteem which Venus attracts to them. They both value the appearance of success as evinced by possessions and the visible signs of affluence. Dressing well is important to both Taurus and Libra; a home to be proud of is essential. Taurus is willing to work hard to acquire these luxurious accommodations; Libra attracts funds almost at will. And each easily grows accustomed to an affluent life style. It is easy for them to justify quasi-devious methods to maintain this status, although each is basically honest and is so considered by those who know them.

Both Taurus and Libra are *self* oriented, concerned with satisfying their own desires rather than with the rights of others. True, Venusian charm smooths the way for them and allows them to use this self-interest in such a way that victims are often unaware that they are being used. The difficulties arise when they try to use these methods on each other.

Taurus is persistent in getting what is desired—through sweetness if possible; through stubborn resistence if necessary. Libra too tries charm first, and if that is not successful, simply goes ahead with what is planned regardless of objections from others, knowing full well that it is often very hard to do anything about an accomplished fact. Fortunately for the relationship, Libra equivocates as often as not, and Taurus stubborn patience can provide time to achieve desired results. By the same token, Libra succeeds often enough in winning the toss in little things which Taurus does not find important enough to fight about so that the situation achieves some kind of balance. Libra seeks fairness—as long as it doesn't place too much strain on personal comfort. Taurus is reasonable—as long as reason doesn't impose on personal convenience.

One thing going for ths union is a compatible love relationship. Both Libra and Taurus are romantics and respond to the overtures of the partner when they are offered. Both are somewhat selfish in this respect also, finding pleasure in the act of *doing for* the other person rather than in *pleasing* the other person. But in a strange way each understands and accepts this benign ulterior motive in the partner's generosity. It is here the combination of romance and material benefits reaches a most successful culmination.

Taurus sensuality is balanced by the Libran tendency to fantasize in romantic matters (which often makes it hard for the real life partner to live up to the imaginings). Taurus can fill this somewhat exaggerated dream picture of what a lover should be without sacrificing the patina of charm which Libra demands.

So throughout the relationship, the opposing traits which in most Signs would bring serious conflict here seem to be softened by the Venus influence to a balancing action. If Libra is inclined to indolence in maintaining the gracious environment, Taurus has the stamina and tolerance to do a bit more than agreed in keeping the home attractive. If Taurus is inclined to hold grudges, Libra tends to be over-forgiving. And it somehow balances out.

Their children will know love that frequently becomes indulgence, yet Taurus will supply discipline which Libra evades; and Libra will restore harmony when Taurus stubbornness seems to be out of proportion to the occasion. Certainly they will be adept in the social graces, and certainly they will be accepted by others for their pleasing manners. Children of these parents will be welcomed wherever they go.

Most quincunx Sign combinations can as easily fall apart as remain together, but this more than any other will probably hold in a lasting relationship. Libra Air provides the atmosphere in which the hearthfire of the Taurus Sun can burn steadily; and the strength of Taurus provides the foundation to support the eternal flame that symbolizes the Sun in Libra. With Venus blessing the union with love and beauty; and with the Taurean sense of family solidarity and the Libran belief in marriage as the natural state, there is a strong probability that the differences here will be worked out for a loving, lasting union.

Taurus-Scorpio

The compelling forces that operate between Taurus and Scorpio had the magnetism always found between opposing Signs. But there is a depth to the interactions between these Suns that goes beyond polarity. The fixed quality shared by these two results in a union that seems fated to endure whether the relationship represents the depths or the heights of experience. And with Taurus-Scorpio it can be either.

Taurus, suspicious of the emotionalism of Water Signs, nevertheless is held by the intensity of Scorpio response; is challenged by a strength of purpose and intent that equals the Taurean unswerving will. Scorpio is fascinated by the force of character that can stand up to Scorpion power.

Each understands the steady drive of ambition which is a foundation stone in both personalities; each has the stamina to endure the inevitable contest of wills which occurs again and again in the interaction of these Suns. As long as each obeys the mutually accepted rules, they will respect each other's motives, however strongly they may oppose in other ways.

Throughout their lives together they will battle and draw blood, and yet the basic force that brought them together in the first place will endure beyond all reason. Taurus stubbornness can never admit defeat; and Scorpio determination never gives up.

Perhaps they do not really wish to sever this bond, even if a way could be found. A strong sensual quality flows through these Signs and will forge a bond of passion which can overwhelm separate conditions that would vanquish Signs of lesser strengths. The stability of Taurus Earth is like virgin prairie; nourished by the depth and magnitude of the powerful flow of Scorpion Water, it flourishes with the dense fertility of the Amazon Basin. All that exists for good or bad in the jungle of the human psyche can come to life here. It depends on individual charts involved which gains ascendency in this relationship.

There is nothing passive or indifferent in this union: Venus and Pluto influences may combine to produce transcendent love, focused on mankind. They may also manifest as grudging revengeful ill temper that tracks its victims through a lifetime and over half a world to avenge imagined wrongs. Somewhere in between these two extremes will be found the temper of this union.

Taurus patience serves to balance out Scorpio intensity to some degree. Once activated, Scorpio anger is hard to re-channel, and it would take a Taurus to even make the attempt.

Taurean tendency to indulgence can be curbed by Scorpio—at least the temptation to fritter talents away in purely social pursuits. Scorpio, given to solitude and secretiveness, can seduce Taurus away from superficial social activities to a more concentrated personal indulgence.

Both Taurus and Scorpio are jealous Signs; they will understand this trait in each other. Its presence may add to the intensity of the relationship. Scorpio desire to keep the loved one in some secret hideaway is at least understandable to Taurus, although the Bull prefers this secretive togetherness after the opportunity to show off the loved one in a social situation.

Each will work to strengthen the relationship in whatever direction it takes. There is little doubt that this union will be financially productive. Both Taurus and Scorpio respect money. The know how to handle it to best advantage. In fact, this can be a highly successful family business team, with Scorpio working behind the scenes and Taurus working with the public. Scorpio enterprises often have the scope of empire, and Taurus has the strength to supply foundations for the far-reaching projects. A business built by these two will be erected from deep foundations. In day-to-day interaction there will be irritations. Taurus will not be hurried should the world come to an end; and Scorpio tends to be a nagger or to adopt a top sergeant attitude with those close.

But these are practical individuals (even Scorpion emotionalism has a utilitarian quality, employed as often as not where it will achieve ends not to be gained by other methods). Rest assured that neither will casually upset a prosperous applecart. When daily contacts rub too abrasively, Scorpio will retire to the den and sulk, and Taurus will take consolation from a hot fudge sundae until the storm blows over.

Children of these two may sometimes feel they are being ground between the walls of a rocky canyon, but one thing is sure: they will learn early that their parents can be depended on. They may feel they are living in the shadow of giants. They may wish for the chance to iron out their own playground difficulties and differences with their teachers. These are the kinds of parents that will pursue the most minute matter to its very beginning if they feel their children are being put upon. Undoubtedly Scorpio at least will frequently feel this is true.

As with all Signs there is a wide divergence between the highly evolved and those still learning how to function in life. Scorpio is perhaps the strongest example of character with two extremes, ranging from the highly spiritual individual to the sadist at the other extreme. The range of this duality is much narrower in Taurus, and it will depend to a great degree upon the level of evolvement of the Scorpio partner what form this union will finally take. At its highest level it can be one of the most beautiful of all relationships; at its worst, one of the most unfortunate matches.

Taurus-Sagittarius

These Suns do not make an easy combination; much effort and much conflict go into making a Taurus-Sagittarius union work. Often the effort is not successful. There are too many areas of conflict to be overcome —too many traits that are in no way complimentary or supportive.

Yet it is a quincux position, and the influences generated by the aspect promise an attraction that makes it hard to leave and harder to remain in the relationship. This is a "damned if you do—damned if you don't" combination.

Taurus, the immovable, stares in awe at the jovial Sagittarius who shrugs under stress and abandons responsibilities to explore the world in a striped balloon—and who seemingly is showered by the largesse of Jupiter in return; protected by unbelievable good luck. Feet firmly planted in the earth, Taurus enjoys special blessings from the Venus influence which lies buried like priceless alabaster in the Taurean character. Taurus seldom suffers from lack of abundance, but the Bull must work and build to amass treasures the hard way. Sagittarius seems guided by a magician who can turn hailstones into silver and moonbeams into gold. Taurus, earth bound, must wait for love to come along, while Sagittarius can embark on a magic carpet and seek love in exciting, mysterious places.

What Taurus does not often realize is that Sagittarius, the carefree wanderer, secretely craves stability, the foundation and fortress strength that is Taurus' lot. The craving is intermittent, however, manifesting itself between adventures; and it is not in the Sagittarian character to sacrifice the freedom of movement essential to the power to function in order to merge with Taurus in a close relationship.

For a while this may happen, if the initial attraction occurs at a time when Sagittarius is in a period of recuperation between audacious challenges to life. Then, depressed by the black moods that sometimes overtake Sagittarians, the Archer finds the down-to-earth gentleness of Taurus a haven and responds with warmth.

Sagittarius represents the physical and the spiritual in man combined in one form. Taurus, guided by Venus, is attracted to both aspects of the character of Sagittarius; however, the physical sensuality of these Signs will provide the bridge that can unite Earth and Fire in a tolerable combination. Venus is a daintier reflection of Jupiter, the Greater Benefic. Both rulers bestow traits that easily, insidiously, drift into indulgence. Together they expand pleasure in the physical side of the relationship for both Taurus and Sagittarius. The union may flourish, with Taurean strength providing foundations for the footloose Archer, who can bring to the fixed Taurus character some of the excitement and mystery of faraway places.

Taurus can provide the focus for the philosophical meanderings of Sagittarius while absorbing some of the gaiety which allows the Archer to function with great good humor most of the time. Taurus has the self-confidence to allow Sagittarius some leeway in the demands for freedom, feeling instinctively that the Archer will always turn toward home once the locks have been tested. Taurus will endure the light-hearted negligence with which Sagittarius shrugs off promises and commitments—for a while, but is hurt by broken promises, and absorbs this hurt without showing it. Sagittarius, who goes into a splendid rage at the first pinch, often does not realize until too late that Taurus may not stamp and scream when hurt, but does not ever forget.

Cautious all the way, Taurus cringes but stands by to help when Sagittarius takes risks that court disaster. Taurus has learned the hard way that a Sagittarian will never be convinced that fire burns until a hand is seared in the bonfire.

And Taurus, who builds in stone, must build in this relationship with the knowledge that if the going gets tough, Sagittarius may take off with little more than a wave of the hand to explore some fascinating corner of the world Taurus can only dream about. Worst of all, the Bull knows that the Sagittarian will probably find the newly-gained position little more attractive than the one that's left behind.

Children of these parents will love them both, and suffer for it. Taurus love and support will attract loyalty; but the exposure to Sagittarian lack of pretense will allow them to realize that Taurus is also possessive in love. Still, these children will feel the strength of family feeling which Taurus feels, and may be able to help the parents understand each other's point of view.

Although this union may hold together for a while, sooner or later Sagittarius will probably fly away, leaving Taurus standing on the home acres trying to keep the leftover love from showing. Fortunately this combination does not too often reach the point of permanence. It's too painful a relationship for either to seek out. If they decide to try, the responsibility for making it work will weigh heavily on Sagittarius.

Taurus-Capricorn

This is one of the most solidly enduring of the Sign combinations. Taurus and Capricorn support each other as prairie and mountain exist together, trusting and depending on the same durable foundations. There is strength underlying this union of Earth Signs: strong cornerstones allow little room for failure.

Both Taurus and Capricorn are ambitious, and their ambitions are amply furthered by industry and self-reliance. These are two of the hardest working of the Signs—they expect to work hard for the good things they want from life. They build carefully, Taurus planning from ideas which Capricorn has learned from previous experience; each accepting responsibility for a full share and both pacing their energies in much the same way to produce the greatest results from their efforts. Taurus desire for beauty supplements Capricorn desire for status to achieve traditional affluence. Both enjoy possessions which others admire.

These conservative Suns value the tried and true. Perhaps it is because they build patiently, slowly; investing much effort to reach their goals makes them reluctant to change course. Taurus resists change with all the stubbornness of the Taurean nature; Capricorn, once dedicated to an idea, clings to it long after it has outlived its value. But these two build for a lifetime and are content to enjoy the classic attractiveness of their choices from one revolution of the cycle to the next. As often as not they are ahead of the parade.

This is not to say there will never be differences between them. Taurus, romantic and sensual, will suffer from the inhibitions under which most Capricorns must labor in their emotional lives. It is almost impossible for Capricorn to express affection freely. The outside of the Capricorn personality resembles the mountain heights which shelter the Goat, the symbol of this Sign. Ruled by Saturn, planet of restrictions, the Capricorn spirit seems encased in a glacier at times. For Taurus, ruled by Venus, the apparent lack of response from the partner can seem rejection; or, conversely, the bluntness of the Capricorn physical response may seem crude. Taurus finds it difficult to see Capricorn's continuing efforts to "do things" for the partner as the expression of love the Goat cannot otherwise express. And Capricorn, extremely sensitive inside the shell of reserve, will be bitterly hurt that the offering of hard work is not properly appreciated.

Since both are self-oriented Signs, they find it difficult to see through the other person's eyes; there will be many misunderstandings between them. Taurus is inflexible, fixed in ideas and reactions by nature; Capricorn dominates as if by decree, as a mountain dominates the plains. No matter how well the Goat maps the action, nor how many lectures are directed at Taurus, the Bull will follow a chosen course with obdurate will. If the path coincides with the one outlined by Capricorn, fine. But Capricorn persistence will not give up in attempts to direct the partner, and sooner or later the legendary Taurean temper will erupt.

Venus bestows a feeling for the social graces on Taurus; Taureans value and practice the small courtesies which often get lost in the shuffle. Capricorn has all the subtlety of a bulldozer in relationships. Taurus, a sucker for tears, draws back when Capricorn demands affection and appreciation. Capricorn feels the willingness to work hard and patiently is worthy of special recognition, even if the hard work is of little value to the Taurus partner.

Still, in spite of Taurus frustration and Capricorn resentment surfacing at intervals, both are too realistic to toss over a relationship that has so many rewarding aspects going for it. Practicality and loyalty work together here to salve whatever hurts they inflict on each other. Capricorn inner suffering is assuaged by gifts which can be paraded with pride before friends; and Taurus finds it easier to forgive apparent lack of response when satisfied with excellent meals and comforted by immaculate surroundings maintained by the efforts of the partner.

Their children will be reared according to conventional standards handed down from their parents, and will be expected to live up to these standards at all times. For so doing they will be blessed with a life of solid comfort as evidence of love and respect from the parents.

Usually these Signs age well; adjustments come easier with the years. Chances are good that this relationship will endure all the way, supported by financial security as genuine as the Hope Diamond.

Taurus-Aquarius

The Aquarian and Taurean Suns square each other, and this aspect sets the tone for the relationship. The complimentary traits of these two fixed Signs are few; the personalities conflict at almost every turn. The fixed element adds rigidity to the challenges working between their natures.

They can and do admire each other, but find it difficult to understand each other. Virgin prairie and clear skies can be mutually appreciative of the fine qualities each possesses, but when Earth and Air come together they usually produce a dust storm.

It is not that one is right and the other is wrong—it is that the two have completely different viewpoints. Aquarian ideas are fixed on distant points of the universe; Taurean ideas are rooted in solid earth. Where Aquarius shows a flexible persistence in aiming for far-off goals, Taurus often wins objectives by simply outlasting the competition.

Both of these Suns are sincere in their attitudes; there is little deception in either Sign. And they share a love of the artistic—although even here the Aquarian will be drawn to the new while Taurean tastes will favor the classic.

Because both Taurus and Aquarius are attractive, friendly individuals they find each other interesting. But a more intimate relationship between the two may have hard going. Aquarius translates every emotion, every action, every idea to the universal; Taurus reduces every concept, every idea, every emotion to the personal. Aquarius demands freedom to explore the universe, physically and mentally; when Taurus looks up at the stars it is to check on the next day's weather.

Taureans are acquisitive; in close relationships they tend to gather loved ones into very small circles to watch and care for them. Restraining an Aquarian in a small circle is like trying to lasso a comet. In a close relationship the detachment of the Aquarian becomes "indifference" to the Taurean; the closeness of Taurus caring becomes "jealousy" to Aquarius.

Aquarians have a chronic irritability just under the surface of the personality which erupts when things go wrong but rarely gains intensity. Taurus will go along for months, seemingly indifferent to daily irritants, until pushed too far; then accumulated wrath explodes like a volcano. The situation becomes a self-feeding cycle of misunderstanding, with Taurus assuming Aquarian irritability is personal dislike; with Aquarius crowding more and more in imposing on Taurean good nature.

Aquarian idealism is all-encompassing: tolerance approaches discrimination. Taurean prejudices become distasteful from both personal and humanitarian standpoints to the Aquarian. But practical Taurus, seeing how often Aquarius is taken advantage of, sees this tolerance as foolhardy.

Trying to build a home together can be a painful process for them. The life goal of Taurus is to acquire, patiently and ploddingly, possessions that are visual evidence of success. The Aquarian goal is to find an attractive life style (which often means a wide circle of attractive friends and freedom to move around among them). Aquarian tastes are as refined as those of Taurus, but possessions can become a heavy burden, symbolic of responsibilities which are not really desired. Aquarian responsibility is to ideas. Taurus accepts responsibility as evidence of security.

Where Aquarius likes to experiment, Taurus resists change. Aquarius is innovative and enjoys moving on to new experiences and fresh landscapes. Taurus, once a base of operations has been established, is inclined to stay there. Taureans would prefer, if possible, to be buried on their own land; Aquarians want their ashes scattered on the wind.

Both these individuals can be fastidious, but in partnership Taurus may be embarrassed by the Aquarian flare for far-out fashion and daring style. Taurus wants to dress in style also—but in conservative, expensive style.

As with the Aries-Aquarius union, these two will be loving parents, but will find it hard to work together. Aquarian ideas of child raising may be eyebrow raising to Taurus, who places great emphasis on appearance and has much respect for public opinion. Aquarius doesn't care what others think, and will work to instill idealistic values that will aid the children's mental and spiritual growth. Taurus emphasis will be on traditional values of thrift, hard work and responsibility. Yet each will cherish and respect their children in very special ways. The children, if they can ignore the cross currents in the parental relationship, will surely profit from the dual conditioning.

It is through the family, most likely, that lasting effects of this most unlikely relationship will be evidenced.

Taurus-Pisces

At first glance one might think the sentimental, elusive Pisces and practical, acquisitive Taurus would have little to offer each other. But the Water element of Pisces mixes with Taurean Earth to mold strong borders which provide direction for both. Taurus Earth needs the flow of water to flourish and be fruitful. Just as Taurus endurance adds stability to the Pisces environment.

The Taurus Sun sextiles the Pisces Sun; traits between the two are more complimentary than similar. And the results counteract areas of conflict.

Venus, the Taurus ruler, is exalted in Pisces, and the two Signs recognize and appreciate the Venus quality in each other; their differences are softened thereby. The endurance of Taurus becomes, for Pisces, a reservoir of strength—not strength which overwhelms but strength to lean on. Pisces lacks vitality, which offers Taurus the opportunity to care for the loved one. Taurus feels a responsibility to care for those close.

Pisces sentimentality, which most practical Signs find embarrassing, is more acceptable to Taurus, perhaps softened by the Venus influence. Taurus understands the sympathy behind Pisces tears (although Taurus would feel the end of the world had come to cry in the presence of another) and can appreciate empathy from Pisces in a crisis (although Taurean emotions seldom surface to interfere with the ability to take charge). Venus here softens Taurus reactions to meet the receptiveness of Pisces even where conflicting traits prevail.

Outright conflicts do exist between these Suns, but Taurean practicality and Piscean imagination combine them to advantage usually. Pisces, empathetic and tolerant, can feel for the unhappiness of others without judging the reasons. Taurus automatically includes loved ones in good fortune as beneficiaries, but, being self-oriented, practicality dictates Taurean need to take of self first and respond to those close from the sense of security that has been established. The two traits interact to the benefit of both.

Taurus works hard to acquire material possessions; is often prejudiced against those who refuse to work hard; who allow weaknesses to defeat them; who hurt loved ones through negligence. Pisces sympathy toward those Taurus considers unworthy bothers the Bull. Pisces forgiveness also runs contrary to Taurus nature. Pisces is taken advantage of time and again; in fact, seems to invite this. And Pisces forgives time after time. Taurus, once convinced someone has taken advantage, will hold a grudge and wait years to get even.

Yet here too the Taurus-Pisces natures can work in harmony, with Pisces empathy persuading Taurus to give a little in such stubborn judgments; and Taurus giving Pisces courage to become a little selfish in relationships.

Pisces is creative, producing ideas as if by magic; Taurus is adept at taking the ideas of others and transforming them to workable plans. Pisces adds lightness to the sometimes heavy thinking of Taurus; Taurus can hold the effusive Pisces optimism down to earth and channel it into successful projects.

Both Taurus and Pisces absorb tensions in contacts with others, and in times of stress suffer physically from hard-to-pin-down ailments as a result. Both these Suns see the home as an attractive haven where they can recuperate in privacy.

In intimate relationship the Pisces-Taurus combination can be potent, with the Venus influence the ingredient that almost assures happiness. Both Signs value quality and beauty, and when they find these in love, will cherish them. Pisces, often too trusting, is hurt frequently by those close. Taurus will go to great lengths to protect the Pisces partner from those who lean too heavily.

Pisces responds to what is received from the partner. Taurus love and consideration will be reflected back in double measure. Pisces can respond to both the romantic and physical sides of Taurus love, and barring afflictions in the natal charts, there will be little conflict in this relationship in the intimate areas.

These Signs make loving parents, respectful of their children. Again, potential areas of friction tend to compliment each other: Taurus stubbornness once a stand is taken will offset Piscean tendency to be too lenient. Children will be cared for; will live in a comfortable, attractive home environment; will be treated with dignity. Taurus will require them to meet certain standards of behavior. Taurus dignity places value on regard for public opinion without being unduly exposed to narrow-minded restrictions. They will be exposed to high mental and spiritual concepts from the Pisces parent, without being condemned for failure to live up to them.

The hearthfire of the Taurus Sun will be sheltered by the rainbow of the Pisces Sun, and the result will be a magical love that lasts a lifetime.

GEMINI

GEMINI-ARIES (Page 15)

A fire arrow generates a lot of excitement on a merry-go-round. Differences seem more corroding than they usually prove to be.

GEMINI-TAURUS (Page 50)

A firefly attacking Ferdinand the Bull. Mutable Air and Fixed Earth find it hard to whip up a successful dust storm, let alone a romance.

Gemini-Gemini

To others this pair will resemble two younsters playing house—a continual round of pizza for dinner, Coke for breakfast, and a dizzying variety of zany interests. Gemini is motion and curiosity and casual contacts and communications. Two Geminis seem like a swarm.

But closer observation will disclose an orbital pattern within this haphazard activity that keeps these two together quite successfully. There is a holding rhythm to the activities of parakeet and dragonfly in spite of apparently aimless dartings and turnings in mid air; the sudden stops serve as launchings for breathless flight in different directions.

Mercury rules, and Mercury is intellect, which strings the colorful activity into a thread of purpose. The resulting series of experiences and unrelated interactions anchors this pair of mutable Suns to its base, substituting for long-range plans to keep them moving toward goals which may seem trivial to others.

Freedom of motion is basic necessity for Gemini; the Twins cannot function boxed into tight routines. Yet these adolescents of the Zodiac also long for parental authority in the background to supply guidelines—invisible but *there*. Gemini frequently looks more for a parent figure in a relationship than for a contemporary, and trouble in their unions with other Signs may stem from the mate's lack of understanding of the Gemini need to move at will.

When two Geminis form a relationship—and they will probably prefer this to a binding union, at least in the beginning—each will fall back on the partner's understanding of this need for independence. If they are enough in tune with each other to even consider a permanent relationship they will probably be able to achieve a working arrangement where each has complete freedom to come and go from a mutual home base.

There is very little possessiveness in Gemini. The Twins enter relationships with curiosity and delight. They neither give nor demand from their mates deep emotional commitment. A relationship here can only endure when there are no rigid demands; no completely closed doors. Where other Signs often place impossible conditions on a relationship with Gemini, these two understand each other perfectly.

Still, in any union there are at least minimal responsibilities, and conflicts in this one will probably come about through the refusal of either one to face up to chores and duties. Because they are versatile, talented people they may be able to afford to pay others to take care of routine responsibilities for them. If not they will be like two kids playing hooky from school—knowing the boom will fall when authority catches up with them, but enjoying there freedom to the fullest right up to the deadline.

If they have children the little ones will be cared for kindly and will be persistently urged toward independence. These are the parents who start their babies taking swimming lessons at the age of three months. But the children will be accorded full dignity as individuals from the day they are born.

Some competition will underlie this union, but it will be friendly; never of the vindictive sort. Geminis seem to be playacting even in their most serious moments. They may indulge in a little jockeying for position at the curtain calls, but they will never be bitter about each other's successes.

They'll have a whale of a lot of fun. This relationship will be a continuous ride on a merry-go-round. How long will it last? Well, merry-go-rounds go around, and around, and around—until the music stops.

Gemini-Cancer

There is a fairy tale quality about a Gemini-Cancer relationship: Tinker Bell and Little Boy Blue getting together; or Peter Pan and Cinderella. And they somehow manage to pull it off, as long as they can maintain the illusion that Story Book Lane really does exist. They work hard at it. Gemini wants to believe that people can fly over the rainbow, and Cancer thrives on the dream that the frog really does turn into Prince Charming of it is protected and loved.

In view of the many conflicting traits which these Suns possess, it seems unliekly they will live happily ever after. But intuition works for them most of the time; and Gemini borrows a little of the Taurus sense of the importance of the home base, and a little of the Cancer love of home, in spite of the imperative need for mobility. These two will enjoy fixing up a home together; Gemini versatility relates to Cancer talents in developing a home that is unique. Cancer, strongly traditional, can influence the flighty Gemini to avoid too much uniqueness; Gemini can persuade Cancer to inject some originality into stuffy notions of what is proper.

But once the fun of decorating is over, difficulties may begin to surface. Cancer will want to settle down and play house; Gemini may grow restless and prefer to sell and begin over. Neither one wishes to deal with the grubby chores that go with living in a home. Cancer, happy to protect and care for the partner in loving ways, nevertheless wants someone else to take care of plugged drains and unmowed lawns. Gemini will deal with such matters if the mood is right, but rejects responsibility on a routine basis. If Cancer can be convinced that such chores fall under the heading of "taking care of" the happy-go-lucky Gemini, and Gemini can settle down to helping often enough to convince Cancer of giving equal time to chores, they manage to keep the menage operating.

Unfortunately they share two negative qualities that

can be devastating in their effects on a happy relationship. Both suffer extremes of moodiness, and both are most sensitive to criticism. The gloom that can descend on this pair when they are plumbing the depths simultaneously can be crushing. If they are lucky enough to alternate their moods, it works out fine. Gemini will find other things to do when Cancer withdraws into a shell, and will keep occupied until the Moon changes and Cancer emerges into the world again. The Cancer desire to protect loved ones will surge to the fore when Gemini is suffering to try to alleviate the misery until Gemini bounces back to cheerfulness again. An intuitive knowledge of when to walk softly will keep these two from wounding each other too deeply with critical comments. Cancer tact helps; Gemini wit can sometimes salvage a tense situation.

There are some supportive opposing traits which can add strength to the relationship. Gemini, blithly self-confident, can shore up Cancerian periods of self doubt. Cancer self esteem is weak and the Moon Child takes courage from Gemini assurance.

Gemini generosity can be a happy influence on Cancer frugality. Cancer's very real fear of poverty—of being without adequate resources—can make the Moon Child apprehensive of Gemini ability to shrug and trust inner resources to provide for needs as they arise. But Gemini is logical enough to admit the benefits of providing for the future, especially if Cancer is willing to assume direction of that area of the relationship. Cancer's willingness to work patiently toward lasting goals can have a calming effect on Gemini impatience, in spite of irritating conflicts. Cancer love of tradition, the interest in antiques, can intrigue curious Gemini into becoming interested also.

Gemini's indiscriminate friendliness can raise Cancer's eyebrows now and then; Gemini impatience with pretense can feel trapped by Cancer's emphasis on status. Keeping up with the Jones is not a game Gemini plays willingly. Still, if Cancer can manage it without placing too many restrictions on Gemini, the Twin won't object. As with all dual Signs, Gemini has a side which can enjoy special privileges as well as sneer at them.

These two Signs seem not to experience much difficulty in the intimate relationship. Gemini is too busy, too curious, to be possessive, or even much involved in the sensual; and Cancer easily sublimates love drives to the home and children. In this combination Gemini becomes the eternal adolescent and Cancer the archetypal parent.

The Gemini partner will not be jealous of parental love superceding marital love, although children of this pair may feel smothered when this happens. Gemini sees children as people, not as rivals. Cancer will see children as children when they are graduating from college. While these parents never quite agree on the fine points of child rearing, Gemini will probably be too busy to make any concerted effort to take over the Cancer parental role. As soon as they are old enough Gemini will include the children in adult experiences (or as soon as the Cancer parent will permit it) and the children will thrive. The disagreement here may take form more as token protest than as devastating confrontations. A whirlwind and ocean swells generate white caps, not tidal waves.

What holds the union together in the face of obvious personality differences seems to be the impracticality of the attraction: they end up in a Never-Never Land of daydreams, playing house rather than coping with a real-life marriage, and manage to convert their fairy tale dreams to a psuedo reality that works for them. And they grow young together in the process. The Cancer partner will determine the holding power of this relationship, especially if Cancer is the woman.

Gemini-Leo

Gemini and Leo find each other attractive; they understand each other. Together they generate a relationship that sparkles and glows. Leo, natural Sign of the Fifth House of Children and creativity, is receptive to the creative talents of perpetually youthful Gemini. Leo relates strongly to youth and can be delighted with the adolescent traits which stay with Gemini into old age.

Both these friendly Signs love people; they work well with the public and desire to help others. Thus Leo can be forgiving when Gemini, caught up in community projects, neglects domestic chores. The elegant Leo is often indifferent to the cluttered condition of the home (except when VIPs are coming to dinner). Gemini, a lackadaisical cook, does not hold it against gregarious Leo for being late for dinner five nights a week because of committee meetings. Often over-enthusiastic, Gemini can understand how easily the Lion becomes involved in impulsive volunteering. Impulsiveness and enthusiasm are—if not twins—at least first cousins.

Gemini also realizes Leo is a trusting baby when it comes to judging character, subject to the most obvious flattery and almost begging to be conned into *anything* as long as the request is sandwiched between compliments. Skeptical Gemini cannot endure insincerity in any form, and quickly puts down attempts by others to gain recruits in this manner. But intuition is an integral part of Gemini thought processes, and the Twin is aware that Leo invites a certain amount of this fawning by pretentious attitudes. Gemini will point this out to Leo on occasion, but carefully. Gemini learns early that the regal Lion has an ego as painfully tender as a new sunburn.

Leo not only likes to take care of loved ones, but insists on it. Gemini appreciates Leo generosity, and is willing to cater to the Leo craving for attention if the demands are neither too insistent nor too frequent. Gemini has better things to do than flatter pomposity, but will comply by paying sincere compliments at appropriate times.

Gemini tendency to be perpetually on the run can lead to friction in this relationship. Leo is possessive of those close and does not take kindly to having the partner flitting from place to place—gone today and gone tomorrow, as it were. It isn't that Leo minds Gemini going when and where whim indicates, but the Lion wants to know all the details, every time, and Gemini hates being called to account for petty reasons. Too close a rein by Leo may contribute to nervousness which can lead to severe physical stress for Gemini. Leo will be indulgent most of the time in this, for Leo is trusting and there is a basic honesty about Gemini that reacts to this trust. The Twin will cut corners in small issues (Gemini is no stranger to the white lie) but when the chips are down will insist on the truth. It isn't the coming and going that Leo minds in the mate as much as not having the mate on call at any given moment; it isn't Leo's persistent interest that bothers Gemini as much as the insistence on accounting for every minute.

The hardest thing for Leo to accept from Gemini will be unconventionality. Gemini likes to experiment; is intrigued by the new. Leo wants the traditional. Establishment status symbols are important to the Lion, who may frown on Gemini attire, especially in social situations. Leo knows full well the importance of social affairs to career advancement and will expect the

Gemini partner to cooperate at these times in dress and deportment. But Leo may be disappointed as often as rewarded in these expectations. Yet in all truth, Gemini has probably warned the Lion before the ceremony that the kingly life style is inhibiting.

The relationship stimulates more intensity in Gemini response than is usual. Leo is ardent in love, but a quality of purity controls the sensual. Still the fire is there, if controlled, and Gemini's intermittent passion is intensified; the blowtorch gains strength from the solar flares. Gemini passion is always filtered through the mental Mercurian influences, based largely on curiosity and a desire to be cared for. Gemini never quite outgrows adolescent emotions—laughing one minute, crying the next. But there is enough fire in the Leo Sun to generate passion for both, and to the average observer this couple may appear to be a satellite rolling across the heavens ringed by a golden hoop.

Neither of these are fruitful Signs; there may be only one child of this union. But any children will be indulged on one hand, reasoned with on the other; they will take advantage of parental indulgence while refusing to tolerate parental interference, and will make their feelings known at an early age. Leo lays down edicts and demands obedience under a loosely disguised system of rewards and penalties. (The Leo parent is the one who gives $5 for each A on the report card when the going rate is 50¢.) But Mercurian cleverness will find ways to outwit the Lion without being suspected, and Gemini will make some demands too.

There is esteem and pride as well as love in this relationship, and there seems little to threaten it. Fire burns steadily in Air, and Air is warmed by Fire, to the fulfillment of both.

Gemini-Virgo

Gemini and Virgo share the rulership of Mercury and the quality of mutability. The Suns are also squared. It makes for a contradictory relationship, with individual planet placements in the natal charts determining the success or failure of these two in establishing a rewarding relationship.

Versatility, strong in both Signs, both adds to and detracts from the chances of them building good interaction. Mercury influence is strong, but Mercury lends detachment. Mutable Signs suffer extremes of moods which, coupled with the Mercury influence, can manifest either as woeful inability to communicate, or as a safety valve which allows both Signs to ride out the thunderstorms in relative safety.

Virgo curiosity is attracted to the provocative Gemini personality in the same way Gemini curiosity *must* investigate anything or anyone that comes into the field of vision. But often this coming together resembles the erratic flights of windblown objects which drift and whirl around each other and never quite make contact: a dragonfly chasing Tel Star. The chances of them reaching a mutual orbit seem remote; and even if they manage that, subsequent barriers to interaction are formidable. For Gemini is an Air creature and the stratosphere seems attainable; but Virgo is an Earth creature and dust can only reach so high before dissipating.

Mercury can help, and when these two Suns succeed in establishing a lasting relationship the Mercury influence will have been strong. Even so, the basic traits of the two manifest in totally different ways.

In restless Gemini, strong demands on nervous energy induce low vitality that can lead to a breakdown, physically and mentally. In Earthy Virgo, the Sign on the natural sixth house of health, this often becomes hypochondria. Mercury mentality coupled with strong intuition makes Gemini very sensitive to criticism. Virgo, strongly analytical, frequently seems to be criticizing when, in fact, Virgo is only trying to point out obvious ways of improving a situation. This doesn't mean that Virgo is *not* sensitive to criticism. However, Virgo's reaction is more indignation that anyone would question the opinions expressed. Virgo is adept at working out the best methods for making things work well but is sublimely blind to negative self traits.

Virgo deals with details and facts and logic and pragmatic experience. While there can be strong spiritual emphasis in this Sign's make-up, it will be coupled with a practical logical coloration. Bent on expanding the spiritual nature, Virgo will go about it as if digging for water—patiently, methodically seeking to pin down the ephemeral to something that can be described. Gemini will give spiritual concepts the same curious once-over that is accorded cherries on a tree sparkling in the sun. Virgo seeks an anchor; Gemini looks for a landing strip on which to put down for refueling.

Gemini unconventionality may keep Virgo on pins and needles much of the time, yet, truthfully, Gemini's lack of convention is, like most other Gemini traits, more on the surface than deeply imbedded. Virgo, taking time to analyze this, will come to realize there is a basic honesty and sincerity in Gemini that will not allow serious deviation from what the partner feels is right. Gemini finds it easier to see the other person's side of the question than does Virgo; intuition allows Gemini to use mental processes in a responsive way. Gemini appreciates the down-to-earth attitudes of Virgo which, even if mutable, have more foundation than the Twin's swaying mental structures.

The effervescent Gemini influence can lighten the Virgo personality and allow release of some of the softness of the inner character. Basically, Virgo seeks the emotional Water Signs to bring the personality to full bloom, in spite of being uncomfortable with emotional responses. Virgo senses the lack of emotion in Gemini, although much more comfortable with this response. The desert may seem proudly indifferent to water—but when desert sands are irrigated, strange and lovely vegetation proliferates, and desert oases are essential to the life of the Sahara.

Children—if there are any—will be self-reliant, efficient youngsters urged toward maturity by parents who value mental processes over emotional ones. Water Sign children of the pair may feel some lack of cuddling, yet will surely profit from the disciplines demanded by the parents. Fixed Sign children may gain some flexibility through growing up in an atmosphere in which reason is the basis for solving problems. This ability to reason will supply the stability that can be lacking in the affairs of most mutable Sign combinations.

The intimate side of this relationship might seem lacking in intensity to some of the more sensual Signs. Here again curiosity will provide common ground from which the final nature of the relationship will derive. If the initial experiences are rewarding, Gemini's appreciation for love will increase responsiveness, and Virgo will respond with loyal and loving concern. Thus grows a self-fulfilling circle, devoid of the passionate conflicts that so often assail the more emotional Signs.

When this union works, it gains strength with every passing year; when it doesn't work, the overwhelming conflicts are apparent almost from the beginning, in which case Mercury will generate a logical decision to forget the whole thing.

Gemini-Libra

These two understand each other, but this often remains a superficial relationship, as if they were riding side by side on a merry-go-round in perfect harmony, yet never quite synchronizing. They wave and smile and hum with the music, but when the caliope slows they find their horses have stopped on different levels. Because the experience is pleasant and there are few obvious barriers to agreement, they will keep trying: Gemini because they're moving and the shifting scene helps hold interest; the mate because the horses have started prancing again before Libra can decide whether or not to get off.

This lack of conflict may be the most damaging quality to afflict the relationship in the end. Strength comes through meeting challenge, as the broken bone is reinforced at the break point by new growth. There is little to challenge either Gemini or Libra in this union, however agreeable it may be.

Both are appreciative; both are sincere. Each is sensitive to criticism but intuitive enough to sense when the other has reached the boiling point. They are self-oriented, but in these Signs potential selfishness is balanced by a desire to look after others. Libra especially is generous to a fault, filling a personal need by giving to the partner (perhaps to balance an equally strong need to take from the partner). Libra gives little thought to pleasing the recipient of gifts—only to satisfying self in the desire to give. But Gemini understands this, having a similar orientation toward giving, although to a lesser degree.

Social interaction is important to both Libra and Gemini. Libra's charm shows easily and naturally in a group of pleasant companions who know the proper responses to Libran overtures, and who make accepted social queries without expecting penetrating answers. Heavy conversation bores both Libra and Gemini after a short time. In general they prefer chit-chat and interesting gossip to intellectual exchanges. Gemini has moments of serious reflections—usually during the devastating moods of despair which sends the Twin into hiding at times. Libra is more apt to refuse to join in when the going gets too serious.

Libra doesn't like being pinned down any better than Gemini does. Gemini desires freedom—mental, physical, emotional—to follow the will-o'-the-wisp of imagination. Libra wants freedom from decisions. Gemini desires change; Libra equivocates. And when serious discussion is involved, it usually demands taking a stand. At the zero hour Gemini will come up with a quick response that will free the Twin from further involvement in a situation that can upset a delicate nervous system. Libra will probably evade the issue by seizing on irrelevant side points, which can be pursued more comfortably; coming up to the wire still weighing pros and cons, and hoping the whole discussion will just go away.

Gemini will find the environment pleasant enough to coast along in the relationship. But Libra will eventually begin to apply pressure, especially if feeling something is lacking in the response of the Gemini mate. The marital partnership is of elemental importance to Libra. However, Librans often have trouble with relationships of all kinds. The basic Libra character demands that every interaction achieve balance. Few relationships come out exactly even in every instance; they must be balanced out over the long haul. Libra demands balance *now*. Being self oriented, Libra's interpretation of give and take often comes out "you give—I'll take." And this is especially apparent in the bedroom.

Everyday interaction of married life seldom equals Libra's romanticized ideas of what marriage should be. The Venus influence is kept within bounds by what the Libran considers "appropriate" actions. But in the bedroom the innate selfishness of Libra distorts the Venus influence and demands the partner live up to a fantasy image of what the mate should be—and this image insists on subservience to Libra's wishes.

Gemini is not basically a sensual Sign (although planet placements in natal charts make a difference). Gemini failure to respond as ardently as desired seems to Libra to be a threat to the marriage itself, and the Libran may begin to tighten the hold on the relationship in insidious ways. In this union, Libra may end up crushing the bluebird in attempting to keep it from flying away. A Gemini cannot be caged, and enslavement by love is as stifling as any other prison.

Frequently the Libran partner will transfer love from the mate to the children, attempting once again to form a binding relationship through love enslavement while achieving balance in the *family* relationship. The parent who holds children at home through their adult years by suffering attacks of illness whenever they show interest in partners of their own is often a Libran, and something of this influence is present in most Libran relationships with offspring. Libra will indulge children as long as they remain dependent, and will often attempt to enforce dependence by giving them gifts—the resulting obligation balancing out the giving. Gemini insistence on children assuming independence at an early age will work to counterbalance Libran indulgence, but there may always be conflict over this issue—as much as Libra and Gemini can manage conflict between them.

As Libra continues to channel affections through the children, Gemini will feel a moral obligation to work against this. But even here Libra is achieving personal ends: forcing Gemini's concern with the problem is, in essence, binding Gemini to the relationship.

Sooner or later Gemini may indulge in passing affairs to relieve the tedium of the unrelenting contest. Libra borrows Scorpio tenacity in the relentless pursuit of balance in relationships. Libra may retaliate with affairs too. The Libran never considers the beginning of this teeter-totter situation, but, rather, balances against the last position of the board which may, in fact, have put Libra high six times in a row. And Libra will not want to let go of the marriage itself. The result may be a marriage of convenience, with an unspoken agreement between the two that a pleasant facade be maintained.

Gemini will stay on the carrousel because of this surface pleasantness of companionship. Libra will remain to avoid ending this relationship that always ends with first one horse up, then the other.

Gemini-Scorpio

A whirlwind does not often form a alliance with the Amazon; if it does, the attraction soon dissipates like mist on a warm morning. The depth and power of the Scorpio personality is fightening to the airy Gemini, whose interests are scattered on the winds. As a rule the deep-flowing river of the Scorpio character pays little attention to this Sign. It is possible in theory for these two Suns, strongly mentally oriented, to achieve a transcendent relationship on that level, but this rarely happens, and depends heavily on power aspect in the natal charts.

Creativity offers a contact point for positive interaction between these two, but they may find it hard going to overcome shared negative traits. Both are impatient, at least in some areas: Gemini with restrictions that inhibit movement; Scorpio with whatever deflects the movement toward personal goals. Gemini flightiness will prove a constant annoyance to the more intense partner. Scorpio demands commitment from partners at every level. Gemini cannot be pinned down without losing identity.

Skepticism in proportion is fine; here Gemini skepticism is heightened by the intensity of Scorpio suspicion far beyond its usual strength. And the Giant nervous system cannot sustain such concentrated reaction for any length of time without collapsing. Scorpio intensity is supported by stamina that keeps this partner moving at high speed for long periods of time.

The moodiness that afflicts both Gemini and Scorpio will be catastrophic to the relationship. Gemini moods plunge to the depths, but the ever-changing personality soon starts to reverse the process when interacting with most Signs. Scorpio moodiness seems to last forever, heavy as a mountain, prohibiting a rise in Gemini's spirits unless the Twin can escape from the Scorpio partner for a time. This may be hard to manage. Scorpio is jealous of the partner; is secretive by nature; wants the mate alone. Gemini will find it hard going to attain the solitude so necessary for the revitalization of energies.

Scorpio will not understand that this intensity injected into the relationship can depress and undermine the delicate gemini nervous system. Too late Scorpio may realize that Gemini resembles Tinker Bell, dependent on others' *belief* in order to stay alive. Gemini cannot endure constant demands for proof; cannot be called upon to justify every movement— every thought—without irreparable damage to the personality. Scorpio can be unyielding in demands in this area. Yet in fairness, Scorpio will be as relentless in efforts to repair the damage to the relationship when realization comes.

Gemini is a social being and soon grows tired of Scorpio isolation. Gemini cannot breathe in the highly-charged atmosphere which nourishes Scorpio. Heavy discussions which probe for gems of wisdom deeply buried in unlikely sources bore Gemini to tears; the Twin is more apt to enjoy the impromtpu get-together than one of the portentious gatherings Scorpio favors.

Gemini is versatile and talented but lacks interest or stamina to take on tasks involving sustained effort. The Twin works well with hovering deadlines and responds quickly in a crisis. Gemini will always come up with some kind of an answer, but once the emergency is past must be alone to recharge batteries. Scorpio, the epitome of endurance, expects everyone to last to the end, and can be critical if the partner falls below Scorpion standards. The Scorpio will have little patience with Gemini's need for sleep; Scorpio can work days on end with a few hours rest now and then, and be none the worse for it.

Many Signs can support each other through conflicting traits, supplementing weak spots in the partner's make up. It doesn't work that way with these two; Gemini appreciation for Scorpio strength is absorbed by Scorpio envy that Gemini seems to receive more compliments and contribute far less to the relationship than the Scorpio partner. Scorpio hasn't learned friendliness leaves leeway for some error, while tactless criticism closes the door on tolerance.

The conflicts will come to painful climax where the affairs of children are concerned. Scorpio intensity will follow the children like a shadow; will keep track of every minute of their day, or try to. Scorpio will keep in close touch with teachers; their questions will probe for minute details of their children's experiences; they will demand perfection—*their* definition—and nag over the smallest breach of performance. Yet their children will be well cared for, and in a way will profit from the vigilance. They may become more confident to pursue the many interests stimulated by the Gemini parent in the process. But Scorpio, being the stronger personality, will cast the longer shadow; and these children may suffer emotional bruises from this parent.

In intimate relations the conflicts are so glaring they cannot be ignored; they can barely be endured. The rather casual sensual nature of Gemini simply drowns in Scorpio emotionalism stifled by jealousy and possessiveness. Scorpio rules sex, and the secretive jealousy of this nature gives a furtive emphasis to the expression of physical love. Scorpio does not understand the fragility of Gemini emotions; cannot believe that the butterfly is expressing love by drifting close enough to touch the surface of Scorpio passion. Scorpio demands commitment from the partner; Gemini hardly knows the meaning of the word.

Wise members of these two Suns will channel mutual attractions through creative enterprises and enjoy a friendly interaction on that level. If they come closer, the Gemini risks being drawn into the currents of Scorpio personality and disappearing, leaving Scorpio to brood over a lost love destroyed by himself.

Gemini-Sagittarius

These are the gypsies of the Zodiac—traveling companions on a magic carpet, daring to risk security in order not to miss a single experience that could add more excitement to their lives. There is no containing them;

they follow their whims where the currents blow them, Sagittarius daring Gemini to fly just a little farther—a little farther; Gemini holding Sagittarius back just a little—just a little. But only enough, in either case, to match paces on their journeys.

Overly enthusiastic, easily bored, they keep each other keyed up; Gemini curiosity supplying a constant flow of interesting information for Sagittarius to take delight in; Sagittarius by readiness to explore Gemini's world of glittering bricabrac. This household has a carnival atmosphere most of the time.

Sooner or later, though, the black mood of Sagittarius will gather and Gemini will be appalled to see the brilliant world of the Archer turn dark. The jovial Sagittarian can turn from court jester to black knight in the time it takes for Gemini to blink.

And what does Gemini do then? Follows right along, generating a matching dark cloud. When these two are in the depths there is no bottom to the gloom that enshrouds them. Sagittarius, normally the jolliest of persons, snarls and lashes out with sarcasm. Gemini, normally light as a butterfly, becomes encased in a cocoon of self pity, activating the processes that drain the nervous system and brings the Twin to the verge of emotional breakdown.

. Gemini's lack of vitality can irritate the Sagittarian who wants to be *doing something*. The Archer's blunt comments will wound Gemini even more, and add to the depression.

They should get along better than they often do in fact. Sagittarius is loyal in a "faithful in my fashion" way. And Gemini is appreciative. Each is intuitive enough to sense what the other feels. Yet often as not they fail to act on their understanding. Sagittarius sees a light on a distant hill and must go exploring; Gemini follows a bluebird to see if they really do fly over the rainbow. However, by the time each gets back to home base the original problem may be forgotten.

For they are drawn to each other as easily as they are driven apart. Gemini mental abilities fascinate the philosophical Saggitarius, who is magnetized again and again by the kaleidoscopic quality of Gemini imagination and creativity. Archer philosophizing is often tinged with humor, which either sets Gemini laughing or catches interest at a deeper level than Gemini cares to explore. It's a near certainty that one or the other will hear a siren song and be up and away to see what's happening before either has a chance to be bored with the subject at hand.

Gemini curiosity can be embarrassing to some of the Signs, but Sagattarius is intrigued by it. The Archer learns by exploring and understands Gemini's picking up information at every opportunity. As conversationalists these two shine—as long as the "mood index" is rising.

Gemini, friendly as a lost puppy, can irritate Sagittarius by indiscriminate fraternizing. The Archer is friendly too, but picks and chooses a little better, although inclined to take others for granted once he's chosen. Gemini feelings can be as sensitive as a weathervane when the gusts begin to blow.

In many ways they compliment each other. Gemini responds quickly in an emergency; Sagittarius takes awesome risks which create emergencies. But some matching qualities work the other way. The Sagittarian dislike of pretense is honed by Gemini skepticism until the two together can fall into the habit of making sarcastic criticisms of others almost routinely.

Sagittarian bluntness when in a down mood has to be experienced to be believed. Gemini can be crushed by these heavy comments when exposed to them too long. It may seem to observers that these two seldom stay in one place long enough for such grievances to build up. But everyone has to stay home once in awhile.

There is a buddy-buddy quality about romance between these two. Gemini, the perennial adolescent, brings something of this youthfulness to romantic encounters; and Sagittarius, while charming the way through any relationship, can be pretty casual about sex. Gemini may not really care too much that Sagittarius occasionally channels affections elsewhere, but deep down may consider this an affront to dignity. While neither requires nor gives a strong emotional commitment, there is a directness in the Sagittarian approach to love and sex that can make Gemini uneasy.

Their children are going to have fun—most of the time. They learn early to keep out of the way of whichever parent is having the dark moods and lay low until Jupiter is stirring up the fun-and-games atmosphere again. Actually, these parents work well together in raising their children. Gemini will support Sagittarian discipline, which can be surprisingly strict considering the casual attitudes the Archer adopts toward most responsibilities. The youngsters soon learn to roll with the punches in this nonconformist household, and generally will grow up none the worse for it.

Neither Sagittarius nor Gemini is strong on staying power; yet there's a good possibility this pair will hold together in spite of this flexibility, or maybe because of it. Polarity has a magnetic power that works in spite of obstacles. Each requires freedom as a basic of survival, and each is willing to give in order to receive it. Each has a kind of magic personality that charms others almost at will. Each has the quality of forgiving themselves their own transgressions, and applies this tolerance to the partner. Don't be surprised to see them celebrating their fiftieth wedding anniversary, even if you're surprised at their choice of celebrations.

Gemini-Capricorn

Except for the surface attraction that seems to draw quincunx Suns together briefly, there is little to support a relationship between these Signs. Unless there are strong supporting aspects in the individual charts, chances for a lasting union are not great.

The initial attraction is there: these are intelligent, self-confident individuals and perhaps recognize these qualities in each other. Gemini, the adolescent of the Zodiac, always retains a childlike orientation in relation to other Signs. And Saturn, ruler of Capricorn, represents the parents in the Circle of the Suns. Thus Gemini may be drawn to Capricorn authority as the whirlwind explores the mountain: and Capricorn can be fascinated by the mobility of Gemini. But the relationship does not often develop to permanence.

There are few bridges to understanding between the two. Gemini imagination supplies the spark for the stimulating Gemini personality. Capricorn practicality stifles the highly imaginative Twin. Ideally, the two should blend and work together, and this is possible if they can overcome the effects of strong traits they have in conflict.

Saturn's influence shapes the character of Capricorn in its own stern image. Self-discipline keeps the Goat trudging along under a heavy weight of responsibilities which can only be handled by industrious application of conservative principles. "Waste not—want not" might be Capricorn's motto, and it is applied to all facets of the Goat's life. Capricorn is uneasy with Gemini enthusiasm which keeps the mate flitting from one project to another, scattering efforts like confetti on the wind.

The inhibited, conservative manner is not a facade,

but is built on traditional foundations that have stood the test of time. Gemini curiosity is indiscriminate, and this irresponsible attitude may shock Capricorn.

Capricorn is self-oriented; is apprehensive of Gemini intuition that can understand motives which the Goat does not recognize as personal. Worse still for taciturn Capricorn, who may secretly long to be a butterfly instead of a stone statue, is the friendly interaction with others which Gemini enjoys in spite of casual promises and light-hearted negligence in social responsibilities. For Capricorn, Gemini may be a constant reminder of youth bypassed. Capricorn is born older than Gemini will ever be.

Age is emphasized in Capricorn. The ruler, Saturn, is the Timekeeper of the Zodiac. Capricorn is the longest lived of the Signs, usually coming to full potential as an individual after middle age. Capricorn often has a difficult time in childhood. Thus the Goat often longs to be a child, and it is the youthfulness of Gemini that is so attractive, and which can seldom be reached in spite of honest efforts within the relationship. The Goat clings to outmoded ideas, fearful of taking the wrong step in trying to escape from imprisoning inhibitions. Gemini, easily bored, tries the new almost routinely.

Capricorn may be resentful that the Gemini partner spends so much energy and interest on others. Gemini lacks stamina to work with sustained effort, while Capricorn vitality sustains physical energy for long periods of time. In this relationship Capricorn may spend a lot of time in physical chores like scrubbing the heelmarks off the hall floor, while Gemini stands around deciding which wallpaper would look best in the front closet.

Thus it may seem to Capricorn that low vitality only afflicts Gemini when there is drudgery in the offing. And there is some truth to this suspicion: boredom will send Gemini into a decline more quickly than a bout of double pneumonia (although this is a possibility also, since Gemini is susceptible to respiratory diseases).

Capricorn's heavy-handed efforts to communicate resentments to Gemini may come across as sarcasm, which wounds Gemini deeply, sending the Twin into a black mood without warning. Capricorn will react by retreating into silence, and the home atmosphere may resemble a morgue for a few days.

In intimacy the chasm between the two will be wide. Deep inside the inhibited Capricorn personality lies a lustiness that is expressed through sex. Gemini is a mental Sign, not given to emphasizing physical expressions of love. With Capricorn the patina of social graces is often missing, and this surface charm is necessary to stimulate interest in the sensual side of the relationship in Gemini. This area of their lives will seldom be fulfilling for either.

As with many Signs, children of the two may be able to draw on the best traits of both and blend them to advantage. Certainly Gemini flexibility and Capricorn stability could compliment each other. There may be problems in their conflicting concepts of child rearing. Gemini will be pushing the children toward maturity and equal status with the parents; Capricorn, as befits the longest-lived Sign, will see offspring as children to be guided and cared for long after their twenty-first birthdays. Capricorn is dictatorial and misses the authority of disciplining youngsters. Gemini doesn't relish responsibilities which go with baby sitting. Somehow the children themselves catalyze these oppositional traits between the parent Suns.

In rare cases this pair can learn to balance each other out to the good of the relationship, but for the most part an enduring union would demand heavy toll from each partner. Tel Star's natural environment is the stratosphere, and the glacier is firmly bedded in stone. The points of contact are too tenuous for most to build on.

Gemini-Aquarius

On the surface this is a delightful combination, and that may be as far as it ever goes. These Signs trine—there is friendly accord between them—but deeper commitment will be conspicuous by its absence. A whirlwind in the stratosphere doesn't generate tension.

The difficulties in this relationship will not come from a lack of complimentary traits. There are far more pluses than minuses in this partnership. The differences are in quality, not quantity. Harmonious curiosity will be the attractive quality between them; a sense of sharing the unconventional concepts they both accept.

Both Gemini and Aquarius like to be where people are. The Gemini personality flits from person to person, from idea to idea, from place to place. Aquarius explores deeper, reaches farther, for mental concepts; makes longer journeys to less accessible environments to satisfy curiosity than does Gemini. Aquarian interest will remain constant as long as a person or a subject challenges. The interest span of Gemini is akin to the roving attention span of a child.

Aquarius observes with the detached interest of an intellectual; Gemini interest focuses on whatever is close at hand. They both like change and tire quickly of the old; and in establishing a home together will adopt the carefree standards of today's mobile society. They will not mind changing jobs and locales—may seek work in foreign countries. Certainly they will be drawn to careers that involve individual freedom, versatility, and contact with people. Neither is the type to settle in on the bottom rung of the organizational ladder and spend twenty years safely edging up to retirement pay. They are far more likely to lead exciting, unpredictable, and to most others rather insecure lives, collecting experiences rather than possessions. Both these Signs have the talent and ability to pull this off without really suffering financial chaos.

"Schedule" will be a dirty word to both Gemini and Aquarius. They will skid right up to the wire on deadlines before taking care of vital matters. They are the kind of people who can decide in mid-afternoon to take off for a week's vacation, and be packed in time to have dinner down the road a way.

They will consider their children as interesting individuals and will treat them as contemporaries. There will be little cuddling, but the children will feel they are an important part of their parents' lives. They will have the type of childhood that will cause grandmothers to wring their hands, and other children to drool with envy—a sort of never-ending afternoon at a carnival. But they'll remember childhood as a time of adventure and joy.

Both these Suns are many talented and probably will share an interest in the arts. Their intimate conversation may resemble shop talk more than romantic chit-chat. There will be little of the sentimental in their private lives; their involvement will be through intellectual stimulation—the rare meeting of the minds that can be as sensually provocative as physical interactin with other Signs.

The shadows that will darken the atmosphere here will be the extremes of moodiness which can afflict Gemini almost on schedule; and Aquarian irritability which will drive Gemini right up the wall. Aquarius may have highs and lows, but will find it hard to comprehend the heaviness of spirit with which Gemini must contend periodically. Gemini is truly not attuned to the kind of bickering that Aquarian impatience inflicts on those close. Since neither Sign is empathetic in the personal sense—both channeling their sympathies on an intellectual level—they may find it difficult to be understanding of each others' weaknesses.

Each is sensitive to criticism, although each will examine the criticism and accept the truth of it after some thought. It is through criticism, however that each is most likely to feel emotional reaction, and the resulting gloom may resemble the dark hours before a hurricane.

But the major drawback in building a satisfying relationship between these two versatile, volatile Suns will be the tendency to scatter their efforts. Highly talented, they fail to live up to potential unless one or the other furnishes stability in the partnership.

Still, the lack of emotional involvement itself can provide the anchor which holds this high-flying pair together, leaving each free to explore personal interests without a sense of guilt and frustration. Certainly theirs will be a relationship that sparkles and glows, and leads them to explore experiences others may not have the courage to seek. Their lives may seem to those around them a perpetual happening, and will, in all likelihood, be exactly that.

Gemini-Pisces

With the Suns of these mutable, dual-signed natives squaring, the question might be how they ever get together in the first place, rather than how they get along together. They do both, of course, aided by planetary placements in individual charts. But the very traits which bring them together may be the most devastating in destroying a lasting relationship before it really gets started.

Both these highly mobile Suns are, of necessity, adaptive. This allows an initial contact to enlarge beyond the hello-goodbye stage. Gemini is motivated to explore the most casual encounter, at least briefly, by an over-active curiosity. Pisces responsiveness furthers the attraction. Intuition works from both Signs to reinforce the magnetism. Gemini senses the many-facted Pisces personality is barely glimpsed on the surface; Pisces senses a wealth of fascinating information is stored up in the Gemini mind. Although neither is quite comfortable with the other personality, neither seems able to ignore the magnetic attraction.

But the natures of these Signs prohibit a deep relationship in most cases. Gemini feels imprisoned by the inner probings of Pisces (even while storing up information the probings reveal). Pisces, in spite of empathy, never quite realizes that Gemini interest is not so much universal as wind-blown, and persists in trying to establish a deeper level of communication than the Gemini cares to pursue.

It is this difference of degree which plays havoc with this relationship. Even the areas in which they agree never quite touch. Pisces is compassionate, literally suffering as intensely as the companion who is undergoing misfortune; Gemini sympathy translates as a desire to help, but without emotional involvement.

Both Pisces and Gemini seem to flit from project to project without apparent plan. The difference between them is that Pisces keeps returning, eventually bringing all of them to completion, while Gemini seldom returns to complete a project once it's been abandoned.

Both signs are super sensitive, but again, with a difference. Gemini sensitivity is directed inward; the slightest criticism can wound deeply, and the same mind that can be overly objective toward another's troubles becomes a veritable litmus paper to soak up personal hurts. The situation is reversed with Pisces: inner hurt will be set aside in empathetic suffering for the other person—friend or enemy. For Pisces, the enemy bleeds the same color as the friend. Coupled with extremes of moods on both sides, the results can be miserable misunderstandings wrench the relationship apart over apparently trivial matters.

Pisces respect for privacy answers a corresponding need in Gemini for solitude. Actually, Gemini doesn't need to be alone so much as opportunity to escape boredom from interaction with those who stay around too long. Pisces privacy can be riddled by Gemini curiosity, goading Pisces to find a place and time to be alone. Sometimes Gemini craves the company of others; Pisces withdrawal at such times can inflict hurts which Pisces understands but cannot avoid.

The closer the relationship, the farther apart the two may be. Pisces cannot accept close involvement with another without emotional commitment. Gemini seems almost casual with the most intimate relationship. Gemini is definitely not a kissing cousin. Pisces wants only to be touched by those close.

As parents these two Signs are at cross purposes from the beginning. Pisces feels an emotional need to protect children; Gemini has an equally strong drive to make them self-reliant. The Gemini parent will teach the newborn baby to fit itself into the family schedule with as little disruption as possible. Pisces will be out of bed at the first whimper instead of giving the infant a chance to go back to sleep on its own. Children influenced by the Gemini parent become independent at an early age; those influenced by Pisces parents never quite outgrow a yearning to "go back home" when things go wrong.

The combination balances out here.

Gemini and Pisces enjoy each other more in social relationships which do not demand constant interaction. The Sun in Gemini resembles a blowtorch, producing an intense flame of energy for short periods of time, then shutting off to move to something else. The rainbow prisms of the Pisces Sun are nebulous and fragile. It isn't so much that they cannot exist together as that they derive from separate sources, and there is not sufficient basis for building deeper, sustaining fire that can withstand the smothering effect of Pisces emotions and the scattering effects of Gemini detachment.

CANCER

CANCER-ARIES (Page 17)

A pressure cooker atmosphere created by elemental Fire reacting to ocean tides in a confined environment. Stresses seldom allow for an easy relationship.

CANCER-TAURUS (Page 53)

One of the loveliest Sun combinations for lasting love and happiness. A down-deep foundation of affection binds them more deeply than they know.

CANCER-GEMINI (Page 83)

Tinker Bell and Little Boy Blue play house in Never-Never land and grow young in the process. A whirlwind and ocean tides generate white caps, not tidal waves.

Cancer-Cancer

These two will embrace each other—psychologically, emotionally, physically—as the ocean waters blend.

Even the fluctuations of moods can harmonize, attuned as they are to the transits of the Moon. When the Moon inhabits their Sign, this union will be blessed with fulfillment; when the weight of Saturn from the opposing Sign lies heavy, they will understand each other's need for isolation.

Potentially this is one of the most rewarding of the double Sign combinations. The family and home will be the heart of this relationship. The protectiveness of Cancer toward the home circle will be doubled, of course, but the possessiveness which can cause havoc in combination with another Sign here will be accepted as a natural state.

Ambition, which often gets in the way of harmony with other Signs, will not only be understood but approved in the Cancer household. The Cancer wife will accept naturally the role of homemaker, devoting her energy to imaginative development of domestic talents, secure in the knowledge that the Cancer husband is moving steadily up the career success ladder. Cancer women who enter careers are often motivated by fear of financial insecurity as much as by the accompanying desire for affluent living. This combination of Suns makes it possible for the Cancer wife to indulge her desire in the one area without fear that she is undermining the other. Nor will she resent the Cancer husband's strong interest in domestic affairs; rather, she will welcome it as proof that his interest is as strongly family oriented as her own.

With today's changing life styles, and the proper distribution of planets, this pair might reverse traditional roles with the man taking on the role of "houseperson" and the woman entering the career world (probably in the role of office wife to an executive or administrator happy to pay handsomely for her devotion to his interests).

Chances are good that these two, so strongly attuned to universal rhythms through the Moon influence, will find themselves almost perfectly attuned to each other. The danger of negative influences in the relationship lies in the possibility that negative qualities in one mate may get out of hand and subtly subvert the other to the same unhappy path. One Cancer sulking in hurt silence for days at a time is bad news; two Cancers sulking is demoralizing. If jealousy invades this household it can undermine the marriage in the same manner as the ocean tides undermine the sand cliffs along its shores— not through being directed toward each other, but because it becomes the lens through which both see the outside world. Cancer suspicion, once loosed in the personality, can quickly dominate.

Children of the pair may feel stifled as they begin to grow beyond the toddler state. It isn't that Cancers deliberately thwart initiative in their children so much as that they smother it through excessive devotion. They provide practically no outlet for children to develop normal feelings of opposition which are an integral part of the breaking-away process in the parent-child relationship.

Cancers will still be trying to coddle their offspring when the grandchildren are going off to college. Often the children have been so conditioned by the protective, possessive parents they accept their own satellite roles as a matter of course. Fire Sign children may rebel; and Air Sign children can be overwhelmed by the excess of emotional blackmail by which Cancer parents often control their offspring.

Still, once the nest is empty, these two will probably draw in the perimeters of their private circle and devote themselves to each other as possessively as in the beginning. These later years may be the most idyllic of all for them.

Cancer-Leo

The magnetism between these two resembles the inter-action of Sun and Moon, rulers of the two Signs. Although they never quite manage precision, they are never quite free to dance their separate routines. Cancer will revolve around Leo as the Moon revolves around the Sun, reflecting the light one moment, lost in the shadow the next.

Which is fitting. Leo will always edge to center stage, while Cancer shines in reflected glory from the radiant Leo personality. Possessiveness is the gravitational pull that will keep them interacting against long odds.

There is little to promote mutual understanding. Both are self-oriented to a degree that blinds them to another's viewpoint, yet each feels a strong need to care for others, and this substitutes for understanding between them.

Leo can only function to capacity in the limelight. Friendly, extroverted, the Lion needs to be at the center of the action. Leo likes people, especially those who admire and applaud. Leo is likely to have a coterie of advisors close at hand most of the time.

Cancer is more aloof, withdrawn, easily hurt in inter-action with others. In a social mood, Cancer prefers a quiet evening with close friends; Leo uses the telephone directory when he asked "a few friends" over for the evening.

Leo's idea of entertaining is dining out at the most expensive restaurant the bank balance allows; Cancer's is to open the home with its cherished possessions to allow friends to share privacy for an evening. Cancer will be appalled at the idea of spending large sums of money to buy the good graces of acquaintances who, in many cases, have little in common with either mate.

Leo's need for admiration often results in the Lion being surrounded by superficial friends. Flattery goes a long way with Leo.

Cancer, frugal and acquisitive, cannot abide seeing the partner spend money for possessions which often are bought to prove the Lion can afford to keep up with acquaintances. Leo often equates "valuable" with "expensive"; Cancer chooses carefully and waits until items of lasting value can be afforded. Cancer is not above reminding Leo—over and over—that "all that glitters is not gold."

Not that Cancer doesn't enjoy affluence; to the contrary. Apprehension over Leo's free spending will be mitigated by the gifts Leo bestows on the Cancer mate. Cancer may carp about the high cost of maintaining a show-place home, but will luxuriate in the lovely surroundings until the bills come in. Both Cancer and Leo have traditional views of luxury: there will be little conflict over the *kind* of lavish possessions they will acquire—only over whether to buy them on credit (Leo) or save until they can afford the best (Cancer).

It is in personal interaction that possessiveness causes real trouble. Here each is fiercely determined to own the other person, although the possessiveness is expressed in different ways. Leo love is a kind of kingly paternalism, and Cancer's is the eternal Mother Love. Both are over-protective of the objects of their affections and demand large amounts of gratitude and consideration for their devotion.

Leo will be generous with the mate but will expect the partner's wishes to be subordinated to personal ones (the king always walks two paces ahead, no matter how beautiful the queen). Only when wishing to display the mate as one more proof of luxurious taste does Leo draw Cancer into the full glow of the spotlight.

Not that Cancer really minds too much. The Cancer

116

mate's focus will always be on the partner. In intimate relations, however, Cancer will feel the weight of Leo's imperious manner. Cancer lacks self-esteem; Leo is self-confident to the point of arrogance. Cancer will suffer agonies in moments of intimacy; even in love, Leo's wish is law.

Cancer is romantic and sentimental; would prefer a special dinner for two at some secluded spot to the spectacular party the Leo will desire. And on special occasions, Cancer would be happier exchanging gifts in the privacy of their home rather than before guests chosen as often as not to advance the Leo partner's career. Even so, ambition will tone down Cancer's protests.

If Leo insists on imposing kingly will in all things, Cancer self-pity may expand to a full-blown martyr complex. Once on the defensive the Cancer partner will resist all attempts at conciliation. The emotional tides within Cancer personality will eventually burst out to inundate the Leo ardor. Leo can dry Cancer's tears for a while, but when they accumulate behind a wall of resentment Leo fire is threatened.

These two will be in accord on the role children play in the family: they are to be loved and protected and sacrificed for and lavished upon—and displayed as model offspring before the world. Many freedoms will not be tolerated by these parents, but the youngsters soon learn that the advantages here outweigh the disadvantages of going along with parental demands. Nothing will be too good for these children as long as they stay within the golden ropes which mark the limits of their playground. This protective parental attitude may hold all through life, with the children falling back time and again on help from home. And in truth, both Leo and Cancer are usually successful enough to indulge themselves in this desire to do *for* their children.

Though Cancer may suffer agonies of hurt feelings through the actions of the Leo partner, the relationship will probably survive, especially if Leo (as usually happens) achieves financial success. Cancer has a sensitive soul, but also appreciates the protection afforded by a lovely home and substantial bank account. Leo may be impatient of Cancer emotionalism, but loves attention; and Cancer knows no peer when it comes to catering to a loved one.

Cancer-Virgo

Cancer and Virgo can build a highly satisfying relationship using shared traits—plus and minus—to support and fulfill each other. But it will be a relationship only a Cancer/Virgo duet would enjoy. This is not a strong, magnetic attraction that will not be denied; it is based on practical considerations that recognize the value of pooling their resources to the benefit of both.

Virgo may feel some reluctance to pursue the initial attraction, but will be drawn to Cancer almost as a dragonfly is drawn to the lantern—almost against the will. Cancer may be reluctant to accept Virgoan attentions, but will recognize the possibility of bringing the Virgo personality to life through emotional interaction, as the desert flourishes under irrigation. Cancer's attitude is always that of the mother who gives life and helps it grow; the Moon Child will water Virgo Earth with tears, but will see it bloom.

They share many traits, and most of these might be negatives for other Signs. They show in better light in this relationship, possibly because they are at home in both Signs. Moodiness for instance, which can spell disaster in some Sun combinations, is simply a way of life which Virgo and Cancer understand. Cancer can be sympathetic when Virgo is down; Virgo can wait when Cancer crawls into a shell until the oppressive weight is lifted from Cancer spirits. It won't matter if the black moods coincide; neither is aware of others when huddling under a cloud.

Worry goes hand in glove with these dark moments, and Cancer and Virgo will be able to share the dubious pleasure of sweating out troubles that never materialize. There is an element of discontent in both Signs; they will be able to dissipate some of this dissatisfaction through talking with each other. Most companions reach a point of irritability after being exposed to a seemingly constant litany of mild complaints which often laces the conversation of these two. The friction will come, if it does, through the manner in which they discuss their troubles. Virgo will shudder when drenched in Cancer tears, and will probably respond with waspish criticisms that cut Cancer to the quick—prompting more tears and sarcasm—and the circle continues until one or the other goes into hiding.

But there will be large compensations also. Both Virgo and Cancer have a frugal streak in their characters, and each appreciates this quality in the other. They are not stingy, but they want value for money spent—every penny of it—and they save for what they want. They will acquire lovely possessions over the years, and they will gloat over them at times. But they will live in elegance at half the cost that others pay. Cancer and Virgo both have the knack of supporting champagne tastes on beer pocketbooks.

Truly their home will be a private place they reserve for themselves and those close to them. A person who is invited to share the intimacy of the Cancer-Virgo home is indeed a friend. Both these Suns are hard workers, and they will not tolerate careless treatment of their treasures by casual acquaintances. A cigarette burn in a carpet may mean the culprit will not be invited back again.

It's likely both partners will hold good jobs, investing their money carefully while following a closely worked-out budget. They will share home chores as a matter of course. Both Cancer and Virgo enjoy cooking; both like to keep the home neat and inviting. There will be no conflict over division of duties.

There may be some adjustment required in the intimate relationship, with Virgo suspicious (maybe scared stiff) of the emotionalism of the Cancer partner. And Cancer will suffer from the apparent coldness of the mate when Virgo is in a detached frame of mind. But Cancer can transfer emotional commitment from mate to children—or home—or job—if a personal relationship leaves something to be desired.

It's probable this pair of Suns will limit the size of their family, which may be too bad, considering the concentration of parental concern that will focus on the offspring. Cancer protection of the children can be all-encompassing, especially if the partner's attention is on other things. And Virgo's critical attitude will place demands on the children almost before they are out of the cradle. Virgo and Cancer both have strict standards for their children, many of which seem petty to others. But these children will usually manage to work their own balancing act in the emotional area, turning to the Cancer parent for consolation and emotional support when the Virgo parent's criticism cuts too deeply; seeking out the Virgo parent when Cancer "smother love" threatens.

A relationship that will last, growing mellower with the years, as possessions accumulate to help compensate for frictions, will be curiously rewarding to both partners as they look back over a lifetime together.

Cancer-Libra

For pure charm this duo is hard to beat. They'll pamper and indulge each other. They will specialize in sentimental gestures, faithfully exchanging valentines through the decades and commemorating anniversaries with long-stemmed roses—one for each year. To those who know them this will seem a perpetual courtship. If Libra feels apprehensive at times in the wash of Cancer emotionalism, or Cancer suffers from a feeling that Libra doesn't care enough, no one else will know.

These two love the traditional trappings of a "successful" marriage: a nice home, a good car, lovely clothes, and a certain social standing in the community. As long as they channel their energies toward realization of these goals they get along beautifully together. These are Cardinal Signs, and they move forward in appropriate ways to realize their aspirations. Libra seems to attract money (often through marriage to a partner who will help further the career). In this union with Cancer Libra has chosen well in finding a mate who knows how to manage their resources to show the most for the investment.

Cancer frugality nicely balances Libra's use of generosity to ensure pleasant relationships with those close. Libra often tries to buy pleasant interaction with others through charm or gifts. Cancer will attempt to buy affection through constant hovering. But Libra will be willing to pay the price of being hovered over to gain the attention so acceptable to Libra.

It is in their intimate relationship that the squared Suns make their tensions felt. Here mutual jealousy comes to the fore; the possessiveness of both Signs conflicts. Here the self-centeredness of both Signs is most apt to emerge as selfishness. Each wants—demands—

first place, and tensions stretch taut as they jockey for position. Charm and tact rub thin quickly when these two square off at each other, as often as not over seemingly trivial differences. Cancer will all but drown in a sea of self-pity if Libra bruises sensitive feelings. Libra will walk away without looking to the left or right if personal rights seem threatened.

Talking things out doesn't work well with these two. Cancer wants tangible assurances of being loved, and Libra wants tangible assurances of being loved, and they will sulk for days waiting for the mate to make the first declaration. Both can be totally self-centered when they choose to be.

And yet the relationship tolerates these stresses. Libra may detest Cancer's tears during arguments, but can appreciate the fact that Cancer does not shout when angry. And if Libra's answer to a pressing problem is to go next door and enjoy a neighbor's company, at least it allows Cancer leeway to luxuriate in self-pity. Deep inside each knows the relationship will assume its pleasant facade once the immediate storm subsides. The home is much too important for Cancer to give it up for the sake of hurt feelings; and the marriage relationship is so important that Libra will, in the end, make what concessions are required to keep it intact.

The jealousy each harbors—a serious detriment in most relationships—works to advantage here. Libra, feeling a relationship threatened, will tighten all holds on the other person—emotional, psychological, economic. Cancer responds to this assurance of being wanted and needed.

Either of these Signs can be jealous of the mate's attentions to the children, however. Cancer may lavish concern on the younsters at the expense of the marital relationship. Libra will retaliate by indulging them with gifts or excessive financial support, to the consternation of Cancer. Over the years this trend may grow to where the two continue their mechanical surface expressions of love over seething inner resentment that has them muttering, "I love you, too" through clenched teeth. Children may use this emotional tug-of-war to play one parent against the other to gain their own ends. What appears to be a happy household may, in fact, be a most unhappy place.

Individual planet placements will play an especially strong role in this relationship, for better or worse. With strength from individual charts, the very traits that work for the union may fall victim to increased influence from the squared Suns, intensifying conflicts without the mitigating influences.

It can be done. These Suns can work out a relationship that is rewarding and permanent. But it will probably fall on the Cancer partner to make the lion's share of concessions. Cancer is hardworking and persevering in protecting the home environment. Libra may insist that they keep trying to preserve the relationship while falling short in making constructive contributions toward that end. But Libran charm will be able to keep Cancer working at the task to the very end in most cases.

Cancer-Scorpio

The emotional interaction of these two Water Signs is intense; it seems to hold forever in spite of forbidding traits that conflict. The magnetic attraction is so compelling that these two often remain together in a relationship in spite of conflicts that torment. Yet they may never achieve true empathy in spite of this fated attraction.

All Water Signs relate harmoniously, but Cancer and Scorpio carry the interaction to deep emotional levels. The Scorpio character is akin to the giant rivers that flow relentlessly forward, cutting strong channels to the ocean. Cancer character is akin to water under tremendous pressure at the bottom of the sea. Both feel more comfortable with privacy than in crowded public places. Each fears exposure of the inner self to others.

In close relationships Scorpio is relentless in the desire to possess the loved one; Cancer is tenacious in clinging to the mate. Each is jealous of the mate in relation to others; both are emotional in their commitment to the partner.

Traits that seem to oppose work here to support the relationship. Scorpio is supremely self-confident and usually takes the lead, once a relationship is established. Cancer often lacks self-confidence and will fall into position and follow Scorpio's lead. Cancer will usually concur with Scorpion opinions; will always defer to them.

They will see eye to eye on finances. Both these Signs have great respect for money and for the ways it can be used to work for them. Cancer frugality will not be challenged by Scorpio's use of joint funds; they will shop carefully and receive full value for their money, and both will be pleased with the results. They will not be too far apart in their likes and dislikes. Scorpio will be attracted to more ornate items than Cancer, but either will give a little without really compromising personal taste.

They may share a common career. They work well together in enterprises that may be a little off the beaten path. Scorpio likes to dig for information that is buried or hidden. Cancer is drawn to the past and is tenacious in pursuing personal interests. They both have stamina to continue their probings long past the point where others have given up. They can work together successfully in matters relating to finance; or in careers related to the past: geneology, antiques, archeology. Cancer intuition sheds light on background information ferreted out by Scorpio. Both are ambitious and will see projects through to conclusion.

Moodiness will hamper the relationship at times, but not as much as with some combinations. For Cancer and Scorpio, moodiness is a fact of life to be dealt with on a day-to-day basis. But emotionalism places a damper on the spirits of these two Suns. Cancer, overly sensitive to criticism, will be wounded often by the tactlessness of Scorpio. There is little of the subtle in the Scorpio make up. Scorpio moves with arrogance and does not give leeway for human frailty. This is a Sign of tremendous talents and little empathy; Scorpio demands the same superlative response from those close. Not everyone can measure up. Cancer can give the Scorpio a run for the money, but may suffer from continuing demands for perfection from the mate.

There will be few problems in the intimacy of close relationships. Cancer may wish for a little less passion and a little more sentiment, but will glory in the possessiveness of Scorpio who desires only to be alone— all alone—with the mate. Scorpio may resent the nagging of Cancer but will hold tight to a mate that is as possessive as the Scorpio variety. These Suns, interacting generate love of great intensity.

Children of the two may feel smothered in the humid atmosphere of the emotionally charged home. They may find it extremely difficult to reserve any part of themselves from the avid concern of the parents. Both Scorpio and Cancer may become so engrossed in the lives of their children they seem to be eating them alive. There is danger here that one parent will become jealous of the deep involvement of the mate with the children.

Pressures then can be almost intolerable for the whole family.

Whichever form the conflicts take, the relationship will hold together in most cases. "Till death do us part" is not just a traditional phrase in the Scorpio-Cancer marriage ceremony. They will have about as much chance escaping the tides of this mutual passion as they would have of swimming upstream against the tides of the Amazon.

Cancer-Sagittarius

What is the magic that draws these two together: a lantern enticing a striped balloon? This romance is more at home in fairy tales—the beautiful princess enamored of a pirate; or Galahad and Guinevere. For Sagittarius, ruled by Jupiter, is a rover, exploring dangerous corners of the world and thought and emotions. And Cancer sees by the shadows of pale moonlight, and is subject to elusive moods. Sagittarian vitality, larger than life and booming with earthy good humor, can frighten the sensitive Moon Child.

Where is the meeting place, then, for these two diverse Suns? An arrow is a poor weapon with which to snare a moonbeam. Lifelines between the two are few and fragile. But they do exist. All quincunx Signs have interconnecting traits, not always obvious, but usable.

Intuition is native to both Cancer and Sagittarius, and allows an exchange flow of empathy. Water and Fire usually have hard going in the emotional areas of a relationship; brought together, the result resembles a pressure cooker. Here, however, there are mitigating factors. The mutability of Sagittarius relates to the Water element of Cancer; and Cancer's protectiveness assumes something of the Fire quality of Sagittarius in its aggressive force. Someway—somehow—the initial attraction leads to an attempt at permanence.

But success may remain just out of reach, no matter how hard these two work at living together. Oppositions are many, and supporting traits few. Everything about Sagittarius is larger than life; minus traits are expanded quite as readily as positive traits, so that generosity becomes extravagance, a gutsy appetite becomes gluttony, bluntness becomes rudeness—or worse, crudeness.

So with Cancer: moodiness can become isolation, thriftiness can become stinginess, self-pity can become martyrdom, protectiveness can become possession. Some of these minuses counteract each other. Cancer frugality can help balance the carefree largesse of Sagittarius; Cancer's love of cooking can produce balanced meals that keep the Jupiterian appetite under control. Cancer tact can help smooth over the blunt Archer approach; patience can soothe irritability. The overprotective hovering of Cancer can sometimes forestall the wild risks the Sagittarian mate takes—both physical and financial.

There is a little of Huck Finn in every Sagittarian man; every Cancer woman is The Mother. In reverse, the Cancer mate can blanket the emancipated Archer woman from some of the more obvious wounds received while challenging established traditions.

But there will always be emotional tensions working at cross purposes between the two. Cancer is a traditionalist; the home is a haven of conventional customs, furnished with antiques as likely as not, and crowded with family heirlooms. Sagittarius has nothing against antiques and heirlooms but they are not to be worshiped. For Sagittarius a hundred-year-old needlepoint footstool is still to be used for propping up feet. If shoes are muddy Sagittarius will kick them off before propping up feet on the stool, but that is about as far as the Archer goes in catering to Cancer "householding."

Cancer is as protective of privacy as of possessions, and will resent the intrusion of spur-of-the-moment friends that Sagittarius brings home without notice. All the tact at Cancer's command will not disguise this resentment when the Archer opens the home to passing gypsies or salesmen. Nor will Sagittarius sit still for the nagging that usually follows these big-hearted gestures. Archer temper will flare time and again as Cancer attempts to pin Sagittarius down to an orderly routine, and sooner or later the blunt sarcasm for which Sagittarius is noted will be turned on the mate, driving Cancer to withdraw behind a wall of frosty silence that takes days to warm up.

What the Cancer mate often forgets is that the black moods of Sagittarius can be as intense as Cancer moods, if not so frequent. If both Cancer and Sagittarius moods touch bottom at the same time, the result could be murder (almost literally).

Sagittarius will keep Cancer on pins and needles most of the time with freewheeling indifference to personal danger. Cancer, who cringes when the children climb a sapling, will suffer trauma when riding with Sagittarius behind the steering wheel. Chances are Cancer will take over the checking account in this union; Cancer hasn't the emotional stamina to suffer through the irresponsibility most Sagittarians show toward finances. But Cancer will never cease to be amazed at the luck which comes the way of the Archer mate as Jupiter seems to rescue Sagittarius from certain ruin time after time.

The emotional area of the relationship should, by all indications, be a disaster; as a matter of fact an almost magical attraction exists between the two. It's hard to reason why—but there it is: Cancerian and Sagittarian

128

romances have powerful magnetic forces working to offset the daily irritations that beset them. Sagittarius, who buckles and swashes through life, and in the process invites many wounds, is like a mischievous child who turns into a cherub when day is done. The Archer will relax gratefully into the arms of the Cancer partner to be held safe until morning. And both are blissfully fulfilled.

Their children may have a rugged time of it, tempted to follow the errant Sagittarius parent to greener pastures; snatched back from the brink of adventure time and again to the snug safety of the Cancer nest. They'll probably never cease trying to sneak out the window, and will never quite escape Cancer vigilance, until they reach adulthood. There should be some balancing of these conflicting parental traits—Sagittarian philosophy counteracting Cancer emotionalism; Cancer patience taking the sting from Archer irritability.

No matter how many times Sagittarius leaves—or threatens departure; no matter how many times Cancer threatens suicide; this duet will probably maintain a permanent relationship. They may live in semi-independence from each other, but Cancer will maintain the home if at all possible, and Sagittarius will not be able to resist the temptation to check in at regular intervals to see if the magic is still operating between them.

Cancer-Capricorn

The extremes of polarity are seen in this relationship: the receptive softness of the Mother opposite the stern strength of the Father; indulgence opposing discipline.

Straight across the board, Cancer and Capricorn are at opposite ends of the crossbar which is balanced on a foundation of ambition and a desire for status. Yet the weaknesses and strengths of these partners focus at the center where the supports are the greatest. This is an enduring combination.

These Suns are traditionalists all the way: established mores and conventions will be yardsticks against which they measure their successes and failures. Although they seem as far apart as the mountain peak from the ocean bed, it must not be forgotten that these two environments spring from the same source. What is now mountain peak was once ocean floor; the rocks at the bottom of the sea once crowned the tops of mountains.

Thus, traits that seem foreign to each other come together in the middle and blend—perhaps after much anguish on the part of both mates—to a workable resource from which to build a firm relationship. Both Signs have the stamina to work hard to reach their goals. These goals will always be substantial, leading to status which is important to both. Theirs is not a craving for the brilliant affluence of Leo, nor the esoteric luxury of Pisces, nor the sensual opulence of Taurus. Theirs will be the solid grandeur epitomized by the fine old house renovated to former dignity, filled with antiques lovingly gathered and laboriously restored to original beauty. The realization of these dreams will be a labor of love, with heavy emphasis on *labor*.

Conflicts appear in personality differences that move like icebergs through their relationship, the apparently insignificant tips signalling larger problems beneath the surface. Capricorn will be annoyed at the unstable emotions of Cancer. (Stern Saturn finds it disturbing to try to pin down the ever-changing shadows cast by the Moon.) Cancer suffers at the inflexible attitudes of Capricorn, apparently impervious to tears. (A lantern cannot melt a glacier.) These traits generate continuing irritants in this relationship. But they represent twin tips of a mammoth ice float. Both Signs are supersensitive to criticism, seeing slights where none were intended. This is a corrosive element in the union which, by some alchemy, becomes a strengthening factor, weakening Sign traits of each enough to allow opposition elements to infiltrate and blend. Cardinal Water combined with Cardinal Earth eventually molds clay cornerstones that are almost indestructable.

All Cardinal Signs are self-oriented, and Capricorn's attitude is, usually, "If I don't look after myself, who will?" The answer of course, in this relationship, is, "Cancer will." Cancer may be jealous of Capricornian self-sufficiency, before learning to trust the intuitive feeling that Capricorn badly needs the softening influence of emotional responses in order to break through inhibitions which keep feelings locked inside. Capricorn, better than most Signs, can tolerate Cancer moods which periodically drive the Crab into a shell to protect sensitive inner feelings.

Both Suns have executive ability, which Cancer expresses in more subtle ways than Capricorn, who is about as subtle as an avalanche in most situations. Standing tall and solid, Capricorn sees the shortest way to the common goal and assumes command. In the face of hesitation or dissention, Capricorn can become domineering and *demand* that the mate acknowledge the superiority of the plan. Cancer tendency is to defer to the mate. Not without sulking—not without tears—but Capricorn won't notice. Cancer may wear a martyred expression, but will usually end up lighting the way as Capricorn moves forward with the confidence of a Sherman tank.

Cancer tact can go a long way toward smoothing the path for Capricorn, who borrows from Sagittarian bluntness at times. Unable to step easily into another's shoes, Capricorn benefits from Cancer empathy. Capricorn may never admit the *fact* of Cancer's intuition, but will learn to "trust Cancer judgment."

The good old-fashioned virtues of patriotism and honesty and thrift will be working standards in this household. Thrift especially. Cancer frugality works well with Capricorn practicality. Neither feels comfortable without visible evidence of status. They are not stingy with each other however; Cancer desires the finer things of life in order to share them with loved ones; Capricorn expresses love through supplying material comforts for those close. Cancer would prefer to have gifts wrapped in gold foil and topped with a red rose at times, but if there must be a choice, will accept a practical gift in a brown paper wrapping, thereby satisfying *two* basic sides of Cancer nature: acquisitiveness and self-pity.

Children here will live the Good Life, exemplified by well-fitted shoes, soft oatmeal with cream for breakfast, neatly made beds, warm hand-knitted sweaters and regular trips to the dentist. They will be pampered by the Cancer parent, disciplined by the Capricorn parent, and imbued with spiritual and ethical values from an early age.

All in all—a good relationship. There may be times when Cancer feels cheated by the lack of romance in the union. There may be times when Capricorn is shaken by the emotionalism of the mate. But there will be little chance of either breaking off the relationship.

Cancer-Aquarius

Extremes of emotional development emerge in the Cancer-Aquarius relationship. The universal quality of

Aquarian emotional involvement is light years removed from the inverted, possessive, individualistic emotional focus of Cancer. Aquarius will channel emotions to the intellectual level, and from that base entice the partner toward an interaction of spirit-sense-intellect. Cancer reduces any relationship to the personal by drawing a circle to include the partner in a very private emotional world.

Traits of these Signs are equally balanced between those which compliment and those which oppose. But either influence is overweighted by the basic conflict between feeling and intellect.

Cancer possessiveness is suffocating to the Aquarian, who is uncomfortable with cuddling and pampering. Cancer can no more resist hovering over those close than resist breathing. In the beginning, Cancer admiration can counteract the Aquarian inclination to run, but Aquarius senses that while the soft words of approval fall gently on the ego, the Cancer is busy trying to reinforce the boundaries of the relationship by invisible cords of dependency and love. Aquarian attempts to loosen these bonds will provoke a wall of hurt silence that would make a steel sculpture squirm.

Cancer self-pity can be as deep and wide as the ocean which symbolizes the Sign element. The martyr complex in Cancer is related to the emotional fluctuations of the Moon rulership, which controls the deep tides of Cancer feeling as the Moon controls the ocean tides. The Aquarian has little room for self-oriented emotions. Jealousy and martyrdom imply a preoccupation with self.

Aquarius hates complaining and nagging and demands for accountings. For Cancer these are automatic responses which correlate with the basic possessiveness of Cancer's nature. It is beyond Cancer understanding that the tighter the hold on the Aquarian, the more pressure Aquarius feels toward flight. Cancer may weep and brood alone while waiting for Aquarius to realize that loneliness is the companion of the one who travels solo. But Aquarius forgets loneliness as long as there is a star in sight.

Perception bordering on the psychic allows Aquarius to catch glimpses of Cancer's motives; intuition allows Cancer some understanding of what makes Aquarius tick; but there are so few common anchor points to strengthen this relationship. Cancer—ambitious, patient, traditional in efforts to acquire the security which is basic to the Crab—will be shattered by the unconcern Aquarius shows for establishing financial cornerstones or for acquiring possessions. Cancer will watch with horror as Aquarius risks the joint bankroll on some experimental undertaking that has, apparently, as much chance of succeeding as a crawdad has of swimming the Pacific. Doubling the affront to Cancer's business sense will be the Aquarian's lack of remorse at having endangered mutual resources. Trying to evoke some evidence of such remorse by silent tears and hurt expressions will get Cancer nowhere. Aquarius isn't much for sackcloth and ashes and the mate's tears will affect Aquarius no more than the rising tides touch the Milky Way.

Trying to establish a home together can be a disaster for this pair. Cancer, oriented toward the traditional, will cling to early marriage furnishings long after common sense indicates it's time to call the Goodwill truck. Strongly sentimental, Cancer will cherish cartons of mementos, move trunks full of out-of-style clothing, scrapbooks, picture albums. Anything that floats into the domestic landscape will be permanently attached as if by magnets.

Aquarius will feel suffocated by this private refuse dump; may even growl at the idea of a permanent home base, preferring to be free to move frequently and keep possessions limited to what can be packed into a U-Haul trailer. Both will want a home that reflects artistic tastes, but they will be oceans apart on ideas of what that means. There isn't much chance of compromise, either. Cancer tenacity for traditional values matches in strength the fixed quality of Aquarian tastes.

Too often the battle of the egos is fought through the children. Aquarius will show anger more strongly in the face of Cancer's overprotectiveness of the children than in almost any other direction. Aquarius has strong ideas of how children should be raised, and feels this responsibility keenly. Cancer will writhe at the unconventional ideas Aquarius brings to this area of their family life. The children will be caught in the cross currents of the conflict between emotion and intellect and may be cut to ribbons by the riptides.

The plus factor here may be the fixity and tenacity of these Signs if they work at maintaining the relationship. Cancer will not give up trying to preserve the family circle as long as there is a spark of hope. A sense of resonsibility to the family may keep Aquarius perservering in the effort to work things out. But it will be a hard pull after the first fascination palls, and the basic conflicts between these two Suns will never be completely resolved.

Cancer-Pisces

Cancer and Pisces have many traits in common. Both reflect the world around them with sensitivity bordering on the sentimental; in both, responses to others are deeply emotional. All Water Signs share the receptivity of their element.

But just as the depth and rhythm of the ocean tides

differ from the elusive clarity of mountain streams, so Cancer and Pisces differ. Because the surface personalities may seem alike, and the deeper reactions are so different, these two Signs are capable of wounding each other deeply at basic levels. It is as if a smoothly flowing river divides sharply at a certain point, one half ending in a hidden lake; the other pushing tenaciously to reunite with the sea.

Both Cancer and Pisces react to their environments with painful responsiveness. At first meeting they react to each other the same way. But neither Sign has self-confidence. Strongly intuitive, they *feel* the rightness of what they do while finding it difficult—even distasteful—to prove their positions with logical reasons. Either is at the mercy of anyone who speaks with conviction and logic, no matter how distorted the logic may be.

Pisces—impractical, idealistic—supports lagging self-confidence through approval from others. Empathy allows Pisces to see a situation from another's viewpoint. Pisces is disoriented without tangible evidence that the mate agrees with and approves of personal actions.

Cancer, while craving approval just as much, is practical and ambitious; learns early that one can move forward much faster by proving a position if it is required. Cancer does this by finding a position which does not violate personal conscience and then works through channels to bring others around to the Cancer's way of thinking. When the two points of view conflict in this relationship, there is apt to be disillusionment on both sides. Pisces will feel shock that the Cancer partner can compromise ideals; Cancer will be hurt that the Pisces mate condemns actions that offer practical solutions to problems. Worst of all will be the intensity with which they will condemn themselves for having hurt each other.

Both Pisces and Cancer accept guilt feelings in relationships, yet Cancer has the edge on Pisces when the chips are down. Both are protective of those they love; both give too much if pressures are brought to bear. Cancer, possessive by nature, is often frustrated in attempts to possess Pisces; the harder the attempt, the more Pisces struggles to escape.

Cancer, self-oriented, is motivated to take a stand when under pressure. Pisces, over generous, allows the mate too much margin, hoping things will settle themselves without confrontation, which only delays the issues.

A little selfishness is an asset for those who deal with life emotionally. In this union Cancer will hurt as deeply as Pisces when things go wrong between them, but will hold to a course of action dictated by practical considerations in spite of the pain. Pisces will give way to save further anguish on both sides; then, accepting this as evidence of personal guilt, will blame the partner for refusing to accept guilt too. It is impossible for either of these Signs to conceal true feelings from the partner, and the hurt deepens, and the cycle repeats.

The result can be isolation for both. Cancer and Pisces fall victim of depression when they know there is trouble in a relationship. Cancer, living in unhappiness, often develops a martyr complex and takes refuge in a place deep inside the self, leaving the surface personality as remote as some alien planet to those close. Pisces, completely adrift in the face of this withdrawal, escapes however it can be managed: physically, if possible; mentally, by work or studies which offer a legitimate excuse for noncommunications; and as a last resort, in alcohol or drugs. And each weeps for the hurt they cause each other.

The home and children offers the strongest base for building a lasting relationship between these Suns. The home is of prime importance to both; loved ones are placed ahead of personal demands. The only intrusion a job can make with either is to ensure necessary funds with which to provide for loved ones. Children have such tight bonds on both these Signs that it is possible for trouble to come through one parent giving preference to children to the exclusion of the marriage partner.

Cancer, possessive and protective, may suffer most in this situation while seemingly less deserving of sympathy. Cancer, isolated from the mate, clings more and more closely to children, fearful of losing all that is dear. Pisces, however much in need of the children's approval, will recognize the necessity for them to go their own ways.

Basic attitudes toward money can bring problems too. Cancer spends wisely, and is willing to wait for the best, but will be very sure the money can be afforded before spending. Very often the "best" here equates with "the most expensive." Cancer, with a basic fear of being without adequate resources, will never threaten the balance in the savings account no matter how much some treasure is desired.

Pisces will also plan before buying, but may not be able to resist spending the last dollar for something that will bring pleasure, on the spur of the moment. Pisces seems to attract resources as needed and does not share Cancer's insecurity when money is scarce. And treasures, being measured in terms of pleasure, will not require the capital outlay, usually, that Cancer's do. Pisces finds the same delight in a beautiful shell as Cancer finds in a rare antique necklace.

If they can somehow keep the emotionalism under control Cancer and Pisces may be able to create a relationship of deep and lasting passion. Both feel a strong need to make others happy. They can bear with each other's moods as long as there is basic assurance of love from both sides.

Neither would enter into nor maintain a relationship for material reasons; but being concientious people, they will hold a relationship together as long as they feel the mate is trying to make it work. This allows them time to work out problems that hang on.

Any relationship between these two Signs will be exceptionally rewarding or exceptionally painful; and there will always be a strong emotional tie whether it lasts or is broken by necessity.

LEO

LEO-ARIES (Page 21)

A relationship built on a base of exploding roman
candles set off by enduring passion. This romance can
set the world on fire!

LEO-TAURUS (Page 57)

These Signs will battle and love with equal passion, and
through it all preserve a larger-than-life relationship
that endures. They balance each other in the small,
important ways.

LEO-GEMINI (Page 87)

Esteem and pride support love here. Fire burns steadily
and warms Air, to the fulfillment of both. A relationship that sparkles and glows.

LEO-CANCER (Page 115)

Interaction of Sun and Moon create magnetism between
these two. Although they never quite manage precision
steps together, they are never quite able to free themselves to dance separate routines.

Leo-Leo

What would you expect from the coming together of two high-tension wires? It usually happens when two Leos are within touching distance. And yet they may find themselves tempted to try over and over. There is so little chance of the relationship surviving that those around them will wonder why they keep at it.

The basic fire of Leo Sun personality is fed by Leo pride, so that what starts out as a good old-fashioned furnace becomes, doubled, a nuclear reactor. Where Aries Suns generate a consuming desire to be *first* in each partner, Leo Suns demand that each mate be supreme commander.

Then what is the force that keeps two Lions braving this potentially destructive relationship? Love. And magnetism. Leos are physically attractive people, and Lions are prone to love at first sight. These two are drawn toward each other the moment they come into the same room. But once they find themselves together in the spotlight—it's almost inevitable that they will—they begin to upstage each other. One may briefly succeed in driving the other into the wings, but even while one is taking a bow, the partner will swoop down from the lofts a la Peter Pan to draw the eyes of the audience away from the mate.

This pattern will be repeated in a never-ending cycle whenever two Leos attempt to establish a relationship. And stimulating this continuing battle royal can be real love that outlasts their attempts to live together under one roof.

If there is money enough and talent enough and forebearance enough to allow them to live their lives in separate but overlapping circles, love may be able to sustain a basic relationship.

They will desire children and take great pride in them whether the relationship holds, or the parents go on to new alliances. These children will have tremendous standards to live up to, but there will be tremendous love to back them up, and tremendous rewards for playing golden sunflowers to the parent Suns.

If both Leo partners have evolved beyond the kingly belief in divine right, the royal jealousies, the vainglorious self-indulgences, to a point where they can tolerate equals, this can be an elegant love story that others remember as a fairy tale romance. If either—or both—mates are of less developed character, the clawing and snarling and battling for supremacy can resemble two challenging jungle beasts.

There's little possibility of "in between" here—it's all, or nothing at all. Which is exactly the way two Leos will want it.

Leo-Virgo

It happens. But when it does, it shouldn't. Earth smothers Fire; and Fire ravages Earth. The Lion and the Virgin trying to find something in common usually come up with temper tantrums, which does justice to neither. Virgo is one of the least social Signs; Leo one of the most social. Virgo is apprehensive of glittering facades; Leo couldn't care less about the details behind grandiose projects. Not that Leo wouldn't appreciate Virgo taking care of all the gritty little chores that must be handled in order to produce the results Leo wants to flash upon the world; the Lion doesn't want to be involved at close range. Leo is apt to look down on the person who doesn't operate on the grand scale. Virgo isn't interested in panoramic endeavors but focuses on the details. It works sometimes as a business partnership: Leo charming the public Virgo balancing the books. As a personal relationship the chances for success are not great.

All Fire Signs have an aggressive, exhuberant tone to their characters. True, in Leo this trait is filtered through self-importance, but it is strong in its own right. Virgo is reticent, preferring to edge into the crowd and remain unnoticed. Leo is always found front and center in any gathering.

They may originally be drawn together by Virgo's desire to be of service and Leo's desire to be waited on. But there isn't enough to back up a lasting relationship as a general rule.

Alone together they will find it hard going. Leo sets the conditions of any encounter by assumption of star billing, and others are automatically cast as bit players. Leo pulls this off in most relationships with such charm that companions are more flattered than indignant and react with admiration.

Virgo social graces are learned according to the book, and that about says it. Virgo simply doesn't recognize Leo's game. Flattery is a word left out of the Virgo vocabulary—Virgo wouldn't know how to go about it. Leo feels most Virgos are rather dull; and Virgo feels most Leos are rather frightening. And both are wrong. But it doesn't make for an easy relationship.

The extravagance of Leo leaves Virgo speechless. There will be constant conflicts over use of mutual funds. Virgo is a statistician; the checkbook will balance to the last decimal. Leo considers credit cards money in the bank. In the flush of prosperity as a result from a salary increase, the Lion may rush downtown and buy luxuries on credit, only to find come payday the monthly payments are substantially greater than the pay increase. Virgo is appalled at the thought of being in debt, even when necessary.

A Virgo trying to keep tabs on a Leo mate's spending will live in hell. For Leo, having the mate demand an accounting of money spent down to the last penny or being put on an allowance will truly be a fate worse than death.

In establishing a home together these two will grind away at each other like stones in an avalanche. Leo is a front man—the epitome of luxury in public—but the home may be a mess. Fastidious Virgo will be driven to distraction by a bathroom splashed with toothpaste spatters; unmade beds that resemble the morning after an orgy; a living room littered with reeking ashtrays and scattered clothes.

Leo, sensitive as a mashed thumb to the suggestion of imperfection, will rage at Virgo criticism. Virgo, knowing whose side the truth is on, will be relentless in trying to reform Leo. To put it bluntly, Virgo becomes a nagger when the environment does not shape up to meticulous Virgoan standards.

Leo's carelessness with food and cooking offends the Virgo, who wants the kitchen antiseptically clean. Most Virgos are excellent cooks and will take over cooking chores if the partner doesn't measure up. Which will bother Leo not at all. The Lion is not given to menial chores, and cooking involves a great deal of work which Leo considers menial.

In intimacy they might—just might—be able to find a meeting ground that would do both Signs justice and allow them to appear at their best with each other. Leo love is of a special quality—the essence of love as the source of life. There is a spiritual emphasis in Virgo love that suggests purity and responds to the special quality of Leo love. Virgo emphasis on sex is not strong; many Virgos never marry. The ardor of the Fire Signs is expressed in Leo as a steadfast belief in love as the basic ingredient in the relationship. They may be able to make it work if they try hard enough.

Children may suffer: overindulged one moment (Leo) and sternly admonished the next (Virgo). Virgo parents are naggers. Their, ''Pick up your coat! Take off your boots! Did you brush your teeth?'' routine has to be experienced to be believed. Virgoes expect their children to be born with the ten commandments and a book of etiquette etched on their souls. The messiness of infants is repulsive to the Virgo parent. Leo is enchanted with the child as a plaything; Virgo will forever be picking up damp diapers (by two fingers, of course) which Leo has dropped on the living room floor.

The Virgo parent will suffer. Guess who's going to seem the good guy to the children: the parent who nags for their own good, or the one who lavishes and indulges their wishes? Virgo, often tongue-tied in expressing love, will suffer at the easy way Leo shows affection. About the only time their thinking will coincide in the matter of rearing children will be in their mutual demands that offspring live up to high standards of behavior. Both Leo and Virgo will expect their children to be models of perfection, especially in public.

With so little in common it seems doubtful the twain would ever meet. They do form relationships. But the divorce papers between these Signs just about equal the marriage licenses.

Leo-Libra

All that is lacking in the Leo-Virgo relationship is abundantly present in this one. Even their minus qualities balance each other out to achieve harmony in the union, so vital to Libra. Each functions to advantage together—and that can be at a very high level.

Social interaction will be a basic ingredient in this successful pairing. Leo will always seek the light of public admiration. An appreciative mate—and Libra is that—is an asset which supports Leo's belief in personal superiority. Fire burns brightly with a steady supply of air. Libra will not be uncomfortable with Leo's desire to make the social scene. Libra doesn't have the avid desire to be socially important, nor use social contacts to further a career, as Leo does; but neither does Libra object to Leo's efforts in that direction. Libra supports and enhances Leo's activities, and enjoys the special privileges that go with the social successes Leo manages to pull off.

Libra, like Leo, enjoys the affluent life, but sometimes has trouble finding it. Libra must always weigh pros and cons, and often misses out on opportunities from taking so long to make decisions. Leo, like all Fire Signs, is impulsive and aggressive in seeking objectives. Libra finds this admirable, especially since Leo retains personal dignity while pushing to the top. Libra has a strong feeling for what is "appropriate" and Leo never violates this feeling. They do each other proud.

They are generous, with each other and with those around them. But they share a common trait of benign selfishness in their giving. Gifts are chosen to satisfy their own feelings of generosity rather than to please the receivers. And neither thinks much of that "It isn't the gift, it's the thought" idea. Unless it is exactly what is desired, Libra will simply ignore it. Leo is apt to be disdainful of any gift that isn't obviously expensive or given by someone considered a VIP. Leo wants to be the giver anyway, never the recipient. It was probably a Leo and Libra who agreed to give each other gifts they wanted for themselves under the Christmas tree, to be exchanged after they were opened.

Leo extravagance may give Libra a few bad moments now and then, but only a few. Libra attracts money and Leo attracts success, and they seldom lack funds to allow them to indulge their champagne tastes.

Their personal relationship is quite as charming as their public image suggests. Leo ardor manages to live up to Ligra's unrealistic dreams of what the marital partner should be. Libra will defer to Leo almost automatically to balance out the relationship, appreciating Leo's innate dignity while responding to Leonine aggressiveness in love. They really do compliment each other.

True, both are sensitive to criticism, and Libra (akin to Virgo or Taurus in demanding an attractive home environment) will be affronted by Leo's indifference to disorder. But to tell the truth, Libra will contribute to the disorder. Libra, usually spoiled by loving parents (charm works as well on Mamas and Daddies as with chance acquaintances), can display selfishness easily when wishes are not granted. Libra will put pressure on Leo to keep the house in order—but charmingly. The iron hand in the velvet glove would rather direct than do the dusting. But subtle hints glance off Leo like tissue-paper airplanes; the Lion doesn't even notice. This may turn into a continuing, low-keyed feud which goes on and on.

Leo's sense of self-importance is as strong as Libra's selfishness, and more noticeable. Leo charm is often laid aside in dealing with those of the inner circle, and the Lion becomes the king dispensing orders. Leo will expect gratitude, approval, and obedience from the mate, all in the name of love. The word "obey" will never be written out of the marriage ceremony in a Leo wedding.

But Leo pulls it off as often as not: Libra, the negotiator who brings the relatinship into balance, will take what concessions can be gained by using charm to flatter the Lion; will stretch the truth if necessary (Libra would never *lie*) to take advantage of Leo's trustfulness; and when indicated, will concede.

Sincerety will counterbalance the effects of this manipulation by the Libran. Both these Signs are sincere in their affection and admiration for each other. They are possessive, too, but that's all right; Libra knows Leo finds the mate important; and Leo knows Libra finds the marriage important. They cater to each other. They are friendly people who are not too often given to dark moods. Leo may sulk now and then when affairs are not to his liking; Libra may refuse to talk for a while. But neither can maintain this isolation for long.

They'll work together well in rearing children, with a tendency to spoil them more than they discipline them. But there will be emphasis on what their children "should" do, and while they never actually lower the boom on obstreprous offspring, they can threaten with a mighty big stick—loss of privileges. Privileges in this household can be well worth the youngsters' efforts to live up to house rules.

Others may find themselves a little envious of this pair as they move through life a little above the crowd, scattering a combination of gold coins and rose petals in their wake. And loving (each other) every minute of it.

Leo-Scorpio

These Suns come together as giants challenging each other, often to the death. There are no weaknesses in the interaction; even the negatively developed traits give them the strength of monoliths as they clash head on. Scorpio has the stamina to stand up to Leo and have something of an advantage. The Scorpion character has subfacets; the Lion never knows whether he will tangle with the eagle, the serpent, the dove, or be stung by the scorpion. This is one of the few relationships in which Leo can be vulnerable.

The Suns square, and even when there are contact points they threaten each other. Leo stalks the banks of secretive Scorpio emotions, in danger of being drawn under and drowned in their depths. The serpent may glide close to trap the Lion, and be burned to death in the act of striking. There is no middle ground. Yet they fascinate each other: fire seeking the only water deep enough to cool the flames within; water seeking the penetrating warmth that only the Sun's energy gives.

Ambition can be the driving force which carries them along side by side, yet the relationship may end up devouring both. Still, each has the power to continue in the union long past the time when it would have destroyed Signs of lesser strengths. The superlative abilities of Scorpio can place powerrful supports under the extravagant productions of Leo. They can achieve goals of such scope that others cannot grasp their significance. Whatever they do will have far-reaching consequences on whatever level. Pluto and the Sun in conjunction can generate profound change and bring about monumental results.

If only there was something complementary with which to balance out the challenging traits which play such an important part in this relationship! They will tear each other to pieces even while they are succeeding beyond their wildest dreams in achieving mutual goals. Sooner or later the Scorpion will lash out and sting the Lion for some transgression; that is, if the Lion doesn't first crush the Scorpio with a swipe of the paw.

They are too self-oriented to consider the other's side in conflict. United they can withstand armies of the world, and they often battle each other with the same strength. Scorpio, secretive and possessive, will bitterly resent the social activity which is the Lion's springboard to success. Scorpio loves with passion; does not want the mate constantly on parade before a spotlight which exposes every facet to the public eye. Leo's exuberance may irritate Scorpio. Envy will burn to match the fire of the Leo personality as Leo successes grow.

But there are compensations. These two love with the same depth as they challenge. Scorpio will be protective when the Lion suffers failure; envious when the mate succeeds. Scorpio will take the Leo to some safe and secret hideaway where the Lion can lick wounds and gather energy; will transfer regenerative power to help the mate recover from the blows against pride. Scorpio will be ruthless in attacking those who have caused pain to the Leo mate, and will never give up until those persons make an accounting.

In the same manner Leo will front for Scoprio and will be loving and generous in caring for the mate. Either of these Signs will help the other when help is needed; it is only when they are on an even footing that the conflicts are crucial.

Scorpio will be critical of Leo's wastefulness, and of careless personal habits; and will criticize, knowing Leo's dislike of being put down in any way. Leo cannot accept personal criticism. Scorpio will pull no punches if feeling the mate deserves criticism, however. And Leo will growl if Scorpio moves in too closely. They are of such different temperaments it is hard to see how they ever reach accord.

Only through love will they be able to come close to each other. Their motivations will be different, but love will provide a mutual emotion through which to reach each other. Scorpio is possessive in love even when it is expressed at the highest level. For Leo, love is the element that fires the life force. Love generated between these two can be all-consuming.

Jealousy is strong in both Signs. Leo and Scorpio are magnetic individuals and draw others to them, and the mates will suffer even while feeling pride.

Their children will have great pressure placed on them, especially if they display their own versions of parental temperament. Neither Leo nor Scorpio will permit outright rebellion, but both will indulge and spoil their children as long as surface regulations are met. If the parents are highly evolved individuals, the tendency to indulgence becomes a wise and loving guidance.

Finances may cause problems in this relationship, but not from lack of resources. Both these Signs attract success. The conflicts will come from Scorpio's resentment over Leo extravagance. And it will not matter that Leo will probably have earned the money with which to be extravagant. Scorpio respects money and handles it wisely, often keeping financial affairs secret even from the mate, and will probably try to control the mate's income. Leo will not accept this type of supervision of personal assets and conflict will be the result. But there will seldom be lack of assets.

If they allow their many opposing traits to take ascendance over their basic love for each other, this relationship will be sheer hell for both. If they can keep these wild horses under control, the love they share will approach the divine.

Leo-Sagittarius

This Fire trine Sun combination can be deceptive in it's apparent attraction. True, trines indicate an easy flow of interaction between Signs, and these two will be attracted to each other. But in the most fulfilling relationships there is a balancing give and take, which often does not develop with this pair. Fire Signs are aggressive, and neither Leo nor Sagittarius is lacking in this trait. They decide what they want and go after it. They use different methods, but neither loses any time wondering how to get started.

Their strong reactions lie near the surface of the personality. A Fire Sign native lights up the landscape when experiencing frustration. Add to this the qualitative conflict between the fixed/mutable elements and it's easy to see how the fireworks get out of control here. This will never be a relaxed household.

A basic honesty in both these Signs may form a foundation for a lasting relationship in spite of unstable surface traits: (i.e. Leo pretentiousness which Sagittarius hates with a passion; and Archer nonchalance over responsibilities which Leo finds reprehensible). Leo expects high standards of behavior from the mate; will first serve notice of these expectations and, if they are ignored, will issue ultimatums. By a system of rewards the imperious, generous Leo can usually impose these standards on those in the home circle.

The Lion may have difficulty in understanding that the other Fire Signs are independent in their judgments, too. What Leo may *never* comprehend is that *no one* dictates to a Sagittarian. Leo's threats to withhold favors, meant as a means to enforce personal wishes, may be taken at face value by Sagittarius. Thus the Leo who announces, "If you don't like the house rules, take off!" may be disconcerted to see the Archer galloping away before there is time to backtrack. Usually Sagittarius will be gone before the mate can be too specific in issuing ultimatums, but if the Lion manages to get in some strong statement like, "And never darken my door again!'' may find that this too is taken at face value by Sagittarius. Let alone, the Sagittarian will probably return to the fold once the initial irritation has worn off.

Actually, Sagittarius doesn't mind Leo taking charge if it's done with a light touch. Mutable Signs chafe under executive orders, but need the direction the Fixed Signs can give them. Otherwise they make false starts and scatter their energies as often as not. Sagittarius may learn to play games with the Leo partner in order to smooth their interaction; the Archer can be delightfully persuasive, and knows Leo can be flattered into almost anything. This helps ease the frequent tensions when Sagittarius' unconventional attitudes affronts Leo's dignity, or punctures Leo's self-importance by a few well chosen words.

Leo can be fooled over and over again by these tactics; will view each compliment, each seeming capitulation, as evidence that the mate has come to accept the Lion's views. Leo will never quite accept the truth that any concessions the Sagittarian partner makes will probably be followed by a direct challenge to other beliefs, if for no other reason than that Sagittarius must forever test the reality of personal independence. The Archer will graze the lush pastures provided by Leo generosity with something near to contentment so long as he is not forced to see the fenceposts. Sagittarius doesn't mind contributing to the partnership, but can't stand a saddle—not even one with sterling silver trappings.

Yet Sagittarius will remain loyal to the Leo mate in Archer fashion. Most Sagittarians retain the affection of past loves. And one way or another, Sagittarians often find themselves separated from their loves.

Opposing traits will be more frustrating between Leo and Sagittarius in the personal relationship than in social encounters. At the same time, there will be a blending of the positive qualities which each possesses. The jovial facade of Sagittarius conceals a center core of idealism and a seeking for higher realms of understanding and spirituality; with Leo this seeking unites with the basic spirit of love which is at the center of the Leo character. An almost sacred concept of love may bind these two beyond the understanding of those around them who witness only the frustrations which result from conflicting traits.

If they can work out some system for soft-pedaling the routine irritations that afflict their daily lives, Leo and Sagittarius work well together as parents. Sagittarius, while disdainful of Leo's indulgence of their children, won't judge too severely, especially if Leo furnishes the money; will supply philosophical guidance that will help balance the possessiveness of the Leo parent. Their aims regarding children will be different. Leo will seek to bind them to the home and family through generosity. Leo will be reluctant to lose this longstanding relationship with his children which clearly delineates the parental role of unopposed authority. Sagittarius will seek to have the children become independent—through acquiring knowledge if possible; will help them discover ways of finding their own pathway to the stars. But they will balance each other out. Sagittarius love is buried deep, but it is always there. Leo's love is clearly visible to loved ones.

It can work if the individuals involved can learn to mesh their positive traits rather than give in to impulses that set their opposing traits clashing head on. Once established, the fire of this love burns steadily for a long, long time.

Leo-Capricorn

It would seem a fire hoop and a mountain have little in common. And yet a ring of fire can become a halo under the right conditions. The frozen strength of Saturn, ruler of Capricorn, can keep the fixed fire of the Leo Sun in proportion.

Ambition is a driving trait of both these Signs, and they respect this quality in each other. Further, their natures work well to advance this common ambition. Capricorn is perfectly willing to work behind the scenes to lend support to Leo efforts before the public, and the Lion appreciates this supportive strength while seeking the spotlight. Leo's lofty attitudes and an almost spiritual concept of love will respond to the inner flame of Capricorn's spiritual orientation. Together they can build a structure of lasting value.

Negative developments of traits, which in another Sign combination would be a detriment, here compliment and blend. Initially there may be some jockeying for position, but gradually the Capricorn will settle down to a power-behind-the-throne position while Leo steps into the spotlight to attract an audience. It is a powerful combination and is almost certainly destined for success.

Leo is creative, innovative; Capricorn lacks imagination. But they both have stamina to carry out their plans, and while Capricorn may brood because Leo is having most of the fun, but will also recognize the truth: that the Leo mate will never willingly take on the more uninteresting chores that must be part of any successful venture. Success speaks louder than hurt feelings in this case. Leo will compensate by generous gifts to the mate in recognition of contributions, which will salve a lot of wounds for Capricorn.

In fact, Leo generosity will almost negate the demanding side of the Capricorn character in this union. Capricorn, with some justification, spends a lot of time brooding because of often ending up with the dirty work while more social Signs end up going to the parties. It is easy for Capricorn to fall into a pattern of demanding just dues, and from there proceeds to demanding gratitude, and affection, and consideration. Leo gives these without having to be asked. A demand directed to Leo is almost certain to be refused indignantly; one does not place demands on the king. But Leo can be quite as practical in recognizing a good thing as Capricorn, and will follow a natural inclination to favor those who measure up to approval.

Conflicting attitudes towards finances may not be dealt with so easily in this relationship. Capricorn will have a hard time accepting Leo's extravagance. Most Capricorns have had to work hard to their money and they want to get value for what they spend. Leo has never really learned that "all that glitters is not gold." The Lion will be attracted to things that bear expensive price tags, and may spend far beyond the capacity of the mutual checking account. Capricorn materialism may fight a losing battle with the need to feel appreciated, however, when Leo brings home expensive gifts. Materialism here takes a back seat to this acceptable evidence of Leo's appreciation.

Capricorn will probably have to work to keep the household in any kind of order. Leo is not only messy, but is also disinclined to perform household chores. Capricorn may be caught up in a never-ending battle with cluttered coffee tables, wrinkled clothes piled on chairs, and lost keys which disappear in the general clutter. Capricorn is an ordered person who realizes the value of time and knows the easiest way to have an orderly place in which to live is to put things away after using—to fold newspapers after reading, and hang clothes in closets after they are worn. With Leo there's not much use trying to make these points. Leo will ignore pointed references to his untidiness and continue to expect the Capricorn partner to tidy up. It usually doesn't bother Leo too much if the house is cluttered. Since it *does* bother Capricorn, the Goat will pick up after the sloppy mate but will brood, and resent, and probably develop a full-blown martyr complex about the whole thing. But Capricorn won't desert the relationship. Because the home that demands so much work will be an attractive one, and the clothes waiting to be hung up will be expensive ones.

The one place where the Leo parnter will feel responsibility in this relationship is in the intimate area. Leo interacts easily with others. Capricorn longs to interact, but in personal relationships Saturnian inhibitions come to the fore and block off easy expression of love. Even when Capricorn tries to make the first move, reticence prohibits overtures. When Capricorn tries to be gentle and loving the actions are often heavyhanded and awkward. Leo may have to assume the lead in the romantic interaction; in this case, will probably want to. Capricorn strength and dignity will be a powerful incentive to the Lion. Leo responds to the earthiness of Capricorn's response with Fire Sign ardor. Dignity rescues Capricorn's bedroom manners from crudeness.

This mutual respect for dignity, for recognized conventions, is a strong binding force in this union. The drive for status is strong in Leo, but is more natural to Capricorn. Leo often dazzled by flattery, may be led down the garden path by unscrupulous acquaintances. Capricorn dignity is a handy attribute to have in Leo's corner.

Capricorn may suffer in the matter of raising children in this relationship, but Saturnian discipline will go a long way to counteract spoiling and indulgence which Leo will show them. And Capricorn will back Leo in demanding they measure up to certain standards of behavior and performance. The children may resent so much guidance, and it's almost certain they will show preference for the Leo parent while they are young. But they will profit all their lives by this combination of love and discipline.

This is a quincunx position; and in this combination there is more strength than usual to support the initial attraction between these Signs. Theirs will be a lasting relationship—not without storms, but in the end highly satisfying as they look back together over the path they've climbed to an enviable position of status and affluence.

Leo-Aquarius

These two Suns oppose and compliment each other. In spite of many conflicting traits, the forces which run both ways along this Air-Fire axis are strong and this can develop into a powerful union. It can also be a demanding one for the self-important Leo and the unconventional Aquarian.

Dynamic Leo will be magentized by the Aquarian while worrying over the unconventional attitudes that set Aquarius apart in a crowd. There is a sweetness about Aquarius, even when in rebellion, that is hard to resist; Leo is drawn to this relationship in spite of characteristics that set the Lion's teeth on edge.

Leo is truly a monarch at heart and exhibits this emphasis in relationships. The Lion does not *do* favors, but *dispenses* them; does not *approve* actions of loved ones, but gives a *blessing*; does not *react* in love, but *bestows* love. Yet this regal paternalism so obviously springs from overflowing generosity and love that even Aquarius, who despises pretentiousness, accept this somewhat admiringly as Leo swashes and bows through life.

All Fire Signs tend toward love at first sight. Leo courtships are launched in a flurry of romantic messages, lavish gifts, impressive gestures designed to sweep the chosen ones off their feet. The Aquarian need for praise is only a shade less obvious than Leo's, and the Aquarian will glory in this visible evidence of personal magnetism; will appreciate the impulsive expression of interst; the spontaneous self-confidence with which Leo moves in to establish claim.

Aquarians, next to the last Sign of the Zodiac wheel, gravitate to those who radiate self-confidence and importance. Leo gives the impression of being a person of prominence whether this is true or not. Aquarius will bask in the glow of Leo admiration and reflect some of this impressiveness back to its source—a subtle flattery which Leo cannot resist.

But for every accord there will be an abrasion in this union. The surprising thing is that they keep working at it. Neither Leo nor Aquarius is noted for compromise. Both these Signs attract admirers with ease. It is doubtful they would make concessions to the relationship if it were not for the fact that strong positive complimentary traits more than match their forceful opposing qualities.

Yet even their friends can generate tensions here. Each finds the easy social manner of the other attractive. Aquarius, always tolerant, will accept Leo acquaintances at face value while separating the superficial from the genuine. Leo is susceptible to "friends" whose main qualifications run to silver-tongued compliments that easily generate approval from the Lion. Leo, to the contrary, may meet the friends of the Aquarian mate with arrogant disdain. Leo relies strongly on the price on the cover in judging the contents of the book.

Still, the two can balance this out if they try. Exposure to Aquarian friendships could induce Leo to consider that what one wears may not be as important as what a person *is*; and Aquarius could discover, with delight, that a conventional cover sometimes hides a text of rare depth and excitement.

Generosity, another sterling quality, can give these two some troublesome run-ins. Leo generosity is unlimited as long as the recipient is grateful, accepting, and does not insist on matching the Leo gifts. Leo wants to be the giver; does not receive gracefully. Accepting gifts from others balances the relationship too equally for comfort to the Leo way of thinking. (Kings do not accept gifts; they accept tribute.) From this viewpoint, Leo feels that the giving of gifts includes the right to express often opinionated views on Aquarian actions. The mate, like Caesar's wife, must be above reproach. Appearance must conform to Leo's standards. Experimentation in dress is not encouraged, and any rebellion will bring a threatened withdrawal of favors—like cancellation of credit cards or, in extreme cases, withholding of Leo love.

Aquarius more than most Signs draws on a personal code of behavior which is as binding as Leo's, but will deal with ethics rather than concrete social conventions. Leo possessiveness is closely related to Cancer's in personal relationships. The only thing that makes it more tolerable to Aquarius is the elan with which the fiery Leo moves to impose demands. High style, Aquarius can appreciate; contact with emotional electric fences can short-circuit Aquarian responses.

Children of these parents may end up with the best traits of both Signs. Leo indulgence in material things will be balanced by Aquarian insistence on an understanding of humanitarian and ethical concepts. The children may be able to combine these two influences in a beneficial way that is felt by the whole family. Leo will feel great pride in the children; Aquarius will feel a deep satisfaction that humanistic concepts have been planted in their consciousness.

In intimate relationship the intensity of response may vary widely in the Aquarius-Leo union. Yet this may be the saving grace which allows it to endure. The core of Leo personality is the purity of the love which is lavished on the mate. Sensual and spiritual love combine in Leo to produce inspiration for focusing of the universal love of Aquarius to the personal.

It will depend on whether Aquarius can maintain this personal focus of universal love toward the Leo mate. The Aquarian will bear the burden here to keep this flame burning. And sometimes even this rewarding responsibility can be more than the fiercely independent Aquarius can endure.

Leo-Pisces

These two Suns are drawn together by an attraction based on complimentary weaknesses. In limited amounts, fire adds vitality to water; water cools the effects of fire. In relationships involving sustained inter-action, the effects may manifest as too much of a good thing. Pisces emotionalism may put out Leo fire; or, as more frequently happens, the fiery reactions of Leo can vaporize the fragile Neptunian rainbow.

The initial responses may be stimulated by excitement —a hint of danger—that carries intriguing overtones of sexual magnetism. But the basic force is subconscious recognition of mutually idealistic concepts of love. And it is on this base that successful relationships between

Pisces and Leo will be built.

These two will gravitate toward each other in the most casual encountes. Both Pisces and Leo are magnetic. Holding court in a crowded room, Leo looks for Pisces again and again, as Pisces listens from the fringes of the circle. The Lion moves in quickly to impress Pisces and may not notice that Pisces also moves in quickly, but more subtly. The Lion stalks boldly, with confidence. The Fish maneuvers in shadowy places to achieve the same goal.

On social levels Leo and Pisces are extremely impatico. Creativity forges an immediate bond. They may be drawn together through an interest in the arts. Leo gravitates to those in the spotlight; the Lion is uncomfortable away from the Sun, and a spotlight can be an effective substitute. Pisces is not really at ease in the spotlight, even when seeming to seek it. Or, if a turn at stage center is sought, Pisces must also have equivalent privacy. This Leo cannot understand. Time spent alone is a necessary evil for most Leos—an interval in which to catch a few hours sleep before changing clothes and getting back where the action is.

These differing attitudes toward seclusion can be one of the buried reefs on which the relationship comes to grief. It is a basic difference at work, much more easily resolved in social encounters than in intimate relationship. And it is reflected in many ways.

Both Pisces and Leo command attention in public. They give much attention to personal grooming, take pleasure in attractive surroundings, and are willing to pay for these things. But each places a special, differing, emphasis on these matters.

What is a sense of quality in Pisces may be, in Leo, a taste for what is expensive. Pisces has a basic need for beauty in the personal environment. Leo's need for attractive environment is related to a need to impress others; to allow for self-evaluation in comparison to those the Lion admires. Leo admiration shines brighter for those whose success is apparent to the world at large. Leo is success oriented; Pisces is value oriented.

Pisces at home may dress even more attractively than in public; will, when eating alone, often set the table with fine china and dine by candlelight. Leo behind the scenes lets the glittering facade dim a little. A Leo's home often resembles a Lion's den. The bathroom from which Leo emerges looking like a page from a high-fashion magazine is often a shambles, with rings in the tub and splatters on the mirror. Dishes may accumulate on countertops for days.

The cultural shock when these two first find themselves alone together can be traumatic. Pisces is sensitive to undercurrents of discord; Leo is sensitive to criticism (and any expression of concern will put Leo on the defensive). Leo's self-confidence is strong but requires constant shoring up by flattery and praise; Pisces needs approval from others in establishing relationships. Pisces expresses approval and assumes Leo will do the same. The Lion may absorb Pisces compliments as a matter of course without reciprocating, feeling the fact of being present should be proof to the mate that Leo finds pleasure in being there.

Both these Signs are generous, but where Pisces gives of the self, Leo expresses generosity through expensive gifts—whether or not they can be afforded. Pisces, who is able to turn to inner resources when material ones are low, may see this lavishness as a form of contempt for values which the Fish finds elemental.

Where Leo is high-minded, Pisces is idealistic. Leonine principles can be sacrificed to practicality in a pinch without undue damage to the Lion's self image. Pisces suffers over compromises to principles, and is more apt to sacrifice practical considerations for ideals than the other way around.

Yet neither willingly hurts others. Leo is truly
163

generous with loved ones, and tries to make them happy by giving them the things that make Leo happy. Leo does not usually understand that for Pisces, things take second place to convictions. Even if understanding were there, Leo would not have a change of mind about what *should* make the loved one happy. Pisces will understand Leo's viewpoint in a conflict, but if the conflict involves personal convictions, will hold out forever while feeling guilty for causing Leo pain.

As parents both Signs are loving, overgenerous, inclined to be protective and defensive of their children rather than firm. Yet somehow the children of this union seem to absorb the loving intentions and take advantage of the weaknesses in discipline without suffering too greatly from the experience.

In the end the success or failure of this relationship must rest with the Pisces partner. Leo loves those close with devotion; but the expression of that devotion will be through material means which demand that the world be aware of this devotion. Pisces empathy will be a strong ingredient in holding the relationship together.

In the case of severe conflict, although both will bleed, it will be Pisces who is destroyed. Leo is blessed with a sense of personal rightness, and will probably blame the mate for the problems even while deploring the trouble between them. Pisces, reacting through intuition, will have self-doubts and suffer doubly through understanding the pain of the mate.

Pisces reluctance to face a confrontation at times of conflict may translate to an act of loyalty in the mind of the Leo partner and soften unbending attitudes. The quality of love between these two can be powerful enough to overcome the destructive forces, and the richness of this bond can compensate a thousand times over for the risks involved.

VIRGO

VIRGO-ARIES (Page 25)

What would a fire arrow see in a dragonfly? Most rewarding as a brief affair, but efforts toward a permanent relationship are worth every minute of it.

VIRGO-TAURUS (Page 60)

A working partnership that will withstand outside stresses while overcoming internal differences to achieve a fulfilling union. Happiness here is a warm sense of achievement.

VIRGO-GEMINI (Page 90)

A contradictory relationship of Signs that share Mercury as a ruler. The flight pattern resembles objects in mutual orbit that drift and swoop without making contact—a dragonfly chasing Tel Star—or vice versa.

VIRGO-CANCER (Page 118)

A highly satisfying relationship which only a Cancer/Virgo duet could love. But it will last, growing mellower with the years.

It seldom happens. And when it does it shouldn't. Earth smothers Fire; Fire ravages Earth. The Lion and the Virgin trying to find something in common usually come up with temper tantrums.

Virgo-Virgo

Two Virgos getting together in a relationship might seem like a lost cause to their friends, but in reality this combination does work out well. Mutability plays a big part in allowing these two Suns to achieve a satisfactory union.

The worst problem may lie in getting together in the first place. Virgos are suspicious of relationships; they move in cautiously, even when attracted by the more magnetic Signs. With both partners backing away from an initial encounter, it may take some time to get them within speaking distance of each other. Ascendants will play an especially strong role here. One partner with an aggressive Ascendant can make the first move and establish contact. A fixed Ascendant can allow one partner to make a decision to meet and stick with it. Once the contact is made, two Virgos will easily figure out the best plan for working things out to please both. Virgos are flexible in dealing with mental problems; once they've pinned down their mutable thought processes, they resort to patient, practical, persistent action that characterizes all Earth signs.

Virgo Suns are among those which show great differences between the highly evolved individual and the less well-developed character. The axis around which the Virgo character revolves is the analytical-critical faculty, balanced by a basic desire to serve others. If this core develops negatively, the waspish, nagging, fault-finding Virgo emerges, with the desire to serve inverted to become a desire to be waited on. At the other extreme is the person who transforms emotional reticence into a spiritual quality of depth, bringing this concept to practical saintliness which serves others in total disregard of self. Somewhere in between are the Virgos who channel their critical abilities in constructive ways—the writers, critics, educators, editors who make full use of Mercury's mental influence in combination with the analytical Virgo Sun.

The success or failure of the dual Virgo Sun combination depends on who is seeking whom. The "middle" Virgos can meet each other quite easily; can interact with either of the extremes of development without too much frustration. Desert sand encompasses Death Valley; it also forms the shores of the Mediterranean Sea.

It is at the extremes of the scale that trouble comes. The waspish Virgo will be just as merciless in using sarcastic comments to sting a Madonna as another martinet; more so, perhaps, because another martinet will make some stings felt also. Worst of all is the Virgo who combines a pseudo-saintliness with carping intolerance. Fortunately the chances of two of this caliber attempting a union are rare. If they do try, the relationship will soon fall apart.

If they can achieve a working interaction, these two can find rewarding fulfillment. Virgos do not find *any* relationship comfortable, allowed to pursue their goals by meticulous methods without irritating less disciplined Signs.

It is unlikely they would have children. Virgo is not a fertile Sign. The preference of this couple may be to remain childless. A tendency toward hypochondria can keep Virgos too occupied with their own nebulous ailments to wish to take on the incessant demands placed upon parents by offspring. A child of this couple would be transformed early to a miniature adult.

It's a good possibility that the Virgo who wants marriage will find it much harder to establish a deep relationship with any of the other Signs than with one of his own.

Virgo-Libra

Virgo and Libra usually get along well together. These are neighbors in the Ring of the Suns, each unemotional enough to allow the other to be himself without exacting penalties. Or, if penalties are exacted, it's almost tit for that, which pleases Libra's sense of fairness, and allows Virgo an advantage often lacked in interaction with more dynamic Signs.

Both these Suns have a low-keyed approach to life, and here probably more than at any other point of the Zodiac wheel Signs borrow traits from each other which give a sort of even-steven ability for each to hold ground when they square off at each other. (No. That's not the way Libra and Virgo do it. These two are more apt to snipe at each other than square off.) But they understand the rules of the game and keep their voices down, and that has the effect of transforming arguments into discussions.

Lack of communication between Earth and Air is largely due to lack of easy contact points between the two. Earth is just there—below; the atmosphere is just there—above, and skyhooks exist only in the imagination. Virgo and Libra sem to build their own bridges to understanding from similar characteristics which blend at the cusp of their Signs. Virgo is more flexible than the other Earth Signs; Libra equivocates. Virgo has the patience to wait until Libra is in an agreeable mood before approaching. As the atmosphere is held by the gravitational pull of the Earth, so Libra has more of an affinity for the fixity of Earth Signs than have Gemini and Aquarius.

The thing is, these Signs also understand each other's minus qualities, and bear with them. Virgo moodiness can be a fearful frustration for many Suns; Libra just ignores it until the whole thing blows over. Libran moods are changeable enough to allow recognition of what's happening, and Libra is self-centered enough to be able to ignore Virgo's depression.

Many of their opposing traits blend to their benefit. Virgo's reticence can be warmed from frequent exposure to Libran social graces. Charm is often a learned attribute for Virgos, who may have a hard time pushing themselves into the center of activity. Libra usually attracts a group, then graciously includes Virgo in the general circle of pleasure.

By the same token Libra can benefit from Virgo efficiency. Librans have a tendency toward taking the easy way out. Charming as children, they are often shamelessly spoiled and well-versed in persuading others to do their chores. Virgo learns early in life that the only way around is through the middle. But Virgo can be as much a manipulator as Libra, and as often as not will exact Libra's share of work from the mate Libra, up against the wall, will be forced to admit that fair is fair, and will buckle down to the task at hand.

Differing views of finances work to the benefit of

mutual resources. Libra is inclined to generosity and Virgo is inclined to thriftiness. Virgo's need to be of service to others does not usually include financial expenditure. But Virgo here cannot help but observe how easily Libra gains desired ends by being a cheerful giver. By the same token Libra cannot help but observe that Virgo seldom loses out by trying to impress someone by reckless financing. Together they can work out a reasonable pattern for handling finances that allows both to exercise basic traits without endangering the relationship.

Their intimate interaction can be beautiful or hellish, depending on whether they share positive or opposing traits. Unfortunately, mutual attributes are not the most rewarding for Libra-Virgo, and are much more apt to errode the relationship than enhance it. Blind to their own faults, critical without being able to accept criticism, intolerant to those who do not see the world from their own rather narrow viewpoints, they are capable of lacerating each other almost at will without even realizing what's happening.

If they blend their opposing traits they can establish points of understanding. Virgo's sensitivity is hidden behind a wall of reticence that often seems unbreachable. Libra charm can find the soft spots in the armor and invade Virgoan affections before the mate realizes it. Virgo love has a strain of spirituality about it which Libra recognizes as appropriate; once given, it is given for keeps—providing the partner responds in kind. These Suns bring out the best in each other and interact with intellectual rather than emotional commitment. They appreciate each other's refinement in intimate moments. Virgo is fastidious and Libra is naturally attractive and charming. Crudeness will never intrude at the personal level.

There will be children, carefully protected and guided

and watched over and pointed upward—ever upward. They will probably not know the delights of exploring woods or creek for hours on end; or making mud pies, or walking barefoot in the dewy grass. They will probably know the joys of participating in the junior symphony; of reading good books and of a well-ordered home and parents who are always there.

There is danger that if these two focus their mutually shared negative traits on the world around them they can become discontented, critical, isolated misfits in their relationships with others. Individual planet placements will, hopefully, combine their basic Sun qualities in ways that help them find happiness together. It can happen. But it will be up to both these Suns to work to make it happen.

Virgo-Scorpio

It can be base; it can be beautiful. And it can be rare. These Suns are not usually attracted to each other. Virgo more than most Signs is immune to the intense magnetism which draws others to Scorpio. But this is a sextile aspect. When they do manage to get past the first, instinctive rejection of each other, they can find mutual rewards in a relationship which draws on deeper levels of interaction.

There are few complimentary traits between them, and many conflicting ones. Their relationship must develop through elemental reaction and interaction of Earth and Water qualities. As the desert sand blooms and produces in abundance when irrigated, so Virgo and Scorpio can transform each other once they recognize the possibility of a relationship together.

Both these Signs react at subterranian levels of the personality. Pluto, ruler of Scorpio, controls all that is buried and hidden. And Virgo moodiness penetrates to the depths of the personality. Yet each maintains a surface reticence that seldom reveals the power of their reactions.

This surface restraint enables them to approach each other in the beginning. Virgo, apprehensive of the emotionalism of Pisces and Cancer, may not realize the quality exists in Scorpio until the relationship is established. With realization, Virgo is able to assimilate and blend this facet of Scorpio personality with personal reactions. Virgo's reserved reactions can have a calming effect on Scorpion intensity. In union they find temperance, to a degree at least. Perhaps self-contained Virgo longs for tears; perhaps Scorpio seeks release from the intensity of self-centered desires.

Both Virgo and Scorpio can be suspicious of new relationships. But once they learn to trust each other they can draw upon each other for support. Virgoan objectivity can help hold the emotionalism of Scorpio in check; Scorpio impatience can stimulate reaction in Virgo.

There is danger that Virgo's analytical view can become criticism—well meant, but anathema to Scorpio, who seldom harbors self doubts. Scorpio does not take kindly to even the mildest suggestion that superior Scorpion abilities can be improved. In the day-to-day routine there can be abrasive irritations. Both are quick-tempered when things go wrong. Both can become naggers when they can't manipulate the environment to their own specifications; feeling they know better than anyone else how things should work, resenting implications that this is not always true.

Scorpio will reject with bitterness to Virgo's repeated advice on how to perform the simplest chores. Still, it's hard to battle a Virgo, who is likely to fade from the scene of controversy and leave the other party throwing a temper tantrum.

Intellectually they are well matched and through this channel will come fulfillment for the relationship. They may not always agree, but they will accept each other's intellectual interests as valid, and support each other in their projects. Scorpio is creative; and Virgo has the analytical viewpoint to evaluate creative work of others. This can be invaluable to the Scorpio partner if resentment of implied criticism can be curbed.

Given the intensity of Scorpio and the reticence of Virgo, it might seem that chances for a fulfilling intimate interaction would be lacking. It may prove to be just the opposite. Scorpio can easily bring too much emotionalism to the relationship, but as with all Water Signs, reflects the quality of the partner. Unemotional Virgo may influence the partner toward a less concentrated approach in this area of their lives. Scorpio intensity may stimulate Virgo to as near an emotional involvement as Virgo ever comes. This may be the only Sun combination in which Scorpio jealousy is not highly activated. Virgo does not stimulate jealousy as a rule. The Virgoan character promises fidelity and loyalty, even when, in fact, evidence doesn't always support the promise.

There is a spiritual quality in both these Signs that expresses most often in interaction with the loved one. This quality is often enhanced between these Signs, and it is through this quality that the relationship is fulfilled to highest potential.

Children may suffer from the concentration of attention to their lives. No detail of their activities will escape the awareness of these often psychic parents.

Youngsters are seldom able to escape the superior supervision of these dedicated mothers and fathers.

Virgo and Scorpio have much to offer each other if they can bring themselves to *accept*. Both are self-sufficient Signs; it is much easier for them to give than to receive. Virgo wishes to serve; Scorpio resents the implication of weakness in accepting aid from others, except at the professional level.

But if they truly try, the dragonfly skimming the surface of the mighty river of Scorpio emotion may surprise a magician; a magician who will direct the flow of deep flowing water through the desert and once there, perform a miracle. Virgo hoards treasure buried in the desert sand of the personality; treasure which may be exposed and rejuvenated by Scorpio emotions. The whole, in this case, well may add up to something much more meaningful than the sum of its parts.

Virgo-Sagittarius

There is little to draw these two together, and less to hold them if their paths cross. At best they usually accommodate each other from necessity, as the desert dunes provide a base for the caravan; as the caravan brings drama and color to the bare-bones desert landscape.

What rapport they achieve must come through blending opposing traits; shared traits are not enhanced by interaction. The moodiness of Virgo will be fired by the heavy black moods of Sagittarius. Jupiter, ruler of Sagittarius, is the planet of expansion, and its influence blows depression out of proportion quite as easily as it encourages optimism.

Both these Signs are worriers. Jupiter's influence interacting with Mercury's influence can multiply small doubts to full-blown storms of morbid despair. Both the Archer and the Virgin need others around who can play down their plunges to the depths of self doubt. But these Suns, squared, are also mutable, and mutability substitutes to an extent for emotional reaction in Earth and Fire Signs.

There are bridges of contact between them, narrow bridges which start from one trait in one Sign and curve to find a possible connecting point in an opposing trait in the other Sign. Virgo discontent—an offshoot of the critical, analytical faculties of the Sign—can be directed to constructive channels through the philosophical optimism of Sagittarius. Fortunately Sagittarian moods appear less frequently than those of Virgo, allowing the two to interact with some ease as long as their temperamental storms do not coincide. Sagittarius takes off when Virgo is hovering under a black cloud and stays away until the mate comes up for air. Virgo keeps occupied at other projects when Sagittarius is sweating out a period of depression until the Archer emerges from the harrowing battle with conscience. Jupiterian enthusiasms, which often seem scattered on the wind, can somtimes draw the Virgo mate into contact with a more active environment. And Virgo skepticism can sometimes help contain the Archer's overblown optimism.

Certainly Virgo objectivity can be a strong factor in smoothing the way for interaction here. It will probably be up to Virgo to do most of the smoothing of the way. Sagittarius like all Fire Signs, is impatient. Desert sand, in spite of mobility, is a basic force which controls whatever comes within its reach: sand dunes in their own way are as impregnable as dams. A caravan crossing the Sahara must follow time-honored trails in order to reach the oases which provide water to sustain life. So with Virgo/Sagittarius unions: although the partners have few complimentary traits, each can and does supply basic direction to the other Sign, which adds strength to the relationship.

This strength is bestowed impartially, through negatively as well as positively developed traits. The independent Sagittarian will take advice from no one. Virgo criticism, meant to give direction to the erractic course of the Archer, instead sparks a fiery temper and sends Sagittarius galloping away from the well-meaning advisor. Nagging in this relationship will get Virgo nothing but an empty house.

However, if they can get past the more obvious barriers, they can find fulfillment together—Sagittarius idealism touching Virgo spirituality to inspire deeply satisfying interaction. Virgo's Earth orientation can accept the sensuality of the Sagittarian mate. These two Suns may find a rare meeting of mind and body and emotion in their love—the oases which gives life to the relationship—with Virgo practicality balancing out Sagittarius idealism. And from this secret source of vitality may come the needed softening to allow these Suns to survive the friction of daily contact. Neither will be really happy with the day-to-day constrictions they place on each other, but they may be able to work out some kind of compromise in little things.

They will respect each other intellectually. Virgo's quick mentality will catch fire and follow the exploratory ideas of Sagittarius, for a way at least (as the sand clouds swirl around the departing caravan for a time before gradually falling to earth as the train moves out of sight.) Sagittarius will delight in the receptivity of Virgo intellect; not every Sign can appreciate the paths along which the Archer's speculative mind impels. Although a rover at heart, Sagittarius will return at intervals to re-experience this exciting mental interaction, even if the relationship does not work out on the physical and emotional levels.

They will draw on intellectual understanding in raising children, and through this channel will balance the negative traits of one against the positive traits of the other, and vice versa, able at second hand to utilize all facets of their personalities by uniting them one step removed from the point of contact. These youngsters will have the practical supervision of the Virgo parent in health matters, school affairs, and everyday routine. The Sagittarian will lift them to an awareness of broader horizons—both mental and physical—encouraging them to explore other environments and take some risks which would almost certainly be prohibited by the Virgo parent.

It will be up to Virgo to sustain the relationship over long periods of time. But this fits in with Virgo need to be of service; and if there is enough flexibility to accept the Sagittarrian need for freedom of movement—of relationship—of ideas—it can become a rewarding union which may leave others wondering what on earth they see in each other.

Virgo-Capricorn

Earth trines produce relationships that are fulfilling and satisfying. Virgo and Capricorn together find security in this one: Virgo giving flexibility to change course where it will be beneficial; Capricorn supplying the stamina to set goals and achieve them. Their conservative personalities understand the paths they will pursue in their common journey without having to spend energy in explanations. Virgo will support Capricorn's regard for status and traditional values; Capricorn will respect Virgo's insistence on attention to detail. Both are practical in outlook, yet together they place emphasis on the spiritual side of their natures. Perhaps it is that, inhibited and reserved as their natures are, they appreciate release from the strain of trying to express themselves with more outgoing Signs. These two Suns are comfortable in their mutual relationship.

They are reliable as individuals and as a team. Virgo knows that Capricorn can be depended on to assume a full share of the chores. Capricorn knows Virgo can be depended on for meticulous attention to routine. They will share pride in their home and both will work to make it a landmark of distinction (in a good neighborhood, of course). They will divide the daily tasks that go with keeping it in order. Both are willing to work for what they want. They realize that in order to *have* one must work. These are ants, never grasshoppers; they are intolerant of those who do not pay their ways.

A shared trait of intolerance is one of the few negative influences to show strongly in this combination. Virgo's critical ability to see good and bad points at a glance can sometimes translate as prejudice against those who can't manage this discriminating analysis. Capricorn concurs. Afflications to individual natal planets can create an atmosphere of habitual criticism of others without these two recognizing the extent of their negativism. Most Signs quickly send up warning signals to keep Virgo criticism in bounds. With Capricorn the feedback indicates approval—until Virgo turns the critical analysis to the mate's affairs. Then Virgo may be astonished at the intensity of the Capricorn reaction. Capricorn is hurt to the quick by criticism from loved ones; may turn on the astonished partner with icy fury—a volcano erupting through a glacier. And having "demanded" recognition of personal sterling qualities, may then sulk in hurt silence for hours. Virgo, usually the one to practice these tactics (if inclined to pettiness) may have to make overtures to reestablish the relative warmth of the relationship—something Virgo does not do easily.

But Virgo will seldom find a relationship so comfortable, and will not willingly sacrifice it. In no other Sun combination are Virgo's positive traits so well supported and the less positive traits so nicely blended to the good of the relationship. Virgo appreciates the strength of the mountain when clouds darken the perspective; if the face of the mountain is shadowed at times, can wait out the periods of self-doubt and martyrdom in which Capricorn indulges periodically. Capricorn, self-righteous in basic attitudes, responds to the changing facets of Virgo thought as to a fresh breeze.

The personal relationship might seem to leave something to be desired from the viewpoint of more romantic or emotional Signs, yet to these two is satisfying. There will be little of sentiment in their relationship, but a bedrock of spiritual values will support their interaction at deeply personal levels. The practical benefits of this union will fill basic needs in these two Signs that will add to the enduring quality of the relationship.

Capricorn vitality will be an asset to Virgo who may be the victim of hard-to-pin-down nervous disorders, and frequently suffers from debilitating headaches. Capricorn, needing to be needed, will care for the Virgo mate during these sieges, if not with tenderness, certainly with competence. Mutual projects will not fall behind because of Virgo illness.

They will set traditional standards for their children, and insist they live up to them. In return these parents will supply the conventional benefits of a good home, a good education, good clothing. These children will have to satisfy their sense of adventure through other sources—they will be encouraged to save their allowances and learn to be reliable rather than to explore new experiences. But they will have solid support all their lives; they will never doubt their parents love for them although they may rebel against the restrictive conditions that seem to accompany the giving of their affections.

An almost ideal coming together of basic personalities to achieve an extremely solid and satisfying relationship, which endures.

Virgo-Aquarius

With an overabundance of conficting traits these Suns would have little appeal for each other, except for the brilliance of the magnetic quality which draws them together. Intellect here is as compelling as the most sensuous contact between more physically-oriented Signs. In quincunx aspect, Aquarius and Virgo find challenge and opportunity to form a relationship that can be exciting for both.

Neither of these Signs is really comfortable with emotion, although Aquarius—experimental and tolerant—can accept it more easily than Virgo. But both have a sweetness in their make-ups that allows them to tolerate emotion in those close. When these two minds meet, the excellence of the intellectual quality permits them to interact mentally with each other without fear of being entangled in an emotional interaction.

Respect will be the keyword in the relationship. Both Aquarius and Virgo have a trace of the ascetic in their characters and can easily adjust to the undemanding emotional requirements of the other. A marriage of convenience could come easily to these two; intellectual challenges can be strong enough to present a channel for interaction through mutual interests and common projects, such as research.

In the wake of this smoothly working intellectual interaction, conflicting traits assume the character of splinters rather than barbed wire. The strong mental approach may allow these partners to regard conflict arising from inharmonious traits as signals to observe and analyze and somehow integrate the opposing forces to the benefit of the partnership.

Thus the more lenient Aquarius will dilute the prejudices of Virgo; Virgo will supply discrimination so often lacking in Aquarius. The sociability of Aquarius will carry them through social situations which Virgo would find extremely trying if forced to face them solo. Virgo benefits in companionship and in turn protects Aquarius from financial and material loss.

They work together well as a team. Aquarius produces highly original ideas which Virgo analyzes and reduces to practical format. Virgo's meticulous work methods counteract Aquarius' far-out work style. Aquarius, helping Virgo (or trying to) may feel he is being neatly sliced by a mechanical razor. The here-today, gone-tomorrow attitude of Aquarius toward intricate jobs can harry Virgo to distraction. Yet shared intellectual awareness reduces possible conflicts to petty annoyances.

But Virgoan criticism can generate real trouble between two. Virgo's analytical mind automatically runs any situation through its checklist in order to reshape it to a more efficient, maneuverable condition. For Aquarius, criticism is the most potently destructive weapon in a relationship. Thinking years beyond contemporaries and companions, Aquarius is constantly subjected to critical remarks that are more reflexive than reflective. Seeing on a wider and more universal scope, the criticisms of less perceptive persons often seem to Aquarius to verge on stupidity. Virgo, keyed to microscopic analysis, can make even a compliment sound critical, and Aquarius can hear a compliment as criticism when it is nothing of the sort. In this area the relationship will meet severe testing, but again, the brilliance of the mental interaction can, in most cases, override this abrasive interaction.

To others this relationship may appear to be a courtship between a jet vapor trail and a dragonfly. That's what it looks like from the outside. Actually, it is more akin to a romance between a flash of lightning and a computer, and it can produce some fascinating brain children.

That may be all that results from this union. These Suns often wait until quite late in life to marry, and neither being oriented to domesticity, as often as not they may choose to remain childless. If they do have children, the intellectual approach to their upbringing will rapidly boost their status from dependents to contemporaries for all practical purposes. Yet the relationship will be loving and the children will benefit in many ways. There will seldom be conflict between these parents in the area of child rearing.

If the criticism conflict can be worked out, an

excellent chance exists for an exciting marriage of the minds.

Virgo-Pisces

Reserved, reticent Virgo finds the emotionalism of Pisces almost intolerable—but is fascinated all the same. Pisces yawns at the idea of the analytical, detailed existence of Virgo—and yet finds strange peace in the order and predictability of Virgo.

How do they resolve these contradictions, since few of the basic traits of Pisces and Virgo even come close to harmonizing? The primary attractive force is the polarity of opposites. These two opposing Suns challenge in several areas, but common mutability gives some flexibility in adjusting.

At the deepest level of personality, there is a bridge of *caring* which allows them contact. For both Virgo and Pisces have strong needs to serve and care for others. Both Signs also have pronounced ethical values—an almost spiritual sense of concern for others—expressed in very different ways.

Where Pisces dissipates emotion in over-reaction, Virgo's emotions may atrophy from being kept firmly repressed. Virgo, the careful observer—analyzing problems and moving to solve them by practical means—will look aghast on the romantic, impractical Pisces, who uses emotionalism in dealing with problems. Pisces, suffering and rejoicing with indiscriminate intensity, may cringe from what appears to be the coldness of Virgo. Yet there is perception in both Signs which allows them to sense that the personality seen on the surface of the other is a masquerade that shelters a core of sensitivity too vulnerable to reveal in any but the most trusted relationships.

It is significant that Pisces, who cannot stand pettiness, intolerance, or discrimination in any other Sign, will forgive all of these to a degree in Virgo. Similarly, Virgo, supremely confident of the rightness of personal moves, with a mind as orderly as a computer, will accept the nebulous thought processes and vague insecurities of Pisces with as near to tolerance as Virgo ever comes. Each will defend, explain, support the other against criticism from outsiders, even while feeling the same criticisms themselves.

If they can get past these surface differences they have much to give each other. But there are so few areas of compatability. Pisces was born wearing rose-colored glasses and seldom removes them except when standing beneath a rainbow. Virgo is apt to be color blind, seeing in terms of black-white-gray.

Thus Virgo may spoil a moment of mutual tenderness for Pisces by a pointed comment; and Pisces can remove the pleasure of a shared tenderness by excessive emotionalism.

Pisces is lenient to a fault, walking in the shoes of the criminal as well as the saint and seldom passing judgment. Virgo is often the first to point a finger, and having decided, usually remains fixed in the judgment. Virgo has very little patience with the Pisces partner who is taken advantage of, feeling with some truth that Pisces has invited the situation by over-responsiveness and an indiscrimnate attitude. Yet Pisces willingness to accept others as they are offers one of the main bridges to communication át the deeper level where lasting Pisces-Virgo relationships must be formed.

Virgo more than most Signs is unaware of personal

short-comings. Virgo's analytical thought processes sort, evaluate, rearrange with such precision that the thought does not occur that these smooth-running life patterns may place pressure on those who are less structured in their habits.

Pisces is not so much disorganized as spontaneous, acting and reacting to developments with instantaneous responses; feeling rather than thinking out reactions. Pisces is overly aware of personal faults and assumes guilt almost as a matter of course when relationships are out of kilter. Unable to refute Virgo criticism with logic, and since Virgo will not accept an intuitive explanation, a habit pattern may emerge in which it is assumed that Virgo is automatically "right" and Pisces is automatically guilty.

This is a basic conflict underlying Pisces-Virgo relationships. There is a nebulous quality about Pisces actions that produces accomplishment without seeming effort; Virgo action is almost an anticlimax after the precision planning. To the outsider it may seem like Virgo does all the work and Pisces takes all the credit. And with this kind of feedback—silent or spoken—it won't be long before the two most involved begin to believe it.

In establishing a home the Pisces will work creatively to produce a place of warmth and charm that is uniqely personal. If forced to explain every move to the Virgo partner and absorb the almost automatic suggestions for improving on the ideas, Pisces may turn off and lose interest. Virgo can be a nag when putting on pressure. Over a period of time, togetherness may produce tensions that can be almost impossible to handle.

Virgo's basic reaction to problems is analysis; Pisces basic reaction to problems is escape. If physical escape is not possible, Pisces will withdraw emotionally until Virgo feels married to a stranger. Efforts to force explanations will only drive Pisces further away. Virgo, unaware that constant advice is one of the major problems, assumes that Pisces emotions have flashed somewhere else. A Virgo-Pisces union can profit from separate vacations.

Money can be a problem. While Pisces is not *really* extravagant, and Virgo is not *really* stingy, they may seem so to each other. Virgo wants money spent to the very best advantage, and will plan and scheme to be sure it goes that way. Virgo also wants it accounted for to the penny. Pisces is not overly conscious of money; is willing to go without somewhere else to buy what appears to be luxuries for personal pleasure. Pisces is adept at making a bargain look like an expensive frill. But Pisces won't want to make accountings and Virgo will be upset at not knowing. It is vital to the relationship that they have clear cut financial rules.

Virgo and Pisces may have misunderstandings in the raising of their children. Virgo will find it hard to stand by while Pisces allows them to out talk the parent to gain advantages. Virgo will see to the center of the situation and no amount of doubletalk will camouflage the fact that the kids are pulling a snow job. Pisces will indulge, Virgo will discipline, and they will both love their children and feel they are working for their happiness. Pisces, who seems the most understanding, may not be helping the children as much as Virgo who requires of them certain specified standards of behavior.

With so many obstacles it may seem easier to just forget the whole thing. Yet, truly, if these two can make it past the surface personalities to the hidden selves that exist in the centers of their elaborate personality defense systems, they can find together a relationship so special it will last forever. For Virgo can supply the anchor point that Pisces imagination needs so desperately; and

Pisces can open the Virgo up to the magic of emotional responses to a degree, and each will respond with the best of their natures. With Pisces and Virgo, this can be a very high level indeed.

LIBRA

LIBRA-ARIES (Page 28)

Aries needs balance; Libra needs ebullience. Spontaneous Fire steadies down with a permanent supply of oxygen.

LIBRA-TAURUS (Page 63)

Libra Air provides the atmosphere in which the Taurus Sun burns steadily; Taurus strength supports the eternal flame of Libra. Venus rulership enhances the chance of a loving, lasting relationship.

LIBRA-GEMINI (Page 93)

An often superficial relationship, as if these two were riding side by side on a merry-go-round, in harmony but never quite synchronizing. May end as a marriage of convenience.

LIBRA-CANCER (Page 121)

To others this may seem a perpetual courtship. In private the passing years may find them faithfully muttering, "I love you, too," through clenched teeth.

Others may find themselves envious of this pair as they move through life a little above the crowd, scattering a combination of gold coins and rose petals in their wake and loving (each other) every minute of it.

LIBRA-VIRGO (Page 168)

They understand each other's minus qualities and bear with them, blending their basic Sun qualities to find happiness together. But it will be up to them to make it happen.

Libra-Libra

This romance is as lovely as the placid wavelets of a moonlit lake on a warm summer night—on the surface. But like the moonlit lake, this charming relationship may hide some snags and boulders. Not that they will be seen by anyone outside the close family circle; it is imperative that Librans maintain a pleasant facade to the outside world. But Librans are also *self* centered people, and what they cannot get by charm they will get by pressure—as much as it takes. Two iron fists in velvet gloves can cast some powerful blows without making a sound.

As if sensing the possibility of hidden obstacles to their happiness together, they may be reluctant to take the final steps, even if those close urge them to end their storybook courtship for a more permanent relationship. Marriage is a serious matter to most Librans. These beautiful, romantic people find such pleasure in social singleness they may find it hard to give up. But marriage is the natural state for Librans, however much side-stepping they do, and sooner or later these Suns will probably take the vows.

They may find, to their dismay, that fairy tales only *promise* happiness ever after—they don't spell out details for achieving it. Librans start charming their way through life while they are still in the maternity nursery; they are much too apt to fall back on charm in trying to solve marital problems rather than face issues and work toward solutions.

But social activities will compensate, and there will be little time to brood over disappointments. It may take them a while to even admit that the connubial bliss they sought is, indeed, something less. They may never face it at all, and go through life murmuring conventional endearments and unholding sentimental traditions while pressuring each other for concessions like two icebergs jockeying for position. The greater the sense of disenchantment the greater the gentle coercion from each.

This marriage will have staying power in the face of hidden stresses. Librans see marriage as the appropriate relationship. Since they seldom require or make an emotional commitment to the partnership they find it relatively easy to substitute a socially pleasurable relationship for a more intense one.

They may have some trouble maintaining the tastefully attractive surroundings each finds desirable. *Self* oriented people insist on tidiness in the home but are not usually eager to contribute to the chores required to keep their surroundings neat.

Children will be expected to be on their best behavior

all the time, dressed in their attractive clothes, ready to be shown off at a moment's notice. But they are not likely to be taught the discipline of hanging up their clothes when they take them off, or to put their toys away when they are through playing with them. Librans don't like nagging and are not likely to "remind" their children over and over again in the interests of teaching them neatness. Children of more aggressive Signs may learn to take advantage of their parents' distaste for upsetting scenes to get their own way, but in the end the quiet good manners of the Libran parents will probably rub off on them to their advantage.

If these two can find in each other the ideals they fantasize in their dreams, the relationship can be beautiful indeed. Usually, however, Librans are too intent on pleasing themselves to work at pleasing others. A lasting relationship here is more apt to be achieved through companionship, held together through appreciation of a congenial home atmosphere and the basic need all Librans feel for acceptable partners.

Libra-Scorpio

Libra and Scorpio, side by side in the Zodiac wheel, often prefer a "live and let live" relationship which does not go beyond the social amenities. It is not that they are unaware of each other, or that they do not find each other attractive at times. But Libra, the planet of balance and harmony, is apprehensive of the inverted intensity of the Scorpio personality which penetrates and probes and works at deep levels to shape relationships to Scorpion desires. So they are apt to coexist, as the atmosphere coexists with the giant rivers of the globe, interacting at points of contact without seeking to further these contacts.

Of course, as individuals these two Signs do interact at the personal level. Libra has a great deal of charm and Scorpio is magnetic, and in social situations they may be drawn together by these qualities.

From the beginning it will probably be Scorpio who pursues the matter, for from the beginning Libra will feel uneasy in the relationship. But Libra may not be able to resist the magnetic Scorpio. This will not be an impetuous romance. Scorpio observes from behind the scenes to find out what can be learned about the other person before revealing an interest. This is fine with Libra, who is leery of aggressiveness. The interaction here resembles the insidious interaction of river mists drawn into the air by evaporation, there to mingle and, later, to be returned to the river as rain. The casual observer may hardly be aware of the responsive currents moving back and forth between these two Signs.

This may be one of the least satisfying combinations of Suns. While it can work smoothly in social or career interactions—almost all Libran relationships move smoothly at the casual level—the requirements of in-depth relationships is painful for these two. Scorpio operates at hidden levels of the personality; Libra moves openly, as the air moves. Drawn into intimate interaction with Scorpio, Libra feels stifled, as air trapped underground becomes stale. Scorpio is uncomfortable pursuing a relationship in public.

The meeting place that causes the least painful reaction is social. At this level each Sign keeps one foot in the natural environment while venturing into an intermediate area between the two extremes. And it is in this area that their complimentary traits blend.

Ambition is a force in both Suns; more so in Scorpio

than in Libra because Scorpio intensity will always bear more forcefulness than Libran equilibrium. Libran ability to negotiate agreements, to give a little, to seek compromise rather than confrontation, seems to attract success and with it, money. The Scorpio personality does not wear as well with the public, but Scorpio is a master at making finances work to advantage. Scorpio has respect for money, and is creative in ways that do not demand public interaction. Libra and Scorpio professional partnerships work very well, with Scorpio serving as manager and mentor for the Libran.

Unfortunately, Scorpio desires to manage the mate's life in the same manner, and the Libran mate only *seems* to be amenable to management in the private relationship. Libran charm and poise is only skin deep; Cardinal Libra borrows intractability from neighboring Signs. Scorpio, intent on probing the innermost facets of Libran personality, may crash head on into an iron fist camouflaged in velvet.

In intimate relationships their conflicting traits seem to be in stubborn conflict, generating negative vibrations instead of positive ones. There is little that balances and blends to the common good; mutually-reinforcing traits tend to work the other way. The cheerfulness of Libra finds hard going in the presence of the taciturn Scorpio partner. Scorpio is almost psychic in perceptiveness, but fails to realize that Libran intuition is more attuned to surface vibrations than to deeply buried feelings. (Perhaps because Libra has little wish to really probe in depth in any situation.) All Air Signs wish to know what is going on around them on the surface, however, and Libra will resent Scorpio's refusal to explain, and the almost pathological dislike of purely social affairs. Libra functions best in this atmosphere, and is displeased by Scorpio jealousy of the mate's interaction with other people. Scorpio possessiveness is akin to the harem concept—Scorpio wants to keep the loved one in a private retreat where the interaction is concentrated between the two of them.

While Libra is fascinated by this focus on *relationship*, Libra is the one who places overpowering pressure in most relationships. Here Libra is outmatched by Scorpio. The two may end up crushing the relationship in their attempts to possess each other.

A competitive spirit at work here prevents a true communion. Libra, who often insists on equalizing a relationship by charmingly forcing the *partner* to move to achieve equilibrium, will find there is *no way* to force a Scorpio to compromise. If any balancing is to be achieved, it will require a giant of equal strength on the other end of the scales. Yet Libra is tenacious, and Scorpio is ruthless in the determination to dominate.

In the end Scorpio will overpower Libra through sheer force of weight. Scorpio, absolutely unforgiving, will take advantage of Libra's over-forgiving attitude. Possessed of great stamina, Scorpio will be intolerant of Libra's need for periodic slow-downs to recuperate from active times, and will use these periods to further personal ends in matters that involve the two of them.

Their children will be torn between these two Signs and may suffer personality upsets from the conflicts. Scorpio is as ruthless in possessing the children as in guarding the mate; opposition, questioning, will not be tolerated. Libra will be of little help in standing up for the children openly, and will seek to balance the situation by using charm to comfort the children behind the mate's back, attempting to undermine the iron control which Scorpio seeks to maintain over their lives.

As always with Suns which are hard to intergrate, highly evolved partners, or those with fortunate planet placements, will be able to work around the basic incompatibility to achieve a working partnership. Still, stress will always be present. In intimacy Libra may feel overwhelmed by Scorpio passion, and tend to shed the patina of charm which helps sheathe the determined steel which lies beneath the surface. Libra will be the victim here. If it is to survive at all, this relationship demands that Scorpio dampen intensity and make some compromises. Even then the union may be more painful than pleasant.

Libra-Sagittarius

This can be the relationship these two Suns have waited for all their lives. The Sign traits interact beautifully to bring out the best in both. Libran Air allows breathing room for claustrophobic Sagittarius; Archer Fire gives some direction to social Libra. And the interaction is achieved with a minimum of stress, allowing the more charming qualities of each to take precedence over the less attractive traits—a striped balloon sailing through a summer sky; a caravan following the morning star.

In this combination, the searching, exploratory properties of Sagittarius are focused on learning and philosophical concepts rather than on self-indulgence. And Libra responds to this higher plane of awareness by striving for true harmony and balance rather than using silent opposition to force negotiation from a weaker partner.

At center of this interaction is shared intuition which allows these Suns to understand thoughts and feelings of each other. From this vantage point they blend potentially abrasive traits to a common good. Jupiter, ruler of Sagittarius, enhances the harmony and beauty of the Venus rulership of Libra. The two, working together in sextile aspect, become alchemists to soften grossly incompatible traits to allow beneficial aspects to work their magic.

Thus Libran charm buffers the bluntness of the Sagittarian approach and the Archer comes to realize through experience that honey does, indeed, attract more flies than vinegar does. Libra's even temper may hold the devastating black moods of Sagittarius at bay for long periods of time, and when they do strike, mitigates their force by allowing Archer optimism breathing room.

By the same token Archer energy can feed the Libran personality to help overcome the tendency to indolence. Libra, used to being catered to by others, is loathe to make the effort to tackle chores. Sagittarian enthusiasm can make even chores exciting and generate cooperation in the Libran mate. The Archer's hatred for all that is false and pretentious can shake Libra loose from dependency on outmoded conventions. Libra plays it safe at all times; Sagittarius seeks the challenge at all times, often taking risks which endanger others as well as self. Through interacting support between these Suns, the Libran can be led to try new methods and embrace more adaptive concepts, and Sagittarius can learn to appreciate a degree of caution, simply because neither wishes to threaten this rewarding relationship.

Both these Signs have difficulty establishing permanent unions. Libra has trouble with relationships: pushing too hard, holding too tightly, demanding too much. The Sagittarian drive for independence is elemental; relationships must be tested periodically to ensure an escape hatch, even if Sagittarius has no intention of using it. Many Signs cannot tolerate this constant movement toward escape; they give up and let go, often to the Archer's consternation. Sagittarius does not crave freedom so much as the knowledge that freedom of movement is possible at a moment's notice. Almost as strong in the Archer character is a basic need for an anchor—a home base—that will always be waiting. Testing this anchor (the loved ones) is also part of Sagittarian nature—as if demanding assurance again and again that they will always be waiting where the Archer leaves them. Through the benevolent influences of Venus and Jupiter, neither of these Suns is so driven to prove the relationship to the last decimal in this relationship as in others.

It's not all wine and roses, of course; the blunt honesty of Sagittarius finds Libran equivocation hard to take. Sagittarius goes straight to the point, and does not spare those close in the process. While avoiding the outright lie, Libra manipulates the truth. Libra's charming manner can usually draw attention of others away from the motives involved; Sagittarius will not be finessed in this manner. And Libra will protest innocence in questionable circumstances to the very end, nimbly moving from one stance to the other in attempts to keep the situation in *balance* (that is, with Libra always looking like Mr. Clean or Snow White). Libra will decry Sagittarius criticism; will try by any means to evade outright confrontation. The Archer, with the spirit of man and the stamina of the animal, cannot be outmaneuvered. There can be bitter hurt on both sides when these clashes occur.

But it will not happen often. Neither of these Signs will risk the special quality of the relationship carelessly, once they have learned the hard way that the other can be pushed too far. In intimacy they find a rare rapport, Sagittarian Fire warming the fantasies Libra cherishes of what the lover *should* be; Libra intellect refining and rarefying the idealism of Sagittarius which, interacting with other Signs, can be overwhelmed by emphasis on the physical. Jupiter enlarges, enhances, expands whatever it touches; here Venus spotlights all that is beautiful and harmonious in the relationship—and this too Jupiter enlarges.

The children of these parents will share in the general abundance of good will that these two generate in this relationship. Sagittarius will give them initiative, courage, a will toward exploring new roads—new ideas. Libra will give them the benefit of established values, conservative virtues—and both will be flexible enough to mingle the best of these two approaches while discarding the unusable. These children will know love and respect, and laughter and beauty and adventure.

This combination offers both Sagittarius and Libra an ideal climate in which to find a fulfilling relationship. With any luck at all (and Jupiter is at work here casting its blessing over the relationship) they will realize this early enough to forego their customary methods which can lead to disillusionment. The conditions are right; with a little effort they'll go through life with everything coming up roses.

Libra-Capricorn

There is basic understanding between these Suns in spite of them being squared. Libra and Capricorn both recognize the importance of foundations. Libra, seeking always to balance, readily senses that practical Capricorn will help steady the changeable Libran nature.

And there is a stronger if less tangible force working between them. Saturn rules Capricorn, Venus rules

Libra. Venus and Saturn in strong aspect can signal sacrifice, and interaction between these Suns contains an element of this influence. Libran efforts to bring harmony stimulate changing the mind almost on schedule. Libra is drawn to the strength of Capricorn and in time can come to depend on that strength to such an extent that independent action becomes difficult. As Capricorn comes to depend on Libran social graces to soften and gentle the Saturnian character. They do not willingly relinquish a relationship that so well provides what each is lacking; they seldom wish to try.

Ambition will give the light that guides these two to a position of status and recognition. They compliment each other in seeking these goals. Capricorn provides the stamina to strive for the highest position, whether social or career oriented. Libran charm smoothes the way in the difficult climb. Capricorn finds it hard, is often unable to empathize with others. Capricorn makes practical use of experience, conquering one step at a time, pushing to consolidate gains before taking the next step. Libra is apt to rev the propeller without ever getting off the ground by cluttering thought processes with everlasting rehashings of pros and cons.

Capricorn domination can be crushing to many Signs, but Libra, who really doesn't like hard work if given an alternative, finds this take-over tendency of Capricorn's strangely comforting, disposing of confusing choices which must be made. Libra also recognizes intuitively that often as not Capricorn's way is the best and quickest road up the mountain. In this union Libra will devote much energy to interpreting Capricorn's decisive actions to others, softening the impact of the Capricorn personality. In other Signs Libra cannot abide aggressiveness and lack of social graces, but will accept them in Capricorn, sensing that beneath the surface of the Goat's personality lies a supersensitive core that requires walls of granite to protect itself from others. By loyalty Libra eliminates the negative tone of this facet of Capricorn character.

Libra—a little lazy, a little selfish—finds it fairly easy to dispense with a playmate in favor of a practical, helpmate who will take over the chores involved in keeping a comfortable home; who will enjoy the challenge of taking care of doctor and dental appointments and balancing checkbooks. Capricorn will keep tabs on the spending habits of the Libran partner. And Libra, even when prefering expensive luxuries instead of practical necessities under the Christmas tree, will not protest the latter too much. Capricorn will cherish any gift that Libra offers; being practical, will have asked the mate beforehand what would be appreciated, and will have set a cost limit on both gifts.

Libra will miss the romantic touch in life with Capricorn, and may even indulge in brief affairs with more pliant partners. But the marriage will not be forsaken. This relationship is too important, the benefits are too rewarding, the status too habit forming for Libra to trade the hard working Capricorn mate in on a new model.

Usually this relationship improves with age, especially in the personal area. Saturnian inhibitions tend to crumble as the Capricorn mate is softened by interaction with Venusian charm. Libra may find that the somewhat frosty intimate relationship warms considerably as Capricorn emerges from behind the glacial facade which shows to the world. For Libra, the mate may not live up to fantasies of harem beauties and sex goddesses. But once released, Capricorn's earthy responses make up in intensity what they lack in finesse. Here again the Signs may blend to advantage—Capricorn responding to the grace of

Libran manners; Libra becoming more practical in expectations, to the benefit of both.

In rearing children, Libra is apt to leave the task to Capricorn, who won't really mind. Capricorn never has opportunity to fully dissipate dictatorial tendencies, and children, unfortunately, must serve as the lightning rod for this overcharge in many instances. But Capricorn will insist on them having the best that can be afforded—it is important to the Goat that the children show up well beside the neighbors—and will instill in them conservative ideas of behavior. Or try to. Libra will serve as intermediary and will relieve some of the inevitable frustration for both the mate and the children.

For highly evolved persons, this relationship can become an almost spiritual union, with Capricorn serving and catering to the Libran mate, while Libra protects and shields Capricorn. It will, in any case, be an enduring relationship, the eternal flame of the Libran spirit interacting with the strength of Capricorn to generate the splendor of the Midnight Sun. A paradoxical but satisfying union.

Libra-Aquarius

The controlling emphasis in this Air trine Sun relationship will be social. These charming, friendly people will be drawn to each other automatically. They are likely to meet at a party and get along famously right from the start, admiring in each other traits each finds especially attractive.

Both Aquarius and Libra are refined individuals who do not appreciate aggressivness. This mutual antipathy toward conflict will make for a pleasing surface relationship. But as the interaction between the two deepens, some disconcerting differences in character and personality will emerge, although each will try to avoid recongition of them. Libra, always in trouble in deep relationships, will feel the frictions first. Drawing on traits borrowed from Virgo, Libra will begin a campaign to bring Aquarian action into line with what Libra expects of a mate.

Libra, while usually doing exactly what pleases the self, will charmingly insist that Aquarian behavior conform to Libran ideas. Libra will be uncomfortable when Aquarian behavior and appearance do not consistently adhere to conventional standards. Libran guidelines for others will hew to a straight and narrow line, while never questioning personal actions.

At the beginning of this relationship Aquarius, always ready to explore a new personality (especially one so seemingly compatible) will accept Libra's soft-spoken criticisms with tolerance. But as the iron hand pinches through the velvet glove, Aquarian tolerance will change to irritation. And unlike Libra, who will avoid direct confrontation at all costs, once the needles begin to slip beneath the skin, Aquarius will voice frustration and stubbornly resist the suggestions of the partner. The more the gentle guidance of Libra is ignored, the harder Libra will push.

Aquarius will *not* accept these all but unstated restrictions on personal liberty. And as Libra feels Aquarian interest slipping away, pressure will be applied more persistently without any overt indication that Libra is indeed determined to force the mate to conform.

The situation goes from bad to worse until Aquarius escapes, one way or the other. And Libra—panic stricken at the thought of coming out the loser in yet another relationship conflict—will continue the efforts to possess the Aquarian without openly admitting there is trouble. Libra will refuse to bring the issue into the open for discussion. Able to negotiate compromise for others with facility, Libra is woefully lacking in compromise in personal contacts.

Libran actions are guided by an intuitive feeling of rightness. Libra seems to possess a built-in radar signal that shows the way that will bring success. What Libra does not understand, usually, is that what is right for one may not be right for another. There is seldom recognition of dual responsibility for settling mutual problems. Libra insists there must be two side to every problem, but often they are "my way" and "the wrong way."

Libra is temperamentally unable to understand the Aquarian need for freedom. More than any other Sign Libra needs the closeness of a partner to balance out and make whole the personality. Once a relationship is formed, it becomes a single unit in Libra's mind. Libra cannot abide a partner making independent decisions, having separate interests, needing time alone.

Yet trying to please Libra (and it's easy to want to; even when being outrageously self-demanding Libra is sweet and soft spoken) is often a losing proposition. Aquarius is flexible enough to try in the interest of maintaining this pleasant closeness in a social sense. But Libra doesn't want compromises; rather, wants to possess the partner. Yet there is no way this desire can be expressed without sounding arbitrary. And so Libra equivocates until even Aquarius, always open to change, loses interest. When Aquarius irritation finally erupts it is likely to be met with hurt silence from Libra, or reprimands for being loud. Yet Libran charm is such that Aquarius will accept this equivocation longer than the other limitations set by the mate.

Aquarian idealism will be lacerated by Libran

domination after a time. Libran reactions are always tempered by what is appropriate. Aquarians don't give a damn what "they" think as long as their uniquely personal idealistic codes are fulfilled.

Libran pressure is cumulative. Aquarius may be driven finally to choose between love and freedom of spirit. Attuned to universal concepts, Aquarius may be appalled to realize, that after a long struggle to reach an equitable solution to a trying situation, that the battle has really been over a hidden ultimatum. Libra will never be satisfied with less than subordination from the partner.

The Libran may win the battle but will never win the war in this relationship. Aquarius will almost certainly place the private self forever out of Libra's reach, if he doesn't disappear altogether. Physical possession is not really what Libra desires most, although that is important. Libra, like Capricorn, craves a devotion and love that springs from the spirit—then squeezes it to death by trying to hold on too hard.

Children of this union will suffer something of the cross currents felt in the Taurus-Aquarius partnership. Each will love the children; each will have definite—and differing—ideas of what is best for them and what the parental responsibility should be. Libra will give lavishly of material things, but always something that the child *should* want or have. Libra sees children as personal extensions of self and not as individuals in their own rights. Aquarius will give few material things, but will give of self in relationships with children. Aquarius wants to plant concepts children can develop as they grow and learn to use guide their lives by and, will grant them the privilege of making their own mistakes. Libra is not tolerant of children's mistakes, once they are past the puppy stage. Yet each of these Signs has something basic and important to impact to their children.

The lack here is one of emotional involvement: the Libran endeavoring to possess without emotional commitment; the Aquarian attempting to fight possession by lack of emotional interaction. These two Suns, which seemingly have so much to offer each other, often cannot communicate at a depth where they can establish meaningful relationships in spite of their best efforts.

Libra-Pisces

There is a mysterious, compelling attraction between Libra and Pisces that draws them together in spite of incompatible Sign elements. Air and Water are not binding ingredients, but dissipate their energies in mists of dissention. With Libra and Pisces, however, the interaction of Venus and Neptune adds an overtone of harmony that strengthens the attraction to a degree that may not show on the surface. Venus, ruler of Libra, is exalted in Pisces; this influence colors the relationship from the beginning. And while the conflicts can be painful, the Venus-Neptune influence can produce a love-martyr coloration that holds the relationship together in spite of pain.

The most detrimental aspect of the relationship lies in the fact that these two are sensitive, pleasant individuals, and the very real conflicts that trouble this union will be buried deep beneath the surface. Since neither is comfortable with confrontations—in fact, will go to any lengths to avoid head-on encounters—they will have great difficulty bringing their problems into the open until deep trouble has developed between them. By the time one or the other is driven to expose the depths of this frustration, it may be too late to heal the breach.

Both Signs contribute to this tension. Libran charm is a velvet cloak that hides the core of self-centeredness in the personality. Pisces, prone to accept guilt for any disturbance in any relationship, will play the martyr far beyond logical limits. Thus, while apparently congenial, they are never really able to communicate. They become glass circles that slide over and past each other without ever meshing to establish meaningful contact. The bitterest thought for these two, perhaps, is their knowledge that this condition exists and to be unable to force themselves to do anything about it.

For their natures do not allow mutual interaction, in spite of good will and honest efforts. Pisces energy goes to making others happy; Libra works to maneuver others to a position where the Libran feels they *should be* happy. The two are not synonymous. Libra works always to bring balance to a relationship; Pisces has neither the will nor the wish to interfere with the attitudes of others. Deeply empathetic, Pisces can be hurt time and again by the Libran partner but will always be able to sense there is "truth" on both sides; Libra will admit to two sides in the conflict but it comes down to the "right one" and the "wrong one." Both are responsive to their environments to such an extent that as, the underground conflicts grow stronger they will react with hurt and resentment at deeper and deeper levels until they must break free or drown in the turgid emotional waters in which they struggle.

Either of these Signs is more lenient with others than with the relationship. They place almost impossible demands on each other and on the union itself. Thus, seemingly trivial conflicts assume the solidity of stone walls; and mildly opposing traits offer never-ending opportunities for dissention. Libra is somewhat intolerant of others' views; Pisces is somewhat over tolerant of others' views. Either trait in opposition with another Sign might blend and support; here they do not make contact from which to interact.

Both Signs are generous, but even this shared quality becomes a potential troubleground. Librans give freely but only those things they feel others should have. Pisces gives impulsively in an effort to please others and win approval. Libra needs only to feel that what has been done "right"; if Pisces feels comfortable with an idea it will not enter the mind that the mate might not approve. Libra, feeling dissatisfaction with the relationship, may withhold approval from Pisces in an effort to achieve balance. Without approval as guidelines to establish accord, Pisces self-guilt becomes overwhelming and the Fish is unable to function in the relationship.

Thus the intimate relationship may suffer from the exaggerated expectations which both these Signs bring to a union. Pisces finds it impossible to remove the rose-colored glasses in this closest, most important relationship. And Libra feels cheated upon discovering that the mystery of Pisces, which seems to promise sensuality, may not deliver in the face of Libran self centeredness. Pisces dreams of love as miners dream of gold; Libra fantasizes sensuality which bears little resemblance to reality. The truth is they long for a beautiful relationship they might not be able to recognize if they found it.

Children of these two will receive love in depth from both, but as with the union itself, this may only be good for them on the surface. Where Pisces tries against stronger instincts to the contrary to help the children develop as individuals, Libra will never willingly relinquish parental authority, but will continue to see offspring as "children" long after they have children of their own. These youngsters may have trouble breaking away from the nest, not so much because they are held back as that these parents make it easy to stay snug and cozy at home.

If Libra can restrain the impulse to hold too tightly to Pisces; if Pisces can damp the simmering emotions long enough to examine the motives beind Libra's equivocation, they may be able to achieve a satisfying relationship. The security of marriage is important to Pisces, however much the Fish may struggle against being boxed in; the *relationship* of marriage is the symbol of life for the Libran. They will both work to maintain at least a semblance of a union, in spite of unrealistic attitudes both harbor.

If—If—If— It all depends. But *if* they can bring it off, the Pisces-Libra relationship can be rewarding.

SCORPIO

SCORPIO-ARIES (Page 31)

Fire is the mover; Water the stable element. Result: oppressive but magnetic—the kind of fated love from which legends derive.

SCORPIO-TAURUS (Page 66)

At its best this is one of the most beautiful of all Sign relationships. A bond of passion can overwhelm separative conditions that would vanquish Signs of lesser strengths.

SCORPIO-GEMINI (Page 96)

A whirlwind does not often form an alliance with the Amazon; if it does, the attraction dissipates like mist on a hot morning. Gemini risks being drowned in the currents of the Scorpion personality, leaving the mate to brood over a lost love destroyed by himself.

SCORPIO-CANCER (Page 123)

They have never achieve true empathy in spite of a fated magnetic attraction. Yet they have little more chance of escaping the tides of this mutual passion than they have of swimming upstream against the currents of the Nile.

SCORPIO-LEO (Page 148)

They fascinate each other: Leo seeking the only water deep enough to cool the flames within; Scorpio seeking the penetrating warmth of the Sun. The forces of passion generated between these two giants can be all-consuming.

SCORPIO-VIRGO (Page 171)

It can be base; it can be beautiful. It is also rare. Once past the surface antipathy, the dragonfly may surprise a magician as he skims the surface of the Scorpio personality. The whole here may add up to something more meaningful than the sum of its parts.

SCORPIO-LIBRA (Page 191)

These Zodiac neighbors often prefer a "live and let live" relationship. If they try togetherness Scorpio may overpower Libra through sheer force of weight.

Scorpio-Scorpio

It will work or it won't. There will be no in between. Scorpios come in two distinct types: one typified by the eagle-soaring, majestic, universal in viewpoint; and the other by the scorpion—inverted, suspicious, deadly in its stinging attack when anger is provoked. It is possible, with forebearance from highly evolved partners, for these two to form relationships that hold together, but they will be demanding and very hard to cope with.

Two Scorpios whose negative traits have taken over are not likely to get together at all. If they do come together they will destroy each other. Scorpios are usually phychic in their perceptions, and these two will recognize the dangerous antagonist in each other and steer clear of interaction.

When the positive traits are developed to their full potential these two Suns will share a relationship of depth and power that transcends most others. The positive Scorpio uses tremendous capacities and superior abilities to achieve goals of universal scope, and this power will touch even the most superficial life levels. Ths shadows cast by two positive Scorpios joined together will touch the lives of others far removed from their immediate locale.

Negative traits of Scorpio are of such strength it takes a powerful individual to control them and allow the positive traits to develop. In the negative Scorpio the viewpoint is directed to the hidden, the secretive; focused toward seclusion and isolation. The negative Scorpio becomes jealous and possessive, insisting the mate turn all emotions toward the relationship and have as little interation as possible with others.

Pluto, the Sign ruler, deals with the underworld and death and dark hidden things; but also with rejuvenation and regneration. But renaissance cannot manifest in these lives as long as the emphasis is toward darkness and isolation. When two negative Scorpios interact the result can be to extinguish the positive traits that can lead to rejuvenation.

Children of negative Scorpio parents would be eaten alive, subjected to the jealous suspicion which Scorpio often turns on loved ones. The demands placed on them from birth could easily be more than some—especially children of Air Signs—could bear. Air Sign individuals, driven too hard, can suffer irreparable nervous and mental disorders.

But with parents of positive development the children would live in Utopia, supported to reach always for their highest goals; encouraged to try for achivements that lie beyond the perceptions of many.

Most Scorpios are successful in anything they try for, but they can be ruthless in their efforts to achieve success. There is little subtlety in the Sign. They often intereact in close relationships in the same ruthless manner in which they make their way in the outside world. Positive Scorpios find detachment by flying far enough above the crowds to get a cosmic view of shared relationships.

A difficult, difficult pairing of individuals which easily degenerates to a continuing power play between the two involved. Few have the strength or the highly evolved character to attempt it without risking defeat.

Scorpio-Sagittarius

Both Suns are independent, both are unconventional, both are intense in reacting against restraints placed on these qualities by others. On the surface they should be able to achieve a relationship that allows each other free reign to move about at will. But *should* and *shall* are miles apart; Scorpio and Sagittarius, side by side, do not make ideal mates. Water and Fire generate passion which too easily reaches the pressure stage. Here it is as if the Amazon were heated to boiling by the fiery furnace of the Sun: the resulting steam could scald the partners beyond saving.

The moods of these two Signs can be devastating. True, Sagittarius succumbs much less frequently to despair than Scorpio gives in to resentment and bitterness; but when and if Sagittarius moodiness coincides with that of Scorpio it is as if the earth opens to release darkness from the underworld. And there is nothing in either to console and support the other during these times; these are self-centered Signs—blunt, independent. They are more apt to leave each other to the mercies of their private pessimisms than to offer comfort.

Neither is patient with the other's traits that do not blend. Yet in practice many of the conflicting traits can soften the negative aspects which develop. Scorpio handles finances carefully, having great respect for money; often working two jobs simutaneously and successfully. Sagittarius has great energy but works in spurts, and in the face of setbacks may toss over all that has been gained, disappearing over the nearest hill in an effort to escape pressure. While not caring a fig for money as such, Sagittarius wants it when it's wanted, and in plentiful supply. Sagittarius, in other words, is extravagant; Scorpio will not find this acceptable in a mate. However, Sagittarius is also lucky, and if these two Suns can bring themselves to work together, can profit from Scorpion handling of Sagittarius finances.

Sometimes they can balance out the Scorpio love of solitude with the Sagittarius love of companionship, or at least recognize a stalemate which forces compromise. In most relationships Scorpio is the stronger, and in this one may be surprised to find Sagittarius is no mean adversary. It is possible to wound a Sagittarius with sarcasm and ruthless willpower, but not for long; the Archer will simply gallop away if the situation becomes too unpleasant. Scorpio, needing absolute freedom while demanding subservience from others, here must concede the strength of the Sagittarian position. If Scorpio wants any relationship at all there will have to be concessions to the Sagittarian's right to freedom. Sagittarius does not recognize jealousy. The Archer will not abide the jealous possessiveness of Scorpio, nor be dragged off to some hidden retreat to be the sole focus of Scorpion emotional intensity. In this instance Scorpio must realize the equal strength of the mate. And it is an uncomfortable impasse for both.

Physically these two may experience a passion of high sensuality. Scorpio is the Sign that governs sex, and Sagittarius has a strong orientation toward the physical. There is danger that this emphasis may dominate the relationship. Scorpio has greater divergencies of development than most other Signs and, may be devil or angel. There is possibility here that the negative side of Scorpio character will interact with the negative traits of Sagittarius to the detriment of both. These Signs demand a strong rein to keep the negative characteristics under control. In this combination it is all too easy to allow them free rein.

Practically, there is no limit to the heights they can reach together if they emphasize the more positive sides of their natures. But it will probably fall on the Sgittarian to lead the way, defusing Scorpio envy and jealousy with loyalty; using a philosophical approach to dampen emotionalism that threatens to inundate the relationship. Pluto is the planet of regeneration, and Jupiter is the great benefic, and the two together can achieve magical results.

It may be that this accord will have to take place one step removed from their own interaction; that is, through the children. Youngsters of these parents may inherit strength to pursue goals of universal scope. They will have courage and stamina to follow through on ideas that leave those around them amazed. They may also find themselves ground to pieces between these personalities who welcome challenge and meet it head on. Certainly theirs will not be an easy childhood, but it can be one that encourages achievement in later years.

Perhaps, when all is considered, these Suns would do better to hold this interaction to a working relationship where each could contribute talents without threatening mortal injury to the other. Side by side, they can present a magnificent partnership: a caravan following the deep-flowing currents of the Nile, serving as contact point for the outside world; the river supplying transportation and food for interaction; neither sacrificing vital energy to the other. A demanding relationship, which will be beyond the capacities of all but the few.

Scorpio-Capricorn

There is power in this combination of Suns—Earth and Water working together to produce solid foundations. Both Scorpio and Capricorn have the stamina and self confidence to pursue their ambitions to the very top, and they support each other in spite of conflicting characteristics that are as strong as complimentary traits.

There is nothing petty in this relationship. These Signs have the vitality of giants. They are ruled by powerful planets whose interaction can change the universal patterns at times. Saturn, ruler of Capricorn, imposes restrictions and moves deliberately; Pluto, ruler of Scorpio, works at deep hidden levels to bring about changes that result in upheaval and ultimate transformation. They interact here to the benefit of the relationship despite periodic upheavals when conflicting traits cannot blend.

The main problem here is that each Sign is so much what it is—so powerful, so difficult to swerve from its purpose. There is little chance for compromise, for negotiation, when Suns of this caliber combine. Still, Capricorn can influence the intensity of the Scorpion involvement toward practical applications; Scorpio emotion can warm the glacial Capricorn facade to release the vitality within.

Scorpio creativity will have to supply the spark for their forward movement, but Capricorn has endurance in building with the ideas of others to produce lasting values. In fact, this will be a relationship that always works behind the scenes to reach goals. And this is good. When forces of this magnitude operate it is easier to control them without others watching every move. Conflicts which develop behind the scenes, as they will inevitably, will be easier to handle.

The emotionalism of Scorpio will create storms in this union: Scorpio intensity will not take kindly to diversion, however practical the results. But the lashing storms of Scorpio emotion will make little impression on Capricorn—a mountain does not flinch from winter gales. Once a stand is taken, Capricorn will remain firm as the mountain rooted in bedrock—and Scorpio reaction will spend itself against a rock face of unbendable strength.

This will be true of all confrontations in this union. Capricorn will stand fast; Scorpio will attack with passion. But somewhere in the process some common purpose will emerge that enlarges rather than diminishes.

There will be intense confrontations at the personal level. Capricorn is as strong-willed as Scorpio is relentless. Both are jealous of the mate's position and stature. There will always be competition closely related to envy working between them, even during their most intimate moments. Worst for Capricorn will be Scorpio's ability to wound with cutting critical comment when sheer willpower cannot win. Capricorns are drawn to Scorpios, conscious of their own inhibited personalities which find interaction with others difficult. Scorpios are secretive, but when they choose can mesmerize those around them with mysterious magnetism. Capricorn moves heavily in social situations and is conscious of a lack of social encounters; Capricorn cannot stand ridicule in any form. Scorpion sarcasm can be the most cruel kind of ridicule.

Still, Capricorn will not mind the possessiveness of Scorpio; this is an affirmation of the mate's love. And Scorpio will be fulfilled by Capricorn's expression of love through sex. The strength of this relationship will be expressed through physical passion. These two will find mutual gratification in physical love that will build on an enduring bond: the glacier melting to feed the deep currents of the mighty river; Plutonian transformation releasing the glory of the Aurora Borealus. In this relationship Capricorn may not feel the need to demand affection and love; may be satisfied with the intensity of the Scorpio mate in this expression of love.

Their children may have difficulty living up to these parents who stand larger than life. Much will be asked of them, but they will be given much support. They may have trouble at times groping their way through the giant shadows cast by the parents Suns, but when they stumble they will be lifted back to their feet before they touch the ground. They may, in effect, feel less like children than miniature adults in the shadow of gods—and this feeling may persist throughout their lives. They may never realize the depth of the love which protects them until they can achieve strength to find their ways on their own.

The home itself will have a heavy atmosphere much of the time. There will be little light-hearted adventure in this household—little frivolity. The house will probably have an air of portentousness. It may be an older home, multi-storied, well-preserved, sitting behind iron gates at the end of a long drive. These Suns do not like being out in the open, vulnerable to the gaze of casual onlookers. By its physical isolation the home will often set the family apart. Children of this pair may find it traumatic to move out into the world at large when they leave the nest.

But once formed, this alliance seldom crumbles. There is too much direction, too much foundational support, to allow it to break up easily. These Suns recognize the strength of their combined abilities and do not want to relinquish their enviable position by destroying the relationship. Having long since realized that they face each other from equal strengths they are intelligent enough to join forces and to somehow achieve a compromise where differences exist. It is easier when both negotiate from power positions.

Scorpio-Aquarius

There is little to recommend this combination in a close relationship. The underlying element of fixity is about the only thing they have in common: the traits which they do share are related to this quality of determination. They are dependable, as would be expected from Signs of superior abilities; they are responsible in performance, but in an almost automatic way, as if they had been programmed at conception to handle demanding assignments without really involving themselves in the action.

In most areas they are strongly, stubbornly at odds. Yet the magnetism of both Signs, as powerful as their squared traits, draws them together as if magic were at work. But the encounter may resemble an eternal testing of willpower more than a love affair. At a distance this projects as a fascinating attractive force. But if Scorpio is doing the pulling, the still deep waters of the personality will surely extinguish the lightning flash of the Aquarian character. And if Aquarius is on the offensive, the lightning bolts will do little more than sting the gleaming surface of the giant river. Compromise is hard to come by in the Scorpio-Aquarius union. Their conflicts will generate a battle to the death.

Aquarius will have a little of the best of the situation; detachment will allow them to rise above the conflict at times and observe the problems from a distance. With Scorpios, the emotional involvement is so intense the battlefield will seem to lie on the surface of their souls.

The humanitarian love which permeates Aquarian character will breed jealousy in the Scorpio partner that fans the fires of revenge which, once lighted by an imagined hurt, will smolder forever. Scorpio love equates to possessive passion—but how does one possess a comet? Aquarian love is diffused through the universe, and even if Aquarius attempted to focus this love on the partner it would be a pale companion to the passion which obsesses the Scorpio mate. Scorpio love is a private love, jealously guarded from others; Aquarian love more resembles the sun's rays that falls as benignly on friends as on lovers.

The social orientation of the Aquarian will be a constant goad to Scorpio, whose ego is so self-sufficient—so convinced of its own superiority—that it has little leeway for casual interaction with others. Scorpio does not do things half way; if another person is attractive enough to get past the disdain with which Scorpio regards superficial contacts, the mate will be pulled headlong into the vortex of love-passion which is the core of Scorpio's emotional relationships.

Aquarian enthusiasms for causes, for groups, for friends, will seem betrayal to Scorpio, who has room for only one involvement at a time. A Scorpio dedicted to a cause will be a loner, without personal attachments in most cases. Having focused the passions on the partner, Scorpio will have little room for other interests; and since Aquarius has, will assume these interests displace the relationship. Actually, this expansion of Aquarian interests may be a barometer which registers the depth of the love for Scorpio; Aquarian love, once activated, can encompass the Milky Way. Scorpio love expands in depth, never in breadth; the deeper the love, the more Scorpio will seek to separate the loved one from other contacts.

It is almost impossible for skeptical Scorpio to feel the idealism of Aquarius. Scorpion perceptions go to the very core of people and situations; it is hard for Scorpio to maintain idealism even if he senses its existence.

Intolerance is the polarization which colors the lens through which Scorpio sees the world and those in it. There is a darkness about the Scorpio character that is reflected in the secretive attitudes toward others; in the desire to work behind the scenes; in the love for solitude; in the desire for revenge. Aquarius sees through the clear prism of the stratosphere; all thought, all interaction, is lifted toward the light.

Aquarius will be drawn by curiosity from one situation to another, from one friend to another, from one idea to another. Each will be examined with tolerance, fixed only in the need to move on as new ideas and situations enter the awareness. Once Scorpio finds a person, an idea, a situation acceptable, it is to alleviate the conflicts, but since no two charts are ever the same, it is possible for these two Suns, given the right conditions, to coalesce to produce a union so intensely pure and brilliant as to challenge the universe.

Scorpio-Pisces

Scorpio and Pisces Suns feel an attraction of great power for each other. Strong physical magnetism is charged by the intensity of emotional response. If intellectual stimulation is also present it can inspire love stories of which legends are made.

In social relationships this may take place as an under-surface force that is compelling even if it is not overtly expressed. In intimate relationships the combination can seem to drown the two with emotional repercussions.

Scorpio plays the mating game at two levels. One is an almost automatic pursuit of any attractive person of the opposite sex, but subtly and secretively. But when it comes to a final choice, Scorpio observes, investigates, and makes far-reaching plans before making a declaration. The uintuitive responsiveness of Pisces can play havoc with this secretive background work, and Scorpio may be startled into revealing the depth of Scorpion rections long before being ready to allow the other person to know the intensity of these responses. Pisces is capable of probing the depths of the Scorpion personality without being crushed by the pressures.

But such intensity cannot be maintained around the

clock, and points of conflict can be as intense as the points of attraction. Both Scorpio and Pisces have an elemental need to withdraw from public contact often. For Pisces this need for solitude is absolute—both physical and mental—and includes isolation from those closest. Scorpio, jealously possessive of loved ones, will see this periodic withdrawal of Pisces as betrayal. Scorpio's idea of withdrawal from public life is to lock the doors of the home for a long and private interval with the mate.

The sexual-emotional involvement is integrated in both these Signs. Yet there is a profound difference that may blow the relationship apart. For Pisces the two are fused: there cannot be one without the other. For Scorpio, the two are separate but interlocked. Scorpio is capable of sexual infidelity which in no way touches the emotional involvement with the mate. Pisces infidelity would require an emotional involvement also. The Scorpio partner would never forgive the suggestion of infidelity on the part of the mate, but would insist on the right personally.

In either case the damage to the relationship would be catastrophic. Pisces would forgive but never forget; Scorpio would neither forget nor forgive and, would in face dedicate all energy to getting revenge no matter how long it took.

The conflicting traits of these two Signs are so many that even the attractive passions may not be enough to withstand erosion. Pisces is empathetic, overly concerned for the other person's feelings even when not in agreement. Scorpio, often arrogant in self-centeredness, can be brutally tactless. Pisces can usually see the other side of a question and qualifies judgment of the actions of others. Scorpio is apt to judge others unmercifully against personal superior abilities. Pisces rejoices in the good luck of others; Scorpio is more likely to be envious of the good fortune that comes to someone else. These attitudes show as strongly with each other as toward strangers. Pisces, united with Scorpio, soon learns that Scorpio's friends bleed the same color as foes.

Pisces, idealistic to the point of unreality, cannot accept the ruthlessness of Scorpio ambitions. This can be a strong factor in undermining the relationship, and Scorpio may never understand what finally caused the walls to cave in. Prepared to defend personal positions to the death, Scorpio cannot really comprehend that Pisces defends *others'* positions to the death.

Even physical makeup can cause a rift between these two. Overly endowed with energy to carry through on several projects at one time, Scorpio is not sympathetic to Pisces lack of vitality, interpreting it as lack of interest as often as not. Scorpio may demand the Pisces mate try harder, and in so doing Pisces will further deplete basic vitality.

In a very real sense the home will be an adhesive force in holding the union together. Both Pisces and Scorpio see the home as a refuge from the assaults made on their spirits by the necessary daily contacts with outsiders. Both will work to build a home of special beauty—a haven which cushions them from outside influences. They will be reticent about opening their doors to others. Anyone invited to this home will be honored indeed and will be one of a select group.

Scorpio and Pisces together make loving, devoted parents, with Scorpio strength underriding Pisces compassion to good advantage. But there will be friction. Scorpio may expect the Pisces mate to direct all energy and interests within the confines of the dream home, refusing to recognize that Pisces needs social encounters as much as solitude. The dual nature of Pisces is nowhere more in evidence than in this fluctuating need for companions one day and utter aloneness the next. Self-sufficient Scorpio, once loved is focused, and the home base established, has little need for social interaction.

In these two Signs are found the greatest extremes between the evolved and negative types of personality. The joining of Pisces-Scorpio on the lower level of development can be disastrous. Pisces, who absorbs and reflects the qualities of the partner in any relationship, magnifies and recycles malefic qualities of an unevolved Scorpio. A union of negative types of these two Signs would truly seem to be made in hell.

The joining of two evolved Pisces and Scorpio partners, on the other hand, would produce a union of magnificent quality, calling forth the highest attributes of these Signs to generate a love that would endure beyond death.

SAGITTARIUS

SAGITTARIUS-ARIES (Page 34)

The excitement of a carnival, starting with a teen-age marriage and lasting through to the Golden Wedding celebration. Aries provides the light; Sagittarius the heat.

SAGITTARIUS-TAURUS (Page 69)

A 'damned if you do, damned if you don't' combination. Taurus may end up alone in the end, fanning the embers of a dying romance, while Sagittarius disappears over the nearest hill.

SAGITTARIUS-GEMINI (Page 99)

These are the gypsies of the Zodiac, seeking adventure on a magic carpet. Don't be surprised to find them celebrating successful anniversaries year after year in a most unconventional manner.

SAGITTARIUS-CANCER (Page 126)

A romance more at home in fairy tales. Lifelines between the two are fragile. An arrow is a poor weapon with which to capture a sunbeam, and vice versa.

SAGITTARIUS-LEO (Page 151)

A deceptive attractiveness camoflages severe conflicts. But it can work if they learn to mesh their positive traits. Once established, the fire of this love burns for a long, long time.

SAGITTARIUS-VIRGO (Page 174)

At best they accommodate each other in a relationship, as the desert dunes provide a base for the caravan which brings otherwise unreachable drama and color to the barebones desert landscape. Occasionally develops to a rewarding union that leaves others wondering what they see in each other.

SAGITTARIUS-LIBRA (Page 195)

Venus and Jupiter are alchemists working together to soften incompatible traits to allow beneficial aspects to work their magic. With any effort at all these two will go through life together with everything coming up roses.

SAGITTARIUS-SCORPIO (Page 212)

Water and Fire generate passion which too often reaches the pressure point; as if the Amazon were heated to boiling by the fiery furnace of the Sun. A demanding relationship beyond the capabilities of all but the very strong.

Sagittarius-Sagittarius

This is the most adventuresome doubling of Signs; the most exciting; the most stimulating. Archers work well as teams—if the team mates are traveling the same direction—and on the physical level at least these independent, devil-may-care rovers may be better suited to each other than to partners from other Signs.

Their home may well be motel rooms or travel vans or mobile homes. It's highly probable that their work may keep them traveling: as airlines personnel, for instance, or as journalists and photographers and entertainers. Even if they settle down to a home in the suburbs, they'll probably be off at a moment's notice whenever an opportunity peeks over the horizon.

They are well-suited to each other in the day-to-day routines that make up a close relationship. By mutual agreement they'll ignore the restricting inconveniences most Signs expect from domestic life. Sagittarians are tolerant of others, because they demand great latitude from others in their own behavior. Archers couldn't care less what "they" think; and being magnetic individuals, are apt to indulge in casual affairs wedded or not. But this insistence on personal liberty seems to be a testing device in a sense; and the Sagittarian who feels free from leashes and fences will be held by the sense of freedom to a relationship which recognizes the claim. Thus these two can understand and forgive infidelities more easily than most.

But the spirit trapped by the animal self may feel uneasy over lack of convention in their lives while demanding utter freedom to defy tradition. Prone to take those who love them for granted, they will make no concessions to the feelings of the other in times of stress. However, a mutual sense of humor will help lubricate the tight spots when one or the other is in the depths of an occasional black mood.

The danger here, as with any doubling of Sun Signs in a relationship, is that as similar traits manifest side by side, undesirable effects will expand in ratio to overpower positive traits. Sagittarians are daredevils; they may take risks together that can be fatal (literally). Jupiter, the ruler, bestowing luck and bountiful success, protects them from disaster so often that they cannot believe there will ever be a point of no return.

In the same way they may indulge minor vices and casual infidelities until not even Jupiter can salvage the relationship.

The philosopher in this Sign may be able to supply a rationalization that will take the edge off the pain of parting, but these two, going separate ways, will always feel a sense of something of value lost forever.

Their children may live a Huck Finn existence of pure delight, at least as seen from the outside. They may develop this sense of adventure themselves. They may also feel deserted by parents that are on the go as often as they are home. In relationships that last with other Signs, the mate helps fill in the security gaps for the child of the Sagittarian parent; here there may be no one to supply this role for the children.

But Jupiter has a way of bringing things to a jackpot conclusion for most Sagittarians, no matter how deeply entangled they become in sticky personal problems. Jupiterian beneficence has a way of raining prizes on those near the Archer as well as on the target Sign. Chances are it will turn out to be a long adventure for all involved from beginning to ending.

Sagittarius-Capricorn

It is possible for these neighbors of the Zodiac to co-exist with very little awareness of each other, as an expedition crawls along the face of Everest; as the mountain stands aloof above the valley trail the caravan follows. But if circumstances unite them, this can be an enduring relationship that offers benefits to both these Suns.

Semisextile Suns have overlapping contact points through which they communicate. They borrow traits from each other which lead to mutual understanding. At the same time there are incompatibilities of element and quality that places challenges before them which must be solved before the union can grow to fulfillment.

Loyalty is a shared trait which goes a long way toward easing conflicts here. Capricorn works hard and is willing to make compromises in order to find a meaningful relationship. But the Goat wants to be appreciated for these efforts. Sagittarius wants to be appreciated *in spite of* of character traits that demand the Archer test important relationships periodically. Sagittarius demands to be taken on faith. Loyalty is the bonding element that will often hold these Suns together in the face of strong conflicts.

Capricorn's stern exterior reflects the quality of Saturn, its ruler. Dignity and traditionalism and status loom large in Capricorn character; in addition this self-disciplined personality does not allow easy interaction with others. It is easy for Capricorn to assume a domineering attitude, especially when dealing with Sagittarius.

Sagittarius is as unconventional as Capricorn is dignified. The need for personal liberty is so basic that Sagittarius cannot function when boxed in by rigid rules. The Archer moves fast and often; at times cannot handle the heavy burdens Saturn places on those close. It is not that Sagittarius does not recognize obligations, but the vital spark of enthusiasm and optimism dies when freedom of movement is curtailed in any direction—mental, physical, emotional.

There will be head-on confrontations time and again between these two on this one point. The bluntness for which Sagittarius is known laps over here into Capricorn; but the impact may be softened by keeping a kind of balance. An onlooker to one of their oppositional encounters may cringe at the force of the arguments they hurl at each other. But these two Suns will have set ground rules and will understand that when it's all over there will be a truce and the battle will be forgotten. For Sagittarius knows deep down that Capricorn will not concede; and Capricorn knows that Sagittarius changes direction without warning and can come trotting home as abruptly as the Archer galloped away in the heat of the argument.

They need each other—Capricorn probably *needing* the most, thus willing to give the most. And in spite of epic confrontations they really want to arrive at some plateau where they can live together without too great a strain on either. There is something missing in the interaction of these Signs that exist side by side. There is no empathy, little intuition, little emotion with which to enter and feel what the other experiences. It is almost impossible for Capricorn to step inside another's skin. The Goat may believe understanding is there, but in truth this is more a process of imposing personal feelings and reactions onto the other person and judging by Capricornian standards. Sagittarius takes others for granted. It is possible for these two Suns to live together without a glimmer of empathy to bridge the gaps in their relationship.

Capricorn ambition will suffer from the scattered enthusiasms of the Sagittarian mate. The Archer will bring fire to projects and will contribute a share of the work. But Sagittarius does not have the stamina to hang in there when the going gets tough. Responsibilities must be assumed by the mate. Capricorn will not mind this too much as long as Sagittarius is appreciative and remains loyal. The Goat will allow the Archer to escape periodically to gather energies, but expects the mate to return more or less on schedule. Capricorn can accept exended "business trips" by the mate, but would be humiliated to admit the partner had deserted forever. Sagittarius can buy loyalty by reappearing when the mood strikes as if nothing had happened, even if the departure took place in the middle of a raging domestic battle.

Capricorn will learn early that it does little good to reprimand Sagittarius for this; it will only touch off the firecracker temper which pops in outbursts of sparks and smoke. Better it is to accept the relationship on Sagittarius terms—it is the only way to maintain contact. And for Capricorn, for whom chances at romance and adventure sometimes seem out of reach, Sagittarius offers some diversion from the heavy burdens which Saturnian rulership imposes.

In the intimate area of their lives they get along very well, the strong emphasis on physical satisfaction mitigated somewhat by a spiritual influence that touches both these Signs: aspiration in Capricorn, idealism in Sagittarius. Both accept the physical side of love with lusty enjoyment. If Capricorn feels hurt at the Sagittarian mate's offhand acceptance of their mutually satisfying relationship there will be no open complaint. There is an element of bawdy good humor to match the Archer's jovial ribaldry. They are well matched on this point.

Their children may have an easier time with this combination of parental Suns than other children with Capricorn parents. Most Signs able to hold their own with Capricorn are pretty heavy themselves in their interactions with children. Sagittarius, who wins by escaping from the shadow of the mountain, will teach the children tricks with which to counteract the strict Capricornian upbringing. Good or bad, this will lighten the load for children growing up in this household, and who knows—maybe for good instead of the other way.

This relationship will probably improve with age, with Sagittarius mellowing to allow good humor to take precedence over irritability; with Capricorn feeling less pressure to dominate as goals are achieved.

Sagittarius-Aquarius

By far the greatest asset this Sun combination has going for it is a mutual need for room in which to move around. Both Aquarius and Sagittarius feel this craving for freedom so strongly that each will concede some personal independence in order to keep the relationship in balance on this point.

Most of the complimentary traits here spring from this insistence on personal liberty. Sagittarius hates pretense; is likely to applaud the Aquarian unconventionality in behavior and dress with good humor even if not following all the way. There is more than a little of the iconoclast buried in Sagittarian makeup, which can seek a vicarious outlet by supporting Aquarian opposition to tradition. At any rate, there will not be trauma in either Sign from embarrassment due to actions of the other. Neither is too concerned with what "they" think. These Signs are self-sufficient. And therein lies the root of potential trouble betwen these sextiled Suns.

Sextiled Suns are supportive to each other; Aquarius can benefit from the self-confident aggressiveness of Sagittarius in taking action and getting started. Sagittarius can use the softening influence of Aquarian social orientation. Sagittarius, like Aquarius, collects friends from many sources. But Sagittarius has friends in spite of outspokenness and a tendency to take them for granted. Aquarius may flit in and out of friends lives without warning, but is genuinely interested and concerned when with them. These two may be often short of money from supplying gratuitous accommodations for friends; they are neither one overly money conscious, and they won't begrudge each other the pleasure of sharing what they have.

Aquarian irritability and Sagittarian temper may clash from time to time, but one thing about it, they don't hold grudges or nurse hurt feelings over these conflicts. They'll probably stay out of each other's way until the storm blows over and there'll be no indication at the dinner table that they've charged through a battle royal before breakfast.

In most cases they will be tolerant of each other's faults, but Sagittarian bluntness can come perilously close to criticism from the Aquarian viewpoint. Aquarius cannot take criticism. Sagittarius doesn't like it, but can shrug it off and go on with a be-damned-to-you attitude under criticism. Aquarian reactions are more refined.

Because Aquarius finds conflict distressing, some effort will be made to avoid it as long as humanitarian convictions are not challenged. Sagittarius may gleefully invite conflict if in the mood for action, relying on a philosophical discussion to set matters straight if the situation gets out of hand.

This couple may battle their way through a happy marriage, turning together to denounce anyone who mistakenly tries to arbitrate. Of course, this tolerance for arguments can become a habit, and it will help if they stay aware of this possibility. It's certain, however, that furious quarreling between them is not as serious as with many other Signs. Those inadvertently caught in the middle of a Sagittarius-Aquarius set-to should remember two points: neither of these Signs cares too much about observing the amenities before others; and each has a built-in safety valve that lets them take off for the wide open spaces when the battle rages too fiercely.

These two are not likely to acquire too much in the way of material possessions. They aren't attuned to the kind of responsibility that possessions demand. Neither can accept monotony, no matter how benign. Both tire of the old very quickly and search for the new. This, plus a tendency to scatter enthusiasms, does not ensure staying power for mutual projects. Chances aren't great for family enterprise here. But this may not prevent them from trying. Aquarian inventiveness combines easily with Sagittarian willingness to explore. It is perhaps the frequent blessings of Jupiterian luck that wipes out caution in Sagittarius. For Sagittarius will take risks. And Aquarian eyes are fixed on far horizons, rarely noticing the stones in the road until tripping over them.

They are mutually idealistic, and Sagittarian philosophy can soothe the bruises suffered by Aquarius more easily than the emotional sympathy of the Water Signs. The moodiness of Sagittarius can profit from the detachment of the Aquarian mate when the black moods strike.

Neither Sign is deeply emotional, yet there may be

conflicts in the intimate relationship. While Aquarius is often experimental, there is a quality of refinement in Aquarian character that may find the bawdy Sagittarian attitudes toward sex distasteful. Where Aquarius does not find it hard to separate sex and love, for Sagittarius love and sex are interchangeable—the ultimate indoor sport. Excesses irritate Aquarius; Sagittarius thrives on them. Individual planetary placements are of great importance in this union. They can soften or intensify the sexuality of either of these Signs to better balance.

Fire and Air children of these parents will probably thrive in spite of the frequent quarrels; Earth and Water Sign children may be torn to shreds. Again it will depend on individual planet placements, more so here than in most families. Aquarius will work to instill enduring values in the children while Sagittarius will shrug off their transgressions, at least until they become an inconvenience. The lack will be in emotional areas. Neither of these Signs will spend much time cuddling their children; they'll spend a lot of time working with them or playing with them or teaching them new skills.

This partnership can be miserable or it can be great; it will never be petty. There will be something larger than life about the relationship. When it's working these two can give the impression they're sailing along in a striped balloon, living an exciting adventure that lesser souls will never experience because they lack courage to risk losing touch with earth. And if things don't work, they'll remain good friends to the end.

Sagittarius-Pisces

The Archer and the Fish have many things in common. Jupiter, ruler of Sagittarius, holds co-rulership of Pisces with Neptune, and one of the bonds that brings these Suns together is an optimistic faith in things turning out for the best. Jupiterian luck, which carries Sagittarius through life with an almost magical power to pull out of tight corners, sheds some of its bounty over Pisces. They both seem to come out on top even in the most doubtful situations.

The Sagittarian's philosophical approach to life is reflected in the ecumenical spirituality of Pisces. Each will give serious consideration to the ideas of the other. Sagittarius is willing to explore new concepts while claiming the right to dissect them with blunt forcefulness; Pisces has extremes of tolerance toward the viewpoints of others while claiming the right to analyze them with emotional intensity. Both Pisces and Sagittarius can divorce other people from their ideas and actions—liking them while disapproving mightily of what they do; approving the actions or ideas of one whom they dislike intensely.

Both Pisces and Sagittarius have the ability to keep many projects moving at the same time, working with cycles rather than by detailed planning. They can support each other through periods of confusing activity that seem to lead nowhere, sensing that the cycles will complete with several projects coming to fruition at the same time. Jackpots tend to come in bunches for both Sagittarius and Pisces. Of course, there is the reverse of the coin to be contended with: trouble comes the same way. But optimism helps them hang in there until—sure enough—they stub their toes over the pot of gold at the foot of the rainbow.

Fortunately this dependence on luck and rose-colored spectacles is supported by a sense of responsibility in Pisces and great capacity for hard work in the Sagittarian. Since neither likes routine, they tend to join forces in a business partnership once the personal relationship has been established. But neither is very practical about finances—Pisces willing to sacrifice financial benefits for principle; Sagittarius willing to give up income for personal freedom. This try at "playing store" to keep away from the chores of "playing house" would be a chancy proposition were it not for Jupiterian luck, which seldom deserts these two as long as they make any kind of effort to work things out.

Still, in spite of strong plusses, there are minuses. Both these squared Suns are so much what they are that points of difference are as forceful as points of agreement. Daily routine causes friction between them more often than not. Sagittarius finds the emotional responses of Pisces embarrassing and irritating; the Archer's philosophical nature has little use for sentiment. While Pisces compassion is strangely comforting when the Sagittarian is caught in depression, it is stifling once Sagittarius has regained a jovial outlook. The Archer is inclined to take the mate for granted, an attitude Pisces cannot endure. Sagittarius understands that bluntness wounds the sensitive partner, but the knowledge seems to inspire a sense of guilt that's expressed as irritability. Sagittarius panics under feelings of obligation. The need for independence demands absolute personal freedom in an intimate relationship.

Both Suns are dual natured, operating on a self-indulgent permissive extreme much of the time while always aware of ethical and spiritual values at the other extreme. Piscean mystical intuition is accorded freer movement within the personality, allowing the two halves of the nature to take turns imposing direction. But the philosophical wisdom of Sagittarius is trapped in the structure of the animal nature and must maintain constant, iron-fisted control in order to give direction to the entity.

The primary attractive force here for the Sagittarian is a sensual attraction based on mystery; the Archer is drawn almost against the will to discover the secret of the magnetism which surrounds the elusive Pisces. Sagittarius follows Pisces as closely as possible—as far as possible—Pegasus seeking a path over the rainbow in search of illusion. Pisces may tease the pursuer with innuendos which the Archer interprets as promises. This fairly tale atmosphere expands under Jupiterian influences working through the immaterialism of Neptune. Sagittarians see only what they want to see; Pisces tells them only what they want to hear.

Once the intimate relationship is established it is harder and harder to keep the facets of these personalities meshing. The Pisces vitality cycle demands privacy at regular intervals to restore energy drained during social cycles. The home is a place of refuge where Pisces can rejuvenate inner resources and physical energies. Home for Sagittarius is apt to be a way station for restless comings and goings. Sagittarius can go for long periods of time without rest; can recuperate with af ew hours sleep. The Archer functions best with friends around. Pisces can become physically ill if forced to maintain constant contact with others. These complex cycles will miss more often than they work together, and the damage can be severe for both.

Each of these Signs has a built-in escape mechanism that is automatically activated when the stress point reaches a danger level. The Sagittarian need for freedom outweighs even the love for the mate. Driven too far, the elusive Fish will disappear forever into a shadowy pool.

Children of these Suns will either be blessed with the

blended positive characteristics of the two, or be plagued by the conflicts that assail them, depending on the parents' level of development. Pisces empathy and compassion can help balance out Sagittarian irritability. The Sagittarian sense of adventure can divert the children from an overstrong attachment to the Pisces parent.

Still, in spite of all the things that can bring conflict, this relationship may glow on and on, a perpetual Christmas tree, with first one and then the other Sun tightening the bulbs to keep the lights burning.

CAPRICORN

CAPRICORN-ARIES (Page 37)

If these two can endure the pressures of opposing wills during the early years, the later ones will find Aries Fire burning steadily from the Capricorn mountain top—a very visible silhouette against the skyline.

CAPRICORN-TAURUS (Page 72)

Solidly enduring; supporting each other as prairie and mountain exist together, trusting and depending upon the same durable foundations.

CAPRICORN-GEMINI (Page 103)

Gemini may be drawn to Capricorn as the whirlwind is drawn to explore the mountain; Capricorn may be fascinated by Gemini mobility. The points of contact are too tenuous to build upon.

CAPRICORN-CANCER (Page 129)

This union represents the extremes of polarity: the receptiveness of the Mother opposing the discipline of the Father. But it endures, with little chance of either mate desiring to break it off.

CAPRICORN-LEO (Page 155)

A ring of fire becomes a halo under the right conditions. There is much strength to support the relationship, and it will be lasting. Not without storms, but in the end highly satisfying.

CAPRICORN-VIRGO (Page 177)

These conservative personalities understand the paths they will pursue in their common journey without having to spend energy in explanations. An almost ideal union of basic personalities to achieve a solid, satisfying partnership.

CAPRICORN-LIBRA (Page 198)

A paradoxical but lasting relationship. The eternal flame of Libra spirit interacts with the Capricorn nature to generate the splendor of the Midnight Sun. More fulfilling as the years roll by.

CAPRICORN-SCORPIO (Page 215)

Influences of this magnitude make compromise difficult. Capricorn will always stand fast; Scorpio will always attack with passion. But they will find fulfillment in love—the glacier melting to feed the sweeping currents of the mighty river.

They often co-exist with very little awareness of each other, as an expedition crawls along the face of Everest. if circumstances unite them, the relationship will improve with age. But it may never get off the ground in the first place.

Capricorn-Capricorn

Solid and permanent, this relationship, once it's established. It may take time to get these two together; Cardinal Earth moves slowly to secure the enduring foundations upon which it builds. These partners may be pst the thirty-year mark before they find each other and may take more time to reach a final decision. But once the marriage is achieved it will be for always. Mountains do not move easily.

As often as not Capricorns choose a mate for home and status. It isn't that they don't love. But not even love escapes the practicality of Capricorn's outlook. "It's as easy to love a rich man as a poor man," was certainly the advice of a Capricorn mother to her daughter. And Capricorns find it so. This pragmatic attitude plays a strong part in holding these marriages together.

In a relationship involving two Capricorns the likelihood of divorce is all but nonexistent. Having chosen theri mates with care, the Capricorn pair begins at once to move toward a traditionally solid position in life, financially and socially. The wife will probably work unless she has small children; it goes without saying the Capricorn husband will have a job with a secure future before considering marriage. With so much invested—in tangible assets as well as physical effort—any Capricorn will think twice before breaking up the union.

Undoubtedly there will be times when the atmosphere of the double Capricorn home will resemble the chill thrown off by a glacier. Capricorn broods over hurts, real or imagined, bestowed by those close. By doubling the Saturnian partners in this domestic drama the opportunities for moodiness are squared. Capricorns have great stamina, and they draw on it to sustain their hurt feelings as well as to achieve more constructive accomplishments. They may go without speaking to each other for days on end, but when the chips are down they'll let the relationship thaw. A substantial bank balance makes a nice security blanket for Capricorns to wrap themselves in to overcome feelings of neglect.

And underlying these surface reasons will be a love that deepends and grows with the passing of time. Most Capricorns are just hitting their stride in middle age; they get better—not older. Their affections grow like the Cardinal Earth which is the Sign's element—steadily, surely—building up over the years in spite of erosion from emotional stress.

Youngsters in the family will achieve adulthood early. Saturn, the Sign ruler, places stern restrictions on children of Capricorn parents. Capricorns are executives by nature who have usually earned their right to insist on discipline by working up in life the hard way. Almost always Capricorns will have severe obstacles to overcome somewhere in their lives. They will not allow their children to escape the narrow rocky path of responsibility. Capricornian love for children is expressed in opposite fashion from the opposing Sign, Cancer: they tend to push the babies from the nest a little too soon in their efforts to prepare them to take care of themselves. But whatever the relationship with their children, their motives derive from love.

This won't be a youthful passion; a wild romance is not Capricorn's thing. But these two Suns will be more apt to celebrate a Diamond Anniversary in good health than any other doubled Sign.

Capricorn-Aquarius

These neighboring Signs have few traits in common. The fixed quality of Aquarius is reflected in Capricorn's persistence. Capricorn is a Cardinal Sign, but keeps trying, often in the face of major obstacles. Aquarian humanitarianism becomes spirituality in Capricorn, but each can understand the related trait in the other. They both want to get down to basics in any situation: Capricorn in a practical manner; Aquarius on a universal level. And neither can stand criticism.

Yet both give criticism rather easily. Capricorn is adept at figuring strategic moves and acting on past experience to achieve goals and, is not backward about telling others how things should be done. While the main target may be large organizations, or society at large, this basic desire to change things for the better is reflected in the Aquarian attitude toward Capricorn.

Signs in semi-sextile aspect will have many traits that conflict to go along with the few that overlap. Yet, working together, they can sometimes produce a unified whole that functions well. The conservative Capricorn may suffer deeply from the unconventional attitudes of Aquarius. Capricorn desires status above all, exemplified by a traditional home in a good neighborhood, a steady substantial income, children who do the parents proud. Aquarian indifference to traditional attitudes is a bitter pill for Capricorn to swallow.

Aquarius is idealistic and shudders over the materialistic orientation of Capricorn with the established order. Capricorn sweats blood over the experimental projects of the Aquarian which seem to have very little practical value. The tendency of the Aquarian to take impulsive action—and then stand firm as the Pole Star—seems sheer folly to rigid Capricorn, inching forward with prudence toward substantial goals. But Aquarian inventiveness can produce some surprisingly good (as well as some spectacularly bad) results if freedom is given to work them out.

Aquarius cannot endure nagging. Capricorn, prone to lecture anyone within shouting distance, will find it almost impossible to resist giving personal views—frequently—on whatever the Aquarian is trying to accomplish. Capricorn is able to plan carefully, fitting pieces together with precision, and come up with a clear, direct plan for achieving specific results. If, as often happens, the Aquarian listens courteously and then continues as before without following the plan as outlined, Capricorn will remind—and remind—and remind—and the difference between reminding and nagging is all but nonexistent.

Capricorn is not usually known for tact. The Goat will decide on a course of action and move forward with the purpose of a bulldozer, and with about as much regard for the opinions of others. Not long on social courtesies, Capricorn accepts courtesy matter-of-factly while rarely reciprocating; may in fact routinely take advantage of the courtesies from others.

This quality of seeming to demand consideration, respect, even love, will place a heavy burden on Capricorn relationships. It is extremely hard for Capricorn to express desires without inhibition; in pushing to get the words out the Goat often appears brash or domineering, and is hurt time and again by the negative reactions received from others.

The blunt exterior of the Capricorn houses a core of sensitivity that burns at the center of the being, however. Capricorn is forever accusing intimates of failing to recognize sensitive personal qualities while presenting to them the thorny personality behind which the vulnerable self seeks protection. The Aquarian responds to this need for tenderness and appreciation as long as the Capricorn does not throw the full weight of practicality and concern for status on the mate. Pushed too hard, Aquarius will prove as illusive as a handful of air; the harder the Capricorn pushes the less will be gained. It is impossible to immobilize an Aquarian. Capricorn would make statues of loved ones, encased in bronze, to stand steadfastly in a convenient corner of the home. Aquarians often give the impression of materializing and dissolving at will in close relationships.

Intimate interaction between these two Signs leaves much to be desired. Saturn, the Capricorn ruler, is inhibiting, restrictive. Uranus, ruler of Aquarius, is the planet of surprises. Aquarius idealism demands an intellectual involvement to balance the physical involvement and make it permanent; and may be turned off by the lusty sexuality of Capricorn, who couldn't care less about intellectual involvement if physical desires are satisfied. Over and over the Capricorn may be stung by lightning flashes. Capricorn may glower and rage and protest, yet is as impotent to crush the Aquarian as the Aquarian is to cause the Goat harm. How can a mountain attack a lightning storm?

Children of this pair may be forced into choosing sides time after time—by the Capricorn. Aquarius will seldom impose restrictions on loved ones, physically, mentally or emotionally. For Capricorn the name of the game is restriction in the form of responsibilities, sworn loyalties, rigid rules. If Capricorn nagging and Aquarian irritability degenerate into habitual bickering it can upset children. Air and Fire Sign children will be drawn to the Aquarian detachment; Water Sign children will escape if possible. Earth Signs will usually tolerate the Capricorn firmness.

Yet, truly, Aquarius could make good use of the steadfastness of solidity of Capricorn character; certainly the Capricorn could use some of the Aquarian social charm. Capricorn will endure much to preserve a marriage. And the burden will be on Capricorn in this relationship. Again, it will require a great deal of balancing through individual planetary placements, to bring out an effective relationship. Otherwise, the best intentions in the world may not be enough to keep these two together.

Capricorn-Pisces

As with the Taurus-Pisces combination, these two Suns can be beautifully supportive of each other. Capricorn is Cardinal—a mountain of strength—but like the mountain face, the Capricorn exterior can be so stern others may find it unapproachable. Pisces warmth can soften and warm the Capricorn while drawing on the solid strength which mutable, emotional Pisces so sorely needs and must find in others.

Both Pisces and Capricorn will instinctively recognize this complimentary interaction in each other. The difficulty may be in maintaining contact until they can get past surface personality traits to allow the Pisces to rech the deeply sensitive inner self of the Capricorn; and to allow the Capricorn to glimpse the inner conviction of the apparently illusive Pisces. When the surface strength supports the inner strength of Pisces, and Pisces empathy slips through to unite with the inner responsiveness of Capricorn, a two-way bond is formed that will last forever.

It is absolutely vital that these two Suns establish these strong bonds in order to use their differing personality traits to mutual advantage. It is not so much working together as bonding together. When this happens, all that is positive in the natures of both these Signs merges and grows in every direction: physical, mental, spiritual, emotional. For it is a strange truth that the strongest traits in these two Signs are oppositional rather than conplimentary, taken one by one. Yet it is this combination of opposing elements that can build such magnificent unity when they come together in a positive way.

The Pisces, intellectually industrious, lacks stamina for sustained physical effort; while Capricorn is the strongest of the Signs physically. Capricorn is ruled by Saturn and is the longest lived of the Signs. Interacting with Capricorn can give Pisces strength to stay in the race; while understanding this, Capricorn may be intolerant of Pisces "laziness." The Capricorn way with a difficult job is to draw on experience and work steadily to rech a first-stage goal; consolidating that position before repeating the process to reach the goal. Capricorn is uneasy with Pisces methods of working at many facets of a project—touching here, probing there—retreating periodically to do nothing at all as far as Capricorn can see. But Pisces does complete projects, and beautifully. Once Capricorn has learned to trust Pisces imagination and intuition, the two can work together to the advantage of both.

The Saturnine Capricorn personality can use the rose-colored glasses of Pisces to pull out of the periods of depression which attack almost on schedule. The restrictive rulership of Saturn is not easy for Capricorn to live with, and Pisces warmth and empathy brings the rainbow a little closer for the Goat.

It's hard at times for Pisces to make headway against the stone face of the Capricorn character, however. The warmth of Pisces qualities can be avalanched by the brusk practicality of Capricorn.

It's accepted that many Capricorns suffer limiting conditions during childhood. They are often self-made individuals who achieve success only after years of struggle against what seem like overwhelming odds. Pisces, on the other hand, seems to attract whatever is needed without much effort. To Capricorn, who has learned to conserve assets, Pisces generosity is little short of frivolous. And Capricorn doesn't hesitate to make these views known. Capricorn generosity usually takes the form of doing something for another which the other person mght well prefer *not* be done. Capricorn, unable to step easily into others' shoes, acts on personal beliefs without considering others' views as often as not. Strong personal opinions supply all the support Capricorn needs, and these opinions can be inflicted on others in very forceful terms.

Pisces is tolerant to a fault and, will go to any lengths to avoid painful conflicts, embarrassing situations, confrontations. The Fish rarely judges others, not so much because of lack of convictions (which Pisces has almost to excess) but because of feeling that no one should impose personal views on others. One of the hardest tasks for the Pisces parent is to discipline children, for instance. Capricorn couldn't care less about stepping on sensitive toes of others if the situation calls for it. The Goat not only has definite opinions about what others should do but will lecture to be sure they understand their obligations. Capricorn's children will have little opportunity to make their own mistakes; the rules will be many and there will be no chance to forget any of them.

Capricorn tactlessness can blister Pisces sensitivity. Empathy makes Pisces extremely sensitive in relationships and this concern for the other's viewpoint often acts against Pisces best interest. Capricorn is at a disadvantage in most relationships. Armed with good intentions, the Goat moves with all the subtlety of a Sherman tank. This lack of consideration is almost intolerable to Pisces in intimate relationships. Absence of small courtesies is especially abrasive to Pisces. However sympathetic to the inability of Capricorn to be gentle, Pisces finds it almost impossible to live with the self-centered demands of the Goat.

Capricorn sees nothing wrong in marrying for money; or in enduring an unrewarding relationship for the sake of affluence and status. Pisces may simply walk away from a life of affluence if personal ideals are consistently violated. Yet Pisces will apprecite the material assets the Capricorn partner supplies as long as they are accompanied by expressions of affection (even if they have to be picked up through intuition).

The Piscean need for privacy is elemental. Capricorn, needing to interact with others, will intrude as a matter of course. There is little reticence in the Capricorn nature. Pisces efforts to withdraw will only induce greater effort on the part of Pisces to remain close. Seeing Pisces slipping beyond reach Capricorn will work harder to "do things" for the partner and feed a sense of martyrdom by imagined proofs that Pisces is unappreciative.

Both Signs are easily hurt by those they love, and both withdraw when hurt: Pisces to restore self-confidence and allow emotional wounds to heal;

Capricorn to brood over hurts in silence. Pisces optimism will return in time, but Capricorn wounds will be nurtured and stockpiled to be drawn out in moments of conflict to prove the mate's ingratitude.

They will both tend to use their children to get back at each other in these conflicts. Capricorn will concentrate on doing for the children and at the same time demanding even more consideration from them than usual. Pisces will ease the sense of aloneness and unhappiness by turning to the children also.

Thus, when things do not mesh for these two it can be a painful union. Given time to establish the bonds that will allow understanding, these two can find a rewarding, enduring life together.

AQUARIUS

AQUARIUS-ARIES (Page 41)

A potent combination of idealism and intellectual
curiosity. But Aquarius, while allowing Aries Fire
freedom to burn at white heat on its own ground, will
not chance a conflagration in the private universe.

AQUARIUS-TAURUS (Page 75)

Aquarian sights are focused on distant points of the
universe; Taurean ideals are rooted in earth. Their
shared love of their children may hold this unlikely
relationship together.

AQUARIUS-GEMINI (Page 106)

A delightful combination on the surface—and that may
be as far as it ever goes. A whirlwind in the stratosphere
doesn't promise much durability. A perpetual
happening.

AQUARIUS-CANCER (Page 132)

It may be hard to pull off after the first fascination
palls. The basic conflicts between emotion and intellect
will never be fully resolved.

AQUARIUS-LEO (Page 158)

This can develop as a powerful but demanding union, but for every accord there will be an abrasive price. The surprising thing is that these two uncompromising Signs make the effort. Aquarius will bear the burden of keeping this flame burning.

AQUARIUS-VIRGO (Page 180)

Others may see the relationship as the consumation of a romance between a flash of lightning and a computer. An exciting marriage of the minds.

AQUARIUS-LIBRA (Page 201)

A lack of emotional commitment contributes to conficts. Although these Signs may seem to have much to offer each other, they find it hard to communicate at a depth where they can establish a meaningful relationship.

AQUARIUS-SCORPIO (Page 218)

Scorpio love is possessive—but how does one posses a comet? Aquarian love is diffused through the universe; focused on the mate, it is a pale companion to the Scorpio passion. Rarely these Suns may coalesce to Produce a union of brilliant intensity.

AQUARIUS-SAGITTARIUS (Page 232)

This pair will often battle their way through a happy marriage, turning as one to denounce those who mistakenly try to arbitrate. If it doesn't work out, they'll remain good friends.

AQUARIUS-CAPRICORN (Page 244)

Capricorn would make statues of loved ones, encasing them in bronze. Aquarius is as elusive as a handful of air. The best intentions in the world may not be enough to hold these two together.

Aquarius-Aquarius

This will be a rare and beautiful alliance if it comes to pass. As with all Air Sign combinations, there is a diffusive quality here which makes it difficult for Aquarians to focus on relationships. These free spirits are attuned to universal concepts—matters of intellect—and they find it difficult to achieve emotional concentration required in close interaction with others. They think in the future, held to the present by tenuous threads of necessity. With the stratosphere for a playground, it will seem a miracle if these two ever met.

But if they do. . .

The attraction here will be inteelectually magnetic, first, physically attractive, second, and will hold more of friendship than of sex. Not that Aquarius are uninterested in sex. It's just more commonplace than exciting intellect and Aquarians are attracted to the esoteric.

Emotional commitment in Aquarius takes the form of community relations. These individuals are the harbingers of a new age coming, and their efforts to help others will be in directions that benefit society.

Visionaries, eyes on the stars, often do not see the needs of those with whom they rub elbows.

Aquarians have a need for physical freedom almost as compulsory as their need for intellectual freedom. This love of freedom extends to their mates as well. Their tolerance in fact borders on indiscrimination.

They have little desire to burden themselves with material things. The real wealth for Aquarius lies in ideas and friendships that allow free interchange of thought. (Not that they won't enjoy luxury if the fates bestow it, but they won't sacrifice independence to the discipline that is usually demanded in acquiring material wealth.)

The detrimental factor in the relationship than is the lack of a cohesive force to hold it together. The passionate drives of most Aquarians are focused on concepts and theories rather than on personal interaction. There may never be open conflict in this partnership—just a drifting apart for lack of involvement deep enough to generate a holding force.

In those rare instances where the two are so finely attuned to each other's mental activities that they can move in absolute harmony, they can find a special kind of intimate communion others seldom experience. They will seem to live in a special world of their own above the human landscape.

Children of doubled Aquarian parents may appear to hold a casual position in the family structure. Yet the bond here can be much stronger than it appears to be on the surface since Aquarians, like Geminis, encourage their children to independence in thought and action from the time they are beginning to walk and, are tolerant of the mistakes they make in learning to know themselves as individuals.

A jewel-like radiance will emanate from this relationship if these two match rhythms—mental and physical—in their continuing quest for freedom. The trick is to come close enough to each other in the first place to allow gravity to take hold.

Aquarius-Pisces

These Suns together create a stimulating union of mind and emotion. Aquarius brings the detachment which emotional Pisces needs in order to function to capacity, while Pisces supplies some flexibility to the ideas which, in Aquarius, can become as rigid as steel coils at times.

They have many qualities in common—both Pisces and Aquarius are endowed with above-average abilities. They are idealistic in all things, with strong ethical and moral values—but these values are highly individualistic and will be unique to each person. Neither of them is overly impressed by public opinion, but each is hurt when their unconventional approach to living is criticized. Pisces, especially, needs approval, because this is the yardstick by which progress is measured. Aquarius is one of the friendliest signs and feels uneasy when discord plagues relationships.

Since both have highly original concepts of life and love and happiness, they are apt to receive more than their share of attention from those who regard their unconventional words and actions with curiosity.

There is little of the malicious in either of these Signs. Aquarius is the Sign of the humanitarian, loving all people but on a universal plane. Pisces feels this universal love for others but refines it to the personal. While in an intimate relationship the Aquarian may be startled by the emotional responses of Pisces, and Pisces may be puzzled by the impartiality with which Aquarius bestows affection, each recognizes in the other the idealism which is the root of the personality and responds to it in spite of its altered form.

Pisces tolerance for others, in the Aquarius can become lack of discrimination. The two together are extremely vulnerable to those who don't mind taking advantage of them. The Aquarian will trust possessions to a likeable stranger and be honestly surprised and hurt at being victimized. Pisces, overly generous, isn't far behind in inviting exploitation. The difference is in emphasis: Aquarians trust others with their possessions; Pisces trusts others with affections. And both suffer loss and both are hurt—and both a few days later invite the same treatment again.

Both feel the need for freedom: Pisces to avoid being smothered by those around; Aquarius to keep from being stifled by small ideas and petty concerns. The Aquarian possesses the intellect of genius—is ahead of the rest of the world in concepts by decades—and interaction with those whose vision does not extend past the end of their noses causes frustration. Aquarians like open spaces—vast reaches of space as seen from mountain tops or high-cruising jets. They like to shake off the restrictions of a highly structured society and move at their own pace with room to stride free.

While Pisces has not the physical endurance for actively seeking open spaces, empathetic responses to the environment keep the Fish attuned to the special places of earth. Pisces intuitively feels the same wonderment as Aquarius in the marvels of the universe. Pisces, most spiritual of the Signs—interacting with the universal through Neptunian influences which take them farther into unknown realms of awareness than other Signs can go—experiences the freedom of spirit which Aquarius lives by, and seconds unconventional means of satisfying special needs.

The hidden reef in this togetherness will be found in emotional areas. The intensity of Pisces emotional responses will at first delight the Aquarian, but as time goes by Aquarius becomes restive under this concentrated focus. Aquarian responses take place in a rarified atmosphere. Pisces insistence on a sustained emotional response at every level will begin to seem like riptides after awhile, and Aquarius will be off to find easier relationships among friends.

The Pisces partner will be shattered to hear of casual infidelities of the partner; as will happen. Aquarius may even do the telling. Friendship is very much a part of love relationship with Aquarius; intellect also. Where either is found, a sexual encounter easily follows. To a Pisces, however, infidelities are neither "friendly" nor "casual"—they are betrayal.

In truth, neither Aquarius nor Pisces is prone to roam from home if the partner shows the slightest responsiveness to their needs. Home is dear to both these Signs although they may differ widely in their concepts of what makes a home. But both are tolerant of the other's views. Sometimes Pisces emotion seems like jealousy. Sometimes Aquarian devotion to friends can cause neglect of the mate. But Aquarius will look a long time before finding another Sign as receptive to unconventional attitudes; and Pisces appreciates Aquarian willingness to allow time to be alone and still supply companionship when the Fish needs to be close to others.

All children should be lucky enough to find this Sun combination for parents. Pisces and Aquarius can offer their children an almost perfect blend of empathy and objectivity; of the personal and universal; of feeling and intellect. Practicality may suffer a little here, but the quality of *caring* these parents show for their children will be so rewarding it will go a long way to make up for that lack.

Both Pisces and Aquarius dislike routine. If they can together summon enough discipline to manage to live in the world as it is (for it is here we must supply our basic needs) then for the rest, these two can conjure up a life of such excitement and enchantment that others will stand open-mouthed in envy. It depends on whether or not they are able to find an anchor to keep them from thumping their heads on the stars.

PISCES

PISCES-ARIES (Page 44)

Aries fire longs for the cooling water. Pisces longs for the warmth of fire. But a heat wave can shrivel a rainbow if they come too near each other.

PISCES-TAURUS (Page 78)

The Piscean rainbow shelters the Taurus hearthfire. The result can be an almost magical love that lasts a lifetime.

PISCES-GEMINI (Page 108)

Better on a social level. In close relationship the Pisces rainbow may absorb the periodic flares of the blowtorch; the frequent, intense bursts of energy may blind Gemini to the nebulous rainbow hues.

PISCES-CANCER (Page 135)

If they can keep emotionalism under control these two can create a relationship of deep and lasting passion.

This union will be exceptionally rewarding or exceptionally painful. But there will always be a strong emotional ties between these two whether or not the union lasts.

PISCES-LEO (Page 161)

An attraction of complimentary weaknesses. Pisces emotion may put out the Leo fire; Leo aggressiveness may vaporize the fragile Pisces rainbow. But the richness of this bond, once established, can compensate a thouand times over for the risks involved.

PISCES-VIRGO (Page 183)

Pisces was born wearing rose-colored glasses; Virgo is apt to be color blind. If they can make it past the elaborate defense systems behind which they hide, each responds with the best of the nature. Best here can be very high indeed.

PISCES-LIBRA (Page 205)

A mysterious attraction draws them together, but they dissipate their energies in mists of dissention. If they manage to bring it off, the relationship can be rewarding in spite of unrealistic attitudes each harbors.

PISCES-SCORPIO (Page 221)

Intellectual stimulation interacting with intense emotional response can inspire love of which legends are

made. But a union of negative personalities here would
be made in hell.

PISCES-SAGITTARIUS (Page 235)

Jupiterian luck gives this union material blessings.
Jackpots tend to come in bunches. But troubles come
the same way. Eventually Archer arrows may sting the
Fish to death.

PISCES-CAPRICORN (Page 247)

Capricorn personality suffers the rigid restrictions of a
glacier; Pisces must deal with riptides of emotional
currents quite as severe. A painful union when traits do
not mesh. Given time, they may be able to establish
lasting bonds.

PISCES-AQUARIUS (Page 256)

A rare and stimulating union of mind and emotion. If
they are able to find an anchor to keep them from
thumping their heads on the stars, they can conjure up a
life of enchantment together.

Pisces-Pisces

It would be best not to pursue this matter, although these Suns may be attracted to each other through empathy and nebulous intuitive understanding which others do not always bring to personal relationships. In the rosy glow of Neptunian romance, they may feel themselves alone in a special universe others will never find. But sooner or later, empathy will not suffice; the nitty-gritty of everyday existence will sprinkle gravel on their primrose path.

And two Pisces depending on each other can be as helpless as foam spinning off threshing sea waves. Who will lead when both would follow? Who will command when both would obey? Which Fish, safe in the depths of the placid pond, will venture to the surface in search of food which, all too often for Pisces, contains a hidden hook. Safer to stay hidden, and sympathize and weep over the conditions of a universe which allows such injustices. These two may seem to move backwards as, clinging tightly to each other, they try to outmaneuver in attempts to avoid a leadership role.

Pisceans learn early that the harshness of the outside world holds peril for them. These two will take turns trying to find a way to navigate the channels of bureaucracy in order to earn food and shelter, retreating back to the haven of the home where they can restore diminished energies after exposure to more aggressive Signs. If they can alternate their advances and retreats the household may survive financially, but it will be hard going. Pisces feels the pain of disappointment and rejection of others as deeply as a personal hurt. For all practical purposes this relationship may degenerate into one long crying jag.

Worse still, it may disintegrate into one long

alcoholic binge. Or drug trip. Or sensitivity session. Or they may grow fat as carp, eating their way to nirvana to indulge their wounded psyches.

Pisces are so dependent on those around them for direction that two Fish, reflecting each other's moods, may finally vanish into a series of diminishing reflections. There may not be stamina enough in Pisces alone to deal with the harsh realities of daily life; another Pisces compounds the fluctuating problems of survival.

Ascendant Signs here would make a great difference. Taurus or Capricorn would lend strength without being rigidly overwhelming. Scorpio could add stamina. But it will take foundations from somewhere else to keep these two Suns from swimming in circles until they disappear. However, if they can find some stability, it's another fairy tale.

This then can be a rainbow romance, for Pisces imagination can bring a glow to the most mundane situations; can turn problems into adventures; can find loveliness in barren landscapes. But it takes a reflecting Sign to generate this beauty. Two Pisces blend together so completely they react as one.

Without some cohesive agent to hold things together nebulous Neptunian troubles can balloon to cover their world with storm clouds. Or the pot of gold may glitter so brightly, seen through rose-colored binoculars, that the foot of the rainbow may seem (eternally) no more than ten feet away.

Generally, however, their children will seem to live in a Walt Disney world. They may feel insecurity at times, but these loving parents will encourage them to keep trying to fly over the rainbow in spite of failures. They will know gentleness and sadness, and may grow up very fast. For it will be obvious to the most naive ten-year-old that a pair of Pisces parents sometimes need looking after.

Maybe it could work. But it will be a kaleidoscopic blend of mysterious shadows and rainbow-hued dreams seen through compassionate tears.

ASTROLOGY FOR THE WORKING GIRL
By Paige McKenzie

PRICE: $1.95 BT51467
CATEGORY: Non-fiction

In this practical guide, Paige McKenzie combines her extensive business experience, her knowledge of astrology and her good humor to help the career woman understand relationships between recognized Sun Signs and a host of personal and career problems. And she offers specific ways for dealing with conflicts, and such specific problems as: When is the best time to make a job switch?

AN UNNECESSARY
WOMAN
Mollie Vesey

PRICE: $2.25   BT51503
CATEGORY: Novel

AN UNNECESSARY WOMAN is a journey through
the heart's wilderness. Alice's children were growing up; her husband's business was prospering.
She had too much time on her hands. Then she
decided to plunge herself into a summer of confrontations—the unexplored territory of her own
emotions, her long-suppressed sexuality, her need
for love and, finally, the years of hidden anger
against everyone she loved, an anger that threatened to destroy them all.

A STAR RISING
Jess Carr

PRICE: $3.50   T51575
CATEGORY: Historical Novel

With the crucifixion of Christ, a new era had
begun. But it was a time of terror and persecution
for the early Christians. Antipas, a wealthy Roman
falls in love with a beautiful young prostitute who
tells him of the new faith. More and more Antipas
questions the bloodshed and debauchery of
Imperial Rome. He gives up his wealth and power
to the woman he loves and a belief that could
cost him his life. **A Star Rising** is the story of a man
caught between Rome's will and Christianity's
struggle to survive. A biblical epic of violence,
passion, and faith in the tradition of **I, Claudius**.

THE SEEING
By William P. McGivern
**(Author of "Soldiers of '44,"
and "Night of the Juggler"
and Maureen McGivern**

PRICE: $2.50 T51493
CATEGORY: Novel (Original)

THE SEEING is a contemporary occult thriller about
a child with profound psychic powers—whose gift
of prophecy becomes a force for evil!

"McGivern retains his stature as one of the very
best writers of suspense novels in the English lan-
guage."

—The Philadelphia Bulletin

THE PASSAGE
Victor Wartofsky

PRICE: $1.95   T51506
CATEGORY: Occult

After the wife and daughter of science reporter Wayne Farley are killed in an airplane crash, his investigation on life after death takes on personal significance. He decides to submit himself to the ultimate experience—to be killed and then brought back to life. If there is a life after death, he will be in a position to prove it.

"...Wartofsky displays literary skills of characterization and description unmatched by present day novelists."
—UNITED PRESS INTERNATIONAL

THE CLAIRVOYANT
By Hans Holzer

PRICE: $2.25 T51573
CATEGORY: Novel (Hardcover publisher:
Mason/Charter 1976)

The story of a beautiful young Viennese girl whose
gift of prophecy took her from the mountains of
Austria to the glittering drawing rooms of Beverly
Hills. She began to exhibit psychic powers at the
age of four. Terrified of their daughter's "gift," her
parents sent her to a remote school. As she moved
from school to school and then from man to man,
she used her psychic abilities to climb to perilous
heights of fame and success!

Author of the best-selling
Murder In Amityville

SEND TO: **TOWER PUBLICATIONS**
P.O. BOX 270
NORWALK, CONN. 06852

PLEASE SEND ME THE FOLLOWING TITLES:

Quantity	Book Number	Price

**IN THE EVENT THAT WE ARE OUT OF STOCK
ON ANY OF YOUR SELECTIONS, PLEASE LIST
ALTERNATE TITLES BELOW:**

Postage/Handling

I enclose...

FOR U.S. ORDERS, add 50c for the first book and 10c for each addi
tional book to cover cost of postage and handling. Buy five or more
copies and we will pay for shipping. Sorry, no C.O.D.'s.

FOR ORDERS SENT OUTSIDE THE U.S.A., add $1.00 for the first book
and 25c for each additional book. PAY BY foreign draft or money order
drawn on a U.S. bank, payable in U.S. ($) dollars.

☐ **PLEASE SEND ME A FREE CATALOG.**

NAME_____

(Please print)

ADDRESS_____

CITY_____**STATE**_____**ZIP**_____

Allow Four Weeks for Delivery